# Peril at Pennington Manor

# Peril at Pennington Manor

## AN AVERY AYERS ANTIQUE MYSTERY

Tracy Gardner

CROOKED LANE

NEW YORK

Published in the United States by Crooked Lane Books, an imprint of The Quick Brown Fox & Company LLC.

Crooked Lane Books and its logo are trademarks of The Quick Brown Fox & Company LLC.

Library of Congress Catalog-in-Publication data available upon request.

ISBN (hardcover): 978-1-64385-906-4
ISBN (ebook): 978-1-64385-907-1

Cover design by Mary Ann Lasher

Printed in the United States.

www.crookedlanebooks.com

Crooked Lane Books
34 West 27th St., 10th Floor
New York, NY 10001

First Edition: June 2022

10 9 8 7 6 5 4 3 2 1

For my dad,
who introduced me to
Nancy Drew

# Chapter One

"Race you home."

Avery Ayers raised one eyebrow at her dad jogging beside her. She brushed the strands of long brown hair off her face toward her high ponytail. "You'll lose."

"Let's find out." William broke into a sprint, kicking up dirt and gravel as he took off toward their lilac-lined driveway down the road.

Four months ago, Avery wouldn't have believed she'd be running with her dad. She'd gone to his funeral a year earlier, after all. She shifted into high gear and joined him, taking the lead as they approached the long driveway to the gray Craftsman-style home. The truck parked outside the garage hadn't been there when she and William left. Avery's sometime beau Art was on the green lawn throwing a Frisbee for Halston, Aunt Midge's majestic black Afghan hound—not so majestic as he launched himself toward the flying disk and missed, fur flying. Halston had been a welcome addition last year when Midge moved in to help out. She was now back in her luxurious Manhattan apartment, but no one had had the

1

heart to make Halston give up the Ayerses' large, fenced-in yard in rural Lilac Grove.

Avery slowed to a walk, letting her dad catch up. She usually used the driveway to cool down, and she wasn't in any kind of hurry to see why Art was here. William fell in step beside her. "I almost had you," he said. "Did you know your detective was coming by?"

"No." *Her detective* had a lot of nerve. It was one thing to stop by unannounced, but then to stay and hang out with their overly friendly dog once he knew she wasn't home? She gritted her teeth. And he had an issue with *her* boundaries. She could feel her dad looking at her.

"Don't worry," he said. "I think he's here for Halston."

She snickered. "Could be." Art was giving the dog plenty of pats and ear scratches before tossing the Frisbee again.

"You still don't want to talk about it?" her dad asked. "Judgement-free zone here."

She linked her arm through his. "Thank you. But no." Art and Halston approached the driveway. "Not now, anyway."

"All right." He lowered his voice. "Do we hate him?"

"Of course not," she said. There was no way she could ever hate Art. She wouldn't have gotten her father back if not for him.

"Well, that's a relief." The three of them met, and Halston wiggled between each of them, soaking up the attention. William held out a hand. "Hey there, Art. Good to see you."

He shook her father's hand. "Hi, Bill. Avery."

She stared at him. He should have called.

William moved toward the house. "I'll let you two catch up. I've got some work to get to." He checked his watch on the way up the porch steps, Halston at his heels. "We'll leave in about an hour to meet with the duke, Avery." He was gone.

She studied the detective as he turned back to face her. At six four, he had five or six inches on Avery, who'd been the tallest girl in every class from eighth grade all the way through grad school a few years ago. A dark-brown scruff covered his angular jawline. His hazel eyes were light today under the bright blue sky. He looked as troubled as she felt at seeing him. "I've missed you," she blurted, cursing her faulty filter.

Relief washed over Art's features. He knit his dark eyebrows, hopeful. "Avery. We should talk."

"Right. That was the whole problem, wasn't it? We should talk, but you wouldn't. Now you suddenly want to?" She heard the cutting edge in her tone, but she couldn't help it. They'd been doing so well, until—she still wasn't sure exactly what had happened.

"You know it's more complicated than that," he said evasively.

Avery stretched her arms high above her head and slowly arced them out to her right, then back over to her left. She drew in a deep breath and blew it out slowly, the way Dr. Singh had taught her to, trying to exhale that sharp edge along with it. "It's not complicated. I'm an open book. You know pretty much everything about me. But you . . . you're a closed book." She reached back and grabbed the toe of one running shoe, pulling her foot up toward her behind to stretch her quads.

"I'm not a closed book."

She did the same with her other foot. "Closed and locked, like my eighth-grade diary."

He didn't crack a smile. "You're exaggerating. This is all only about one thing—"

"One apparently life-altering thing." She bent at the waist and pressed her forehead to her knees, blowing out an aggravated breath before straightening back up again. "And when I tried to pick the lock, you changed the combination, and then you set the thing on fire to make sure I'm really shut out."

He frowned. "Um. You're losing me. You're making too much of this, I promise." He tipped his head. "I'll unlock the diary. Or give you the code. You can read me." Her eyes were drawn to his lips, where the faintest hint of a grin threatened to break through.

"So . . . you're an open book now?" Was he capable? Could the deeply guarded Detective Art Smith really let her in? She searched his eyes for some clue that he meant it.

He held her gaze intently. "Completely. I'll prove it. How about tonight? Let me take you out. I'm a much better date than some stuffy duke."

Avery laughed. So he'd caught that. "It's a work thing. We're going to meet Aunt Midge's friend who just flew in from Europe, from this small kingdom called Valle Charme. He wants to discuss hiring us to appraise an entire mansion full of antiques in the Hudson Valley before he sells the place. Some of it goes back centuries."

Art's eyebrows went up. "Nice. Then I guess you definitely have to meet with the duke."

"Yes, we do. But . . . maybe next weekend?"

Disappointment colored his features. "Oh. Sure. Are you busy all week?"

Avery had moved home from Philadelphia to take over running her parents' business, Antiquities and Artifacts Appraised, after the accident. She and her younger sister, Tilly, had been in the back seat of the family car on the way home from dinner when sabotage had caused the car to plunge into a ravine, killing both their parents. Or so they'd thought. Four months ago, when Avery had discovered that the priceless ruby she was authenticating was linked to the accident, she'd learned her father was still alive and in protective custody. She and Art had followed the clues to her mom's killer, and William was finally able to return home, knowing his family would be safe. The horror of believing he was dead was instantly forgiven by William's daughters and his two business partners, and eventually by tiny but mighty Aunt Midge.

Now Avery nodded in response to Art's question. She had an inkling he'd hoped to take her out sooner than a week from now, but it couldn't be helped. "We still get a steady influx of assignments from the museum, and ever since Sir Robert won us the auction house contract, it's been nonstop. I'm not complaining," she added.

"Sounds like it's been great for the business," he agreed. "Are you free next Friday night?"

She cringed. "I, uh . . . I can't Friday. How about Saturday?" She wasn't trying to be difficult. She couldn't tell him what she'd be doing Friday. A stab of guilt prodded her, but she shrugged it off. They hadn't dated in almost two months; she had nothing to feel guilty about.

"I'll take it. I'll let you get to your work thing."

The space between them, the lack of a hug good-bye, punctuated Avery's unrest and mixed emotions about the detective. She raised a hand in a wave as he drove away and then headed inside to shower.

* * *

Two hours later, Avery and her father turned onto the long, winding driveway that led to Pennington Manor. She'd first met Nicholas Pennington IV this summer in London when they'd been settling Tilly into school at the voice conservatory. Aunt Midge had brought her and William along on a lunch date with the duke, who was delightful. Avery leaned forward in the passenger seat, craning to take it all in once they were through the gated entry. The approach was beautifully lined with rosebushes and perfectly manicured gardens. A man in jeans and a wide-brimmed hat worked with pruning shears near one of the enormous stone pillars at the edge of the circular parking area. The manor's elegant gray brick-and-stone exterior was a study in authentic Old English architecture, complete with tall parapets overlooking the spectacular river and valley and conical spires rising above circular turret staircases. To call it a manor didn't quite do it justice. It was a castle, right down to the pretty lily ponds flanking the east and west wings. There was even a greenhouse and a large stable. A long tan building opened onto a fenced corral leading out to a rolling green pasture, where a young man was walking a horse that towered over him. Several other horses grazed peacefully. Pennington Manor reminded Avery of something out of a fairy tale, beautiful and serene.

William pulled around the circle and parked a few car lengths away from two black town cars with trunks standing open, midway through being unpacked. Avery nodded in greeting to the middle-aged couple pulling suitcases from the cars. She knew the duke's children were flying in but doubted the son of a sovereign leader would unpack his own suitcases. And besides, these two bore no resemblance to any of the family photos Avery had found online in her research. She'd spent last night reading up on the Penningtons in preparation for today's meeting.

Avery and William climbed the stone steps to the entryway. He put a hand out to knock just as tires squealed behind them.

A red Tesla Model X came to an abrupt stop alongside William's car. The young man who climbed out was oddly dressed in expensive-looking black trousers and dress shoes and a gray T-shirt bearing the words *Bowling is right up my alley*. He sprinted up the steps to where Avery and her dad stood, brown paper bag in one hand. He flashed a grin, and Avery recognized his striking good looks from her research. Twenty-two, recent Cambridge University grad, and award-winning polo player, Percy Pennington was the younger of Duke Pennington's two sons.

He held out his hand. "Lord Percy Pennington. You must be here to do the photos for the real estate company. You'll want to fetch your equipment, won't you?" His words held the same inflections as his father's. Avery recalled that Valle

Charme, the island the Penningtons were from, was somewhere off the southern coast of France.

"We're, uh, from the antiques appraisal company," Avery offered. The man looked exactly like what she'd expect of royalty, except for his attire. "Duke Pennington is expecting us." She extended her hand. "It's so nice to meet you, Sir Percy—um, no, sorry—I mean, my lord, er—"

William interrupted, saving her from further butchery of the man's title. "I'm William Ayers, and this is my daughter Avery. Your father arranged a meeting to discuss the appraisal of the manor's items."

Percy Pennington nodded. "Right. He mentioned something about that." He pushed the heavy door open and led them inside to a stately, two-story-high vestibule. The couple with the suitcases skirted past them and made their way to the wide, curving staircase. A younger woman entered from an adjacent room, and Percy stopped her. "Suzanne." He held the paper bag in the air. "Put this in the freezer. God forbid my mother doesn't have her gelato before bed."

"Oh!" The woman's eyes widened, her gaze moving from him to Avery and William and then back to Percy. "I would have sent Roderick if I'd known the duchess needed something, Lord Pennington. I'm sorry you had to be inconvenienced." Suzanne's pretty, delicate features were made even more so by her large blue eyes and blond bangs. She was treating the duke's son with such deference, Avery guessed she was also an employee at the manor.

"No need to apologize." He winked at her. "It was a good excuse to take the new toy for a spin. Oh, Suzanne—"

Avery thought he was about to introduce them. Percy continued, "Take the Ayerses up to my father." Suzanne was definitely staff. There were no niceties, and Percy apparently didn't feel it necessary to introduce the manor's employees to . . . well, Avery and her father were also employees now, weren't they?

"Of course," the young woman said in response, turning her attention to Avery and William. "If you'll please follow me?"

Suzanne led them in silence up the staircase and down a long hallway. Along the way, Avery slowed and tapped her father's arm, pointing to an alcove with a sitting area overlooking the entryway below. Displayed upon a pedestal was one of the pieces the duke had mentioned, a handsome bronze sculpture of a man with his hound. *Companions* was a rare creation by Famke from the 1840s, the life-sized piece larger than Avery had expected. Beside it was a stunning French provincial–style Gustavian sofa done in royal, textured tones, a polished trumeau mirror above it. Even the ornate crystal chandelier hanging overhead must be highly valuable. This place was an antiques appraiser's dream.

A high-pitched shriek of laughter burst from the large room on their left, followed by more giggles. Avery spied two adorable little girls running in circles around and underneath a sheet draped across a couch and an armchair in the room—a makeshift tent. A petite brunette in khakis was unpacking an open suitcase on the four-poster bed, the bedding lavish and plush in deep burgundy and cream. A second woman, tall, thin, and dressed head to toe in black, stepped into view near the doorway. Ignoring Avery, she made eye contact with Suzanne. The woman's gaze dripped with so much contempt, Avery shuddered. The woman placed a well-manicured hand on the heavy wooden door and slammed it. Suzanne made no comment.

Avery widened her eyes at her dad, finding him equally bewildered.

"Here we are," Suzanne announced when they'd reached the open door at the end of the hallway. At his desk, Duke Nicholas Pennington IV was deep in conversation with a younger man opposite him in a leather armchair. He smiled as Suzanne announced Avery and William. "Your Grace, your guests have arrived." She held a hand out for them to enter.

Both men rose, the duke coming around his desk. In his late fifties, Nicholas Pennington IV still possessed the build of a much younger man. His dark hair showed only traces of gray at the temples, and it was easy to see where Lord Percy's good looks came from. He immediately put Avery and William at ease with his warm welcome, shaking William's hand and greeting Avery with the briefest kiss on each cheek. "Avery, William, I so appreciate you coming today. This is my eldest son, Nicholas. Nico, William is our good friend Midge's brother. And this is Avery, Midge's niece."

Percy Pennington's older brother wore jeans and a black button-down. Nico appeared to be around thirty or so. He was taller and broader than Percy but graced them with the same dazzling smile. "Good to meet you. I see the resemblance to the lovely Midge. Your aunt is always a welcome guest in Valle Charme," Nico said. "I do hope we'll see her while we're in New York."

Avery nodded. "I'm certain you will. She probably would have come with us today if she hadn't had a prior commitment."

"We'll have her out for dinner," the senior Nicholas Pennington said. "How was your drive in?"

"Not bad at all," William said. "Under an hour."

Nico spoke as the duke ushered them over to a sitting area. "Father, William, Avery, please excuse me. I have that four o'clock with the broker," he said to his father. "I'll leave you three to talk antiques."

"It was nice meeting your sons," Avery said, once Nico was gone. "We met Lord Percy when we arrived. You must be pleased your family was able to travel with you."

"Yes. It isn't always easy to coordinate schedules, but they wanted to be here," the duke said. "Especially as we begin discussing plans for some of the heirlooms and antiques in the manor."

"Of course." It made sense. The duke and his extended family would need to keep things equitable. "Your home is absolutely stunning," Avery said. She'd seen only a fraction of the manor and was already wowed.

"Thank you. Though it's by no means my home. In years past, we'd come on holiday now and then, but my late mother was much more attached to it than I ever was."

Avery spoke. "Duke Pennington, please accept our condolences. My aunt Midge says the duchess—I mean, the dowager duchess—was a lovely, sweet woman." She frowned at her flub. She'd read up on the Penningtons of Valle Charme in preparation for today's meeting and Googled *proper etiquette around royals* during their drive here, but now she wished she'd done a more thorough job preparing. The duke's mother's title had the elder designation, as the duke's own wife, Mariah, was the duchess. Should she have addressed him as Your Grace, the way Suzanne had?

He leaned forward, speaking earnestly. "Please. Might we dispense with the formalities? I understand it's difficult for the staff here to alter the manner in which they address my family. My mother was a stickler for procedure. But my friends call me Nick."

Avery smiled. "Are you sure? How about Nick unless you're with your family or the staff? I'll feel too disrespectful otherwise."

"I've got to agree with her there," William said. "I do want to say, your mother passed so recently. If you decide to have us handle the manor's appraisals, it will take a while. Several days at least. And we hate to intrude. If you feel your time in the Hudson Valley is better spent enjoying the company of your family, Avery and I assure you we'll make your contract a priority whenever you decide to start the process. Even if it's months from now."

Avery stared at her dad. It hadn't occurred to her to suggest the duke wait. It should have; she and her father were still working through all the emotions that came with losing Anne last year. Grief didn't resolve itself quickly. "My father's right. We can do this anytime. It's up to you."

"I appreciate that," Nick said. "But it's time. I'm tasked with deciding what to sell and what to ship back home to Valle Charme before the manor goes on the market. I believe we're all ready to say good-bye to the place, save Percy. But he'll have to come around to the idea."

"I'm sure he will," Avery said. Changing homes—even summer homes—was always an adjustment. She thought of her own moves, first out of state after college and then back home last year. She still missed her friends in Philly.

"I'll show you around a bit so you'll know what you'll be dealing with when you begin on Monday. Assuming Monday works for you?"

Avery glanced at William. She'd been under the impression they were being interviewed for the job, but it seemed they were already hired. "That will be perfect," Avery said. "We'll start Monday morning."

"Your Grace?" The middle-aged woman who'd been carrying the suitcases appeared in the doorway of the study. "So sorry to interrupt. I have the inventory pulled up, as you requested." She held an iPad in her hands.

"Mrs. Hoffman, please come in." The duke took the tablet from her. "You have perfect timing. Meet William Ayers and his daughter, Avery. They're half the team that'll be handling the appraisal process. Avery, William, this is Lynn Hoffman; she and her husband, Ira, have been caretakers here for—how long now?"

"Twenty-two years for us, sir, and my parents for thirty before that," she replied. She gave Avery and William a small smile. "It's so nice to meet you. Please let me know if you need anything while you're working."

"Would you like to accompany us, Mrs. Hoffman?" the duke asked. He tapped the screen and scrolled, perusing the list. "You must know some of these pieces better than I do."

"No, sir. I wouldn't impose. Your Grace, I don't want to forget—the Wolfs were hoping for a moment of your time later today. I believe they've run into a few questions about transferring two of the mares."

"Certainly. Please let them know I'll come out to speak with them in a couple hours."

When she'd gone, Avery spoke. "We saw the horses when we drove in. They're beautiful. What will happen to them when the manor sells?"

"It's somewhat complicated," Nick said. "The majority are my son's polo ponies. He's been competing since his teens on both sides of the pond. He'll still have his string of ponies in Valle Charme, but the groomsmen—Jerry Wolf and his son Bryan—are helping Percy coordinate all of the rehoming."

"Ah. I can imagine that being a little tricky." Avery understood now why Percy in particular wasn't thrilled about saying good-bye to the manor.

Duke Pennington sighed. "This entire process is. I may have underestimated the impact of selling. Many of the staff here have been with my family for decades. I'm not simply putting them out of a job; Mrs. Hoffman and her husband live on-site. So do the Wolfs and the housekeeper," Nick said. "Yet they're each as cordial as ever. Even with reference letters and generous severance packages, I'm certain it'll be an adjustment for everyone involved."

The displacement of the employees hadn't occurred to Avery either. "Well, I expect it will all work out."

He nodded. "Of course." He looked down at the iPad. "Let's begin with the crown jewel in my family's collection, shall we?"

Avery was practically tingling with anticipation by the time Nick had led them through the mammoth house. She spied one fine antique after another as they passed a library to die for, a gorgeous formal dining room right out of an old movie, and a regal personal theater done in royal reds and golds. He pushed open the double doors they'd arrived at and stood to the side, allowing Avery and her dad to enter before him.

"We call this the reception room. This is where my mother took her afternoon tea and entertained guests."

Avery turned in a circle, then looked up, tipping her head back. The space was decorated in white on white with varying textures, skylights intersecting the arced panels in the high, domed ceiling. The room took up one end of the estate, the floor-to-ceiling windows offering a panoramic view of the Hudson Valley and the river. "Breathtaking."

The duke nodded. "It is. Thank you." He moved toward the far side of the room, where a glass case sat beneath an overhead spotlight. "My great-grandfather, Prince Albert, passed this pocket watch down to my mother, a gift to him from his father, King Albert III of Valle Charme. It's part of a set." He pulled a key ring from his pocket, glancing over his shoulder to be sure Avery and her father were following him. "It will stay in my family, of course, as the sentimental value alone would make it impossible to part with. But the Viktor Petrova timepiece is priceless. I suspect you've never seen it's equal. The gold—"

The duke stopped short, staring down into the case. On either side of him, Avery and William immediately saw why.

The pocket watch was missing. Inside the case, the black velvet display tray held a pair of gleaming De Grisogono cuff links, a slim diamond-inlaid tie tack, and a gold chain and monocle. There was no void where the watch would have been.

Duke Pennington tapped the screen on his iPad, scrolling through. "This doesn't make any sense," he murmured.

Avery spoke, her tone reverent. "It was . . . you're certain it was in this case?" It was a stupid question. She knew it before she finished asking.

The duke didn't reply. He unlocked the case, opened the top, and reached a hand inside—

"No!" Avery shouted, stopping him with a hand on his arm.

He stared at her, surprised. His gaze moved to her hand, her fingers wrapped around his forearm.

She gasped and let go abruptly. "I'm so sorry. I just—if you think someone has—if someone's stolen it, you shouldn't touch anything. What if they've left fingerprints behind?"

His eyes grew larger than they already were. "Bloody hell. I didn't think of that. Oh Lord. I hope this isn't what it seems."

"Is it possible that it was taken out for some reason? Cleaning?" William asked.

"Not likely. I'd have had to authorize that," Nick said. "And there's only one other key." Using the tip of one finger, he closed the glass lid and locked the case.

She had to ask. "Who has the other key?"

"My son." He sighed, his brow furrowed. "Let's hope that's all it is—perhaps he took it to be polished, knowing we were hiring appraisers. I'm sorry. I've got to look into this; it can't wait."

"No problem at all," Avery said. "We understand."

"We'll see you Monday morning," William said. "I'm sure there's a reasonable explanation," he added.

Avery was the first to speak once they were in the car on the way back to Lilac Grove. "I don't think the watch was sent to be cleaned."

Her dad glanced at her from behind the wheel. "I don't either."

"The items in the case must have been moved around. Did you notice that? Whoever took the pocket watch didn't want there to be an empty space in the display."

William nodded. "Right. I thought the same thing."

"Well, then Nick probably noticed it too. Was he just trying not to panic in front of us?"

"Probably," he said. "When you were researching the Penningtons, did you see anything about the Viktor Petrova pocket watch?"

Avery shook her head. "No. But I'll look it up. And which son has the other key? He never said, right?" She picked up her phone. "Oh no. What in the world? I have three missed calls and a whole bunch of messages from Tilly."

William stared at her in alarm. "Something's happened."

Avery was about to phone her sister back when Tilly called her again via FaceTime. Her little sister's normally adorable face filled the screen. Her nose was bright red and her blue eyes were puffy. Avery frowned, holding her phone so her father could see too. "Tilly, what's wrong? It must be midnight there!"

Tilly's voice cracked as she spoke, threatening to break into more tears at any moment. "I've been trying to get ahold of both of you for hours!"

"Honey, what happened? Are you all right?" William's gaze darted between the road and the phone, his brow furrowed. "Are you crying? Are you hurt?"

"Yes," Tilly wailed. "Well, no." Her head whipped around as she looked behind her, and she disappeared off the screen for a moment before popping back on.

"Tilly?" Avery heard panic in her own voice. Her sister was prone to drama, but this was extreme. "What's going on?"

"I need you to pick me up tomorrow morning at the airport. I'm coming home, and I'm not going back."

# Chapter Two

A very spotted Tilly while she was still making her way out of the cordoned-off security area at JFK Airport in Queens. Tilly waved wildly, bouncing up and down, but it didn't make the crowd ahead of her move any faster. She pulled an exasperated face, her long, curly blond hair flying out in all directions from her messy topknot. She looked a whole lot better than she had the night before. At least she wasn't crying anymore.

At nineteen, Tilly was seven years younger than Avery. They couldn't be more different, in both physical appearance and attitude. But in the past year, after losing their mother and believing they'd lost William too, they'd grown closer than ever. While William had fretted and worried all of last night about his youngest daughter and what might be wrong, Avery knew her sister. In spite of her tears, if anything had been truly, devastatingly wrong, like life-or-death wrong, Avery would have felt it. Seeing Tilly now, her usual silly grin and infectious energy in place as she threw herself into their arms, Avery was reassured her sister was fine. Obviously upset enough about something to fly all the way home from London a week before her autumn break, but still fine.

William frowned down at her, standing back to search her face. "What happened, Lamb? I hate the idea of you flying all those hours alone and upset. I could have come to you."

Tilly looked sheepish. The nickname had been given to her as a child, her parents' tongue-in-cheek nod to their youngest daughter's wild, rambunctious demeanor. She was anything but a lamb. "I'm okay. I'm sorry I worried you, Daddy," she rushed on before William could get a word in. "I had to see you guys. I just *had* to. Can we go home? Please? We can talk later. I'm tired and I just want to go home."

Avery picked up her sister's bag. Had she seriously flown across the ocean because she was homesick? Tilly had been ecstatic to begin her freshman year of college in Europe. The London Conservatory of Music had been her dream school since tenth grade. In the car, their dad behind the wheel, Avery turned to face her sister in the back seat. "Tilly. Are you really all right?"

Tilly glanced up from her phone, where she was speed typing something to someone. "I'm good."

"Because Dad and I were supposed to pick you up from the airport a week from today. You used your savings to pay for your flight change?"

"Yes. I used *my* savings." She sighed dramatically and dropped her phone into her backpack. "Don't worry, A, you're not my guardian anymore. You can drop the bossy act."

Avery was taken aback. "Damn." She turned abruptly in her seat, facing forward. That was sassy, even for Tilly. She gave her father a sideways glance. He was staring in the rearview mirror at his daughter, his jaw set. Tilly was going to have to explain herself sooner or later. William would have to deal with her; Avery doubted her sister would be as rude to him.

Finally home in Lilac Grove, Tilly dropped to her knees and threw her arms around Halston. The happy Afghan hound wiggled and whined excitedly, nearly knocking her over. Tilly kissed the top of the dog's head and straightened up.

William cleared his throat. "Let's go make some lunch, and we'll talk this . . ." His voice trailed off as Tilly sprinted up the stairs.

"I'm not hungry and I don't want to talk," she yelled over her shoulder. Her bedroom door slammed seconds later.

William's brow rose in bewilderment. "What was that?"

Avery shook her head. "I don't know. Has she finally hit her rebellious teen phase? I mean, I kind of expected it after the funeral. But it never happened."

"Well. Let's give her some space. If she doesn't come down by dinnertime, I'll go talk to her," William said. "I'm starving. How does grilled cheese sound?"

Avery followed him into the kitchen. There had been times, since he'd been back, when she'd wondered what she was still doing living at home. What with her trips two or three days a week into their Manhattan office, it'd make sense for her to start looking at apartments. She and William worked from their home office about half the time, but sitting across from Micah and exchanging research tidbits and thoughts with him and Sir Robert always made her more productive. With all of the changes in the last several months, she felt tied to Lilac Grove. Her father was finally back, and Tilly was still here part-time. And then there was Art, who lived nearby. The Springfield County Sheriff's Department had a residency rule. Avery knew she shouldn't factor him into her musings on future plans. Their short-lived, budding romance had imploded in spite of their chemistry.

She simply wasn't ready to move. Being in Lilac Grove allowed her the best of both worlds: quiet, small-town coziness interspersed with the bustling pace of Manhattan, only an hour away.

Sunday evening, when Avery and her dad went upstairs to talk with Tilly, they found her fast asleep, sprawled out on her bed still wearing her shoes. Avery gently took them off, pulled a blanket over her, and turned out the light. She closed the bedroom door behind them.

"She's going to have to talk with us tomorrow," her dad said. "She must need the sleep."

"She must." Worry needled Avery. "At least she was her usual sassy self today. She really did seem okay." She wasn't sure if she was trying to convince herself or her father.

The kitchen was filled with the aroma of pancakes and coffee the next morning when Avery came downstairs. Tilly was wide awake and perched at the kitchen island. She smiled brightly, no trace of yesterday's angst or attitude. "Good morning!"

Avery poured herself a cup and joined her. "Morning. Thanks for breakfast. You look better."

"I feel better. So, why didn't you tell me you're working for royalty? You and dad were talking in the car yesterday about some King Albert guy."

"We just got the job. It's Aunt Midge's friend, the duke, the one Dad and I met in London when you were in freshman orientation."

"I know," Tilly said. "I just hung up with Aunt Midge. We're coming for dinner tonight! Does the place really look like a castle?"

Avery widened her eyes. "Wait, you are? You and Aunt Midge?"

"Auntie's coming over today. Dad's making her babysit me," Tilly said, rolling her eyes. "He told her I shouldn't be alone. God, I'm nineteen! But since she got invited to dinner at the castle, I get to come too."

"It's not actually a castle. Though it kind of looks like one," Avery said. "Tilly, listen. What the heck happened? Why are you home a week early? Can you afford to miss that much school?"

Tilly slumped, leaning on the counter top and groaning. "It's not a big deal." She rested her head on one hand, turning to give Avery a sideways glance. She lowered her voice. "Do you know if the school's emailed Dad? About . . . anything?"

Oh, snap. What kind of trouble had Tilly gotten up to? Avery shook her head. "I don't think so. He'd have said something." She narrowed her eyes. "Why do you ask?"

Her sister shrugged. "No reason. Hey, I'll be here for the marathon now! Are you ready? Maybe I should've made you eggs instead of pancakes. Aren't you supposed to be like, trimming or cutting or something? No fat or carbs before the race?"

"I can have a pancake, don't worry. Don't change the subject. Come on, we've always been able to tell each other anything. Is it your grades? The courses are harder than you expected?"

Tilly straightened up and looked down her nose at Avery. "My grades are first-class in all my courses. That means I'm doing great, in case you don't know how grading works in the UK."

"I didn't. But I'm not surprised—you've always been a good student. So then what is it? Is it Noah?"

"No! What? Why would you assume that?" She pushed away from the counter, grabbing her cup of coffee. "Can't you just be my sister? Stop trying to parent me! I'm going to take a shower before Auntie gets here." She nearly ran into William on her way out of the kitchen.

He turned and followed her. "Tilly."

Tilly spun around. "Morning, Dad."

"Family meeting tonight after work. No arguments. Agreed?"

"Agreed." She opened her mouth to add something but then seemed to think better of it. She abruptly came over and hugged William. "I'm glad to be home. I made pancakes for you guys." She turned and went upstairs, Halston on her heels.

William ran a hand through his thick, fair hair as he joined Avery. He piled a stack of pancakes on his plate. "And I thought it'd get easier as you two got older."

Avery tipped her head. "Hey. You're talking to the good one—at least at the moment." She smiled. "She's working through something. It'll come out. I'm glad Auntie will be with her today."

"Well, we'll be gone a while. Without knowing what on earth brought your sister home in such a rush, I didn't feel comfortable leaving her alone. Midge will call us right away if anything's amiss—I promised we'd be reachable."

"Good." She added just the teensiest bit of syrup to her pancakes; she shouldn't be eating them at all, and she knew it. "So what do you think is up with that pocket watch? There are so many people in that house, anyone could've taken it."

"I suppose you're right," her dad said. "But how? Which of Nick's sons has the other key? And even if someone found a way to pick the lock, I'd think it'd be tricky in that busy house to steal something so valuable."

"True. Hopefully one of the sons really did send it to be polished or something. Though that wouldn't be necessary, not for our appraisal."

William shrugged. "A layperson wouldn't necessarily know that. I'm with you. I hope it's back in the case and we'll get to see it."

\* \* \*

As they rolled through the gated entrance of Pennington Manor, Avery felt lighter, relieved to focus on work for a while instead of her sister. Though Tilly's attitude was amped up, she truly seemed to be all right. It had been smart of William to set a deadline for a good heart-to-heart. Avery didn't want to parent Tilly any more than Tilly wanted her to.

They were climbing the front steps when Micah's car pulled into the circle drive. Avery and her father waited for their colleagues to join them. In his midfifties, Micah Abbott was dapper in a brown suit, his hunter-green pocket square matching his bow tie. His attire always held a midcentury modern vibe that Avery knew was unintentional. Sir Robert Lane followed him up the steps, dressed as if he were about to meet the Queen of England, right down to his navy-and-gold paisley ascot tie. The *Sir* portion of Sir Robert was an affectation rather than an actual title. He handled the finance and marketing end of the business, while their partner Micah was Avery and William's right-hand man and history expert with the appraisal process. Micah was a longtime friend of the family and had become something of a father figure to Avery in the last year when she'd believed her father was dead. When Avery'd discovered Micah bleeding out from a gunshot wound in his Harlem townhouse four months ago, she'd been terrified she'd lose him too.

"Stunning," Sir Robert said. "If the antiques inside are as impressive as the facade, you two win the prize for best assignment of the year."

William rang the bell. Avery raised her eyebrows at Sir Robert and Micah. "Brace yourselves. You won't know where to begin, there are so many high-end pieces," she promised.

The young blond woman from the other day opened the door. "Good morning, Mr. Ayers, Ms. Ayers." She nodded cordially to Sir Robert and Micah. "Please, come in."

The flurry of activity they'd walked into on Saturday was a stark contrast to the quiet this morning. In the stately vestibule, Avery gestured to the housekeeper—she'd located a record of Pennington Manor employees online, and she'd been right in her assumption of the woman's role. "Robert, Micah, this is Suzanne. Suzanne, these are our associates, Micah Abbott and Robert Lane." Leaving the *Sir* off of his name felt strange on her tongue, but it seemed disrespectful to use the unofficial title here.

Surprise crossed the housekeeper's features. "It's so nice to meet you all. I, um . . . I'm afraid Duke Pennington was called away. Was he expecting you?"

Avery exchanged a glance with William before speaking. How strange of the duke to schedule them and then not be here. "Yes, he'd asked us to begin the appraisals this morning. I wonder—" She stopped abruptly as the doors behind them swished open again and a man in a black suit and chauffeur's cap rushed over to their little group.

He swiped his cap off and smoothed a hand over close-cropped brown hair. "Duke Pennington has just now returned. I saw your group arrive and wanted to catch you. He sends his apologies for his tardiness." His gaze moved to Suzanne. "He asked if you'd escort their party to the reception room."

The housekeeper nodded. "Of course. Thank you, Roderick. If you'll all follow me, please?"

Entering the elegant, white-on-white room at the end of the long hallway where they'd discovered the Petrova pocket watch missing, Avery's group was greeted by a slender middle-aged man holding an iPad. "Good morning, Ayers and company!" He smiled widely.

Avery narrowed her eyes as she cast a glance toward the lighted pedestal at the far end of the room. She had no time to inquire about the watch, as the man continued. "I'm Mathew, Duke Pennington's personal assistant. His Grace will join us soon. He asked me to show you to your temporary work space." He crossed to the wall closest to them and touched a small square panel, and a white door that hadn't been noticeable before slid open, revealing a darkened room.

"Fascinating," Micah murmured beside Avery.

Mathew switched the lights on, illuminating an enormous, empty ballroom. "Duke Pennington thought perhaps you'd like to use the room as a makeshift appraisal lab. The lighting is adjustable, from full dark, to lighted with dimming, to daylight." He touched another panel and the entire ceiling began to shift, the sections sliding outward and accordioning into an unseen recessed space. Within a minute, they were staring up through glass at the bright blue sky. The assistant held an open palm out toward the dance floor. "Would you like to put your equipment down?"

Four long tables occupied the space, complete with power strips, chairs, two laptops, and additional lighting. The ballroom's bar was set up as a coffee station, stocked with flavored creamers and teas and a huge basket of snacks that Avery could only admire from afar. She had plenty of protein bars and raw nuts in her purse. It was all lovely.

"Now this is antiques appraisal done in style," Sir Robert said. "Perfectly presented, Mathew. We appreciate the hospitality."

The man's wide smile returned. "I'm so glad it's acceptable."

Avery clasped her hands. "I can't wait to get started. We'll need to take another trip or two out to the cars for a few things."

"No problem," Mathew said. He tapped his iPad. "The groundskeeper will meet you outside to help carry items in."

When Avery, her trio of colleagues, and the groundskeeper made it back, laden with cases that held their tools of the trade, the duke was waiting for them and his assistant was gone. He rushed over to Avery, taking the box she was balancing on her briefcase.

"Thank you! That's our spectroscope. I was about to drop it." She turned and motioned to the groundskeeper. Deeply tanned, he seemed to be around the duke's older son's age. She felt a little guilty pulling him away from his work just because they needed some extra muscle. "Would you mind putting that right here, please?"

The man obliged, setting the oversized case on the table beside the other equipment. "Would you like me to bring in anything else?" he asked.

"No, I believe we got it all in one trip. Thank you," Avery replied.

The duke stopped the groundskeeper as he was on his way out. "Gregory, would you let me know when the locksmith arrives? They confirmed with Mathew for today, but we don't know what time. I want to be out at the gate when they change the locks."

"Sure, Your Grace, I can do that." He turned, pulling the gardening gloves from his pocket as he left.

Avery introduced her colleagues to the duke and waited until the round of handshakes was finished before finally asking her burning question: "Duke Pennington, I'm dying to know. Were you able to discover what happened to your great grandfather's Petrova timepiece? Had it simply been sent out to be cleaned?" Since he was having the locks changed on the gated entry to the estate, she likely already had her answer.

Nick shook his head, his mouth turned down. "I do wish that was the case. Percy hasn't ever used the key I gave him. There's no other explanation but that it's been stolen, and I'm stymied as to how."

"Oh, I'm so sorry!" Avery exclaimed. "I was able to find a picture of it online, and I filled in my colleagues. We'd all hoped to see the piece in person; it's gorgeous. I know it held great sentimental value for you, aside from its worth."

"Yes." The duke knit his brow. "Well. You two saw me unlock the case. Even if someone had picked the lock, could they have locked it back up again after the theft?" He stared off toward the reception room through the doorway, lost in thought.

Avery raised her eyebrows at her father, her gaze moving to Micah and Sir Robert. "I, uh . . ."

"I doubt it," Nick said, answering his own question. "But they'd have had to, or else someone borrowed Percy's key. But he says it's been in his possession since he arrived."

Avery's mind raced. "Have you called the police and reported it stolen?"

"I did, yes. They're sending a detective out sometime today or tomorrow to look around and take my statement. The authorities seemed less than optimistic." He sighed. "That watch has been in my family for generations. I may never see it again."

William spoke. "Let us ask around a bit in our circles. We've worked with items of historical significance before; I wouldn't think it'd be very easy to sell a well-known Viktor Petrova timepiece. Not unless the thief faked provenance—certificate of authenticity—too, and that'd point to a professional, wouldn't it?"

"Good point," Sir Robert chimed in. "My Barnaby's connections might have heard something. The auction house keeps an ear to the ground for high-profile items."

"Avery mentioned you received the pocket watch as part of a set," Micah added. "Have you verified the remaining items are intact and genuine?"

The duke's complexion went even paler than it's natural tone. "No. You all make excellent points. You can check the set over today, yes? Perhaps now?"

"Of course," Avery replied.

Her team dove in to examining the cuff links, tie tack, and monocle after Duke Pennington had retrieved them from the locked display case. He took Avery's suggestion of using his pocket square to lift the top and remove the items, in hopes of preserving any possible fingerprints left by the thief. Nick hovered for a while, watching over their shoulders and murmuring about beefing up manor security, until his wife came to find him.

Duchess Mariah Pennington was a lovely, well-preserved woman. Her silky straight auburn hair fell just below her shoulders, complementing high cheekbones and lips that were too full to be natural. She wore a black-and-tan dress cinched tight at the waist, accentuating her generous curves. From the doorway, she addressed the duke in a low tone. "Nicholas, a word, please?"

"Of course, my dear." He moved to her side, making introductions as he went. "This is my better half, the duchess Mariah Pennington. Sweetheart, say hello to our appraisal team: William and Avery Ayers and their colleagues Micah Abbott and Robert Lane. They work out of Manhattan."

Avery took a step in their direction, meaning to greet the woman, but stopped as the duchess gave their group a quick dismissive smile and then turned to the duke. Avery craned to hear their exchange, but the duchess was so soft-spoken it was a wonder even her husband could hear her. He nodded and excused himself.

When Nick and his wife had gone, Avery glanced at Micah beside her and whispered, "I can't keep track of all these people!"

He straightened up from the spectroscope he was using to examine the tie tack and leveled his gaze at her. "That was the duke's wife. Her name is Duchess Mariah Pennington."

Avery rolled her eyes at his deadpan sense of humor. Micah was one of her favorite people. Which was good, because it was usually the two of them side by side on any given case— or it had been, before William returned from the dead. Even now he still hadn't fully reintegrated into the business he and his wife had created over a decade earlier.

"Funny, Micah. But I was talking about the sheer volume of people. The duke's assistant and driver, his extended family—both his sons are here, plus the wife and children of one of the sons, not sure which. And all of the manor employees. Not to mention the outdoor employees, like the stable guys and the groundskeeper."

"Well," Sir Robert said from his stance at the bar, sipping his cup of gourmet coffee. "It's par for the course with some royal families. When I was dating Francesca, we vacationed with her childhood friend's family in Europe, on an island with one of the oldest monarchies. You've probably heard of her? Princess Elzbieta Venla."

Avery obliged with a white lie, giving him what he wanted. She didn't have the heart to burst his bubble of self-importance. Sir Robert was always dazzled by the intrepid Francesca's world. It had been four months since she'd vanished into thin air, and he was still slightly smitten despite what they now knew about her. "I have heard of Princess Elzbieta! How cool."

"Lovely woman. But, as I was saying, Princess Elzbieta has her own attendants, her husband has his, the castle itself has an extensive staff. What we're encountering here isn't so unusual," Sir Robert said.

"Wow," Avery said. "Sounds like the detective they're sending to look into this will have his work cut out for him—trying to find the thief among family and staff. I don't know if changing the locks on the gated entrance is worth the trouble; it seems like it was an inside job. Though I'm sure it makes Nick feel as if he's doing something positive."

To her left, her dad pushed his chair back from his make-shift workstation and spoke up. "The De Grisogono cuff links are genuine. The particular cut of the diamonds is one give-away, and you can see just with the loupe that the setting is a match for the brand in the early 1900s. Here, take a look." William passed the loupe—an appraiser's simplest and most frequently used magnifying tool—to Avery.

She leaned in to check out the cuff links and saw that her dad was right. "Want to see?" she asked Micah.

"That's all right. The tie tack appears to be authentic on preliminary examination as well. I wouldn't imagine anyone going to great lengths to create a fake anyway—it's valuable but not Viktor Petrova pocket watch valuable."

Avery added notes to the spreadsheet she'd started on her laptop once she'd downloaded the duke's inventory document. They'd work through the antiques and heirlooms and create a detailed report of each one for the duke's records. And if he needed help finding buyers, Sir Robert was Antiquities and Artifacts Appraised's in-house king of connections. He knew everyone, either through his and Francesca's circle or through Barnaby's Auction House. She closed her laptop and stood. "Let's secure these back in their case and get started with the rest of the house. We've got five hours until dinner." The duke had extended his generous invitation to their four-some along with Aunt Midge—and now Tilly.

The modern-day castle was three stories, not counting the dizzying parapets. Avery could hardly imagine how many rooms there were, or the wealth of fascinating antiques each held. They split up, Sir Robert with Avery's father and Avery with Micah, who was game to begin on the second floor with *Companions*, the rare Famke sculpture that had grabbed her interest the other day. The size and weight of the bronze man and his dog prevented them from moving it to their temporary lab, but it didn't take long to set up an appraisal area in the space overlooking the vestibule and chandelier.

She had lost all track of time when a delicate chiming sound resonated through the manor, startling her out of her research. Avery's graduate degree in cultural anthropology with an emphasis on gemology fed her fascination with the history of the artifacts she was fortunate enough to be working with, and she'd fallen down a rabbit hole on a website detailing the sculptor's thought process when he'd decided on a pearl-inlaid collar around the hound's neck. She glanced up from her computer. Micah sat on the floor, examining the base of the pedestal.

"What was that? It didn't sound like the doorbell," Avery said.

"I don't know. It came from the intercom system." He pointed to the hallway wall above them, toward Duke Pennington's office.

As he pointed, the two little girls Avery'd seen the other day burst through the doorway of one of the bedrooms. The younger one, a tiny thing, squealed and slapped at her older sister. "Mummy! Lucy won't share!"

Lucy—a girl of five at most—held a doll over her head and scrunched up her face. "Don't be a baby, Ava! Mummy! Make her stop!"

The tall, thin woman who'd slammed the door on them as they passed by the other day stepped into the hallway. She scowled down at the girls. "You'll both stop, or I'll tell your father." She plucked the doll from Lucy's outstretched hand. "Go find Nanny Gretchen. I've had it. Now!"

Without another word, the girls linked hands and ran past Avery and Micah and down the stairs. The woman followed and paused when she reached their setup near the statue.

"You're the appraisers, I take it?" She looked down at them.

"Yes, I'm Avery and—"

The woman cut her off. "My husband said we're having guests for dinner. It's in half an hour. In case you want to . . . clean up." Her disdainful glance was easy to read—Avery imagined she was taking in the bit of clutter they'd created, the fifty-something-year-old man sitting on the floor, Avery's ponytail and complete lack of adornment in stark contrast to her own gorgeous black ensemble. She must be Nico's wife. Percy seemed too young to be married with children, though—being in his early twenties—he wasn't, of course. But Avery couldn't fathom the cocky, exuberant young man from the other day being paired with this woman.

"Thank you. We wondered what those bells meant," Avery replied. They watched the woman continue down the hallway. She turned at the stairs but went up rather than down.

"Chilly," Micah murmured.

She laughed. "You're always so kind. That lady is . . ." She couldn't think of any word she could use to describe the duke's daughter-in-law, not out here in the open where any-one could overhear. "Chilly, I guess. Not a happy camper," she said, matching Micah's quiet tone. Her phone buzzed beside her, and she grabbed it. "Tilly!"

"How is she? Let me say hello," Micah said.

"It's just a text. You'll see her. She's coming with Aunt Midge for dinner." Tilly and Micah's son Noah had dated until Tilly left for London. They'd all grown even closer this past summer, reunited with William and with Micah's son being around more to help during his father's recovery after he'd been shot. "Tilly's just letting us know they'll be here in a few minutes. We should probably finish up for the afternoon."

On their way back down the hall to the lab, the caretaker woman from the other day rushed through a double swinging door off an adjacent hallway. Beyond her, Avery caught a glimpse of the enormous kitchen. "Oh my, I'm so happy I caught you," Mrs. Hoffman said, drying her hands on her apron. "I believe there are six in your dinner party, is that right?"

"Yes, thank you. Something smells delicious!"

Mrs. Hoffman beamed. "It's Beef Wellington, Duke Pennington's favorite. We rarely have him here, so I took the opportunity to make it for all of you. With that and raspberry parfaits for dessert, it will be divine, I promise!"

"Wonderful! We can't wai—" Avery broke off as a piercing shriek came from somewhere outside. She sucked in her breath, staring wide-eyed at Mrs. Hoffman and then Micah. A clamor of footsteps came from the vestibule behind them. Duke Pennington ran past them toward the front door, and Avery and Micah followed.

Outside on the expanse of gray stamped concrete that ran between the house and the lily pond, a little group was already huddled in a circle. Avery spied Aunt Midge's powder-blue classic T-Bird coming up the drive. Whatever had just happened, she had a feeling Tilly shouldn't see it. She began to move toward the group but hesitated, letting Micah go ahead of her. She wasn't sure she was prepared to see what had happened either.

The duchess Mariah clapped both hands over her mouth, and Nick pulled her close, turning her toward him protectively. The groundskeeper, Gregory, knelt over a figure sprawled on the ground; Avery glimpsed one black-stocking-clad leg, the shoe missing. The younger man she'd seen in the horse paddock, the son, Bryan Wolf, came racing up to the group and stopped short, his face white, at the same time a door on the side of the manor swung open. Lord Nico came out.

"What's all the—" Nico stopped where he was. "Oh no."

Avery's father appeared at her side, Sir Robert behind him. "What happened? We thought we heard a scream." He closed the last few yards to the scene of the trauma, and Avery's feet moved against her will, following him.

The groundskeeper in the center of the group sat back and let out a painful wail. Avery's line of sight was suddenly clear. She gasped, her gut flipping over with a nauseating lurch. Suzanne's mangled, lifeless body lay broken and bleeding on the ground.

# Chapter Three

The sound of a car door slamming got Avery's attention. She jogged across the circular drive to Aunt Midge and Tilly. "Hey, Tilly. Hi, Auntie." She gave her aunt a quick hug. "Not a bad drive, right? What do you think?" She turned and made a sweeping motion in the air, encompassing the manor and grounds. Her voice sounded forced and fake-cheerful to her own ears.

Tilly spoke. "What are they doing over there?" She took a few steps toward the growing gathering on the south side of the manor.

"What's all the kerfuffle about?" Aunt Midge asked. She opened the trunk of the Thunderbird and began pulling out gift bags, hanging the first couple on her arm and then handing the others to Avery.

"It's, uh, an accident. Tilly, don't," Avery warned, shooting a glance at her sister. "It just happened, right as you were pulling in. The housekeeper—well, I don't actually know yet. She might have fallen from the roof." She tipped her head back, her gaze moving along the parapets three stories above poor Suzanne's body. Why would she even have been up there? How could she have simply fallen? Had she jumped?

"I see Daddy," Tilly said, and strode boldly away from Avery and Midge.

"Matilda Marie!" Aunt Midge's tone was sharp, leaving no room for argument.

Tilly slouched and huffed her breath out dramatically, but she turned around and came back over to them. "Oh my God! You two have to stop treating me like I'm a child."

Fortunately, William and Micah were headed toward them. Avery saw that the family's driver, Roderick, had joined the circle surrounding Suzanne, and now Lord Percy came down the front steps and trotted over to them. The crabby, chilly woman—Lord Nico's wife—stood on the top step. She remained where she was, arms folded over her chest. Nick's assistant, Mathew, brushed past her, his phone to his ear, likely calling an ambulance or the police, or both.

"Hi, honey," William greeted Tilly, hugging her around her shoulders. "Doing all right? How was the day?" His gaze went to his sister, as petite as William was tall.

Midge answered for Tilly. "Our day was lovely. We went for mani-pedis and took Halston to pick out a new toy. And we talked quite a bit." She closed the trunk and straightened her flowing lavender chiffon caftan over smart white cropped pants and top, the long hem fluttering about her bejeweled kitten heels. At sixty-one, she was as eclectically elegant as ever. "I'm thinking the duke may wish to reschedule, in light of this tragedy. If so, the least we can do is leave them with some treats—especially for Nick's granddaughters."

"That's a good thought, Auntie," Avery said. "It's awful. We'd chatted with the housekeeper a couple times. She seemed like a sweet person."

Micah spoke. "It's so sad. What a horrible accident. There's no surviving that kind of drop." He was studying the parapets along with Avery.

"I wonder . . ." William mused, not finishing the thought.

"Are you thinking what I'm thinking?" Avery asked. She lowered her voice, even though they were nowhere near the group of family and staff. "What if it wasn't an accident?"

Micah stared at them. "Do you think she was pushed? Why? By whom?"

"I have no idea. But you have to admit it's strange, right after the Petrova pocket watch going missing," she replied. "Nick's heading over here."

"Remind me to fill you in on what Sir Robert and I discovered in the library. It could be related," William murmured, as they moved to meet the duke in the center of the circle drive.

Nick held his arms wide, and Midge stepped into them. A hug and a kiss on both cheeks later, they stepped apart. Aunt Midge kept hold of his arms for a moment, looking up at him from her five-foot-one height. "Are you quite all right, my friend?" Her tone held deep concern as she searched his face.

He nodded. "I am, thank you. I'm in shock." He turned back toward his family and staff, who were milling about, talking, and pointing upward toward the parapets. "I think we all are. My housekeeper Suzanne appears to have fallen to her death not twenty minutes ago. We heard her scream.

I—I'm so sorry you had to see her that way," he said, his gaze moving to Avery, William, and Micah.

"Don't apologize," Avery said. "It is shocking. I mean, why was she up there? Does anyone know?"

"No. I can hardly fathom all of this. She was such a kind young woman." Sirens sounded in the distance, approaching quickly. "Oh, that's a relief. Maybe the police will get to the bottom of this."

"Nick," Midge said, "I'll call you and we'll reschedule dinner. I believe you're going to be tied up for a while. We brought some little gifts for the girls and your family. I'll leave them in your foyer, and we'll get out of your way."

"You could never be in the way," he replied. "The timing is a shame. And my goodness, forgive my manners," he said, as if suddenly realizing Tilly was with them. "You're Midge's niece Tilly, aren't you? Happy to be on school holiday for a bit now?"

"Yes, sir, thank you," Tilly answered, suddenly still and quiet.

"I promise we'll make a second attempt at this soon, Tilly, before you head back to London. Oh my, here they are," he said as two police cars and an ambulance came through the gated entrance.

While the duke showed the authorities to Suzanne's body, Avery led the way to the manor entrance so they could leave the gifts. On the wide top step, Nico's wife cleared her throat. "Excuse me. What are you doing?"

Avery smiled sweetly at her. "This is my aunt Midge, a close friend of the duke's. She's just leaving the gifts she brought since dinner's canceled. Midge, this is—I'm sorry," she interrupted herself, gaze moving back to the woman. "I don't believe we've formally met."

"Lady Annabelle. I'm Lord Nico Pennington's wife." She exchanged a glance with Midge. "It's lovely to meet you. You may put those on the bench inside the door." She stepped aside.

While Avery and Micah set their packages inside, Midge handed two glittery polka-dot gift bags directly to the woman. "It's terrific to finally meet you, Lady Annabelle. I've not met your daughters, but Duke Pennington speaks about them constantly. I do hope they enjoy these. I'm very sorry for your family's loss."

"Thank you. We're fine. It doesn't affect our family; she was the housekeeper."

Avery bit her lip, her eyes wide. Holy cow, that wasn't just chilly, it was brutal. She headed down the steps without another word to the woman, Tilly following. She stopped at her father's car, looking back at Aunt Midge, who was still engaged in conversation with Lady Annabelle. How could she stomach it?

"Dang," Tilly whispered to her. "Harsh."

"Seriously." She pulled open the driver's side door.

"I'm afraid I can't let you leave." A deep voice came from behind Avery, startling her. She spun around to find one of the officers looking sternly at her. Behind him, an unmarked car rolled up and parked with the police cruisers.

William spoke up. "Officer, we're outside contractors. We've only just started working for the Penningtons today."

"Which reinforces why you can't go yet. Nobody leaves the property until we've gotten everyone's contact information and taken statements." He turned to include Aunt Midge as she joined them. "We'll start with what time you each arrived today and go from there."

After Avery gave her statement and details, she peered over at the flurry of activity around Suzanne's body. The clusters of family and staff had spread out, giving the newly arrived forensics team space to photograph and document the grisly scene on the concrete. Uniformed officers were speaking separately with each person and taking notes. A man and woman in dark suits—detectives, she assumed—had exited the unmarked car and were conferencing with their heads close together while gazing up at the roof. As Avery watched, the duke joined them, and then he and one detective went indoors. Within minutes, she spotted them on the roof. The detective held a tape measure up to a parapet, which appeared to be a few feet taller than the short skirting wall that made up the perimeter.

Avery drifted over to William, who was talking quietly with Micah. "Dad. While we're waiting, what did you find in the library?" She kept her voice low. Aunt Midge and Tilly were speaking with the officer at the moment.

Her father matched her tone. "Nick's inventory shows a set of French empire nineteenth-century gilded bronze candlesticks that should be displayed on the mantel over the fireplace. But that's not what we found. I'm sure it's possible they were moved to a different room, but the candlesticks there now are very close in appearance to the French set, though obviously much newer. It's a little odd."

She frowned. "That is strange. We'll have to ask him about that. If the French empire set was replaced for some reason, I'd assume Nick would've removed it from the list."

"Right, that was my thought too."

The other detective joined Avery and William, holding his badge out for them to check. Micah, Aunt Midge, and Tilly moved closer to hear what he had to say. Sir Robert seemed to have made friends with Lord Nico; they'd been chatting animatedly for a while now.

The detective pulled business cards from his pocket and passed them out. "I'm Detective Carter. I need to ask you folks not to leave the state for the next forty-eight to seventy-two hours, until we have the autopsy report back. It's a formality, no worries," he added, meeting Tilly's gaze. "It doesn't mean any of you are in trouble."

"Does this mean Suzanne didn't fall? It wasn't an accident?" Avery asked. "How will you be able to tell?"

Detective Carter registered surprise. "I'm, uh, I can't discuss details of the case, ma'am. One other thing. Duke Pennington mentioned in his statement that your team is scheduled to do antique appraisals on-site for the next week or two?"

"That's right," William answered.

"You'll want to discuss this with your employer, but I'd suggest postponing your assignment until we know what happened here."

"Oh." Avery's gaze moved from Micah to her father.

"With the recent theft and now Ms. Vick's unexplained death, I assume you wouldn't want your team in peril." He

45

paused, making eye contact with each of them as he made sure his point was received. "I'll be in touch."

Avery shuddered as they watched him head back to his partner, now standing beside Suzanne's sheet-covered body and aiming a red laser pointer up at the roof. "I'm done. It's been a long day," she said. "Are we ready? I'm starving and exhausted. We all probably are."

They left in a caravan together, William driving Avery and Tilly, followed by Midge, who was heading back to Manhattan, and Micah and Sir Robert last. Micah had to tear Sir Robert away from his new friend Lord Nico, as he was as hungry and exhausted as Avery and ready to leave.

In the car on the way home, Tilly leaned forward and tapped Avery's shoulder. "So are you going to listen to that detective and cancel the job?"

Avery turned sideways in the passenger seat to look back at her. "Not cancel. But . . . we've agreed we all need a good night's sleep before we decide to postpone. I hate to slow down our momentum, and Dad has already made an intriguing find. Around the end of the eighteenth century—"

Tilly's yawn reminded Avery that her younger sister had just traveled all the way from Europe the day before. She'd also never found the family profession even the slightest bit interesting. Avery couldn't really blame her. Tilly was an amazing singer, knew every single word to every single Broadway musical from the last three decades, and was brave enough to go to college across the ocean. She was on her own path. Their mom would've loved to see how Tilly had grown up in the last year and a half.

"Hey." Avery changed the subject. She softened her tone and tried to sound casual. "How are things going at school, really? Not your grades or getting through the work. But being there. I don't know if I've ever said it, but you're way braver than I was at your age. I never could have gone that far away from home."

Tilly turned and looked out the window. Her profile belonged on a nineteenth-century cameo pin—the small, slightly upturned Ayers nose, strong jawline, stubborn chin, curling tendrils cascading down her neck. She abruptly covered her eyes with one hand and dropped her chin to her chest, arms drawn tightly in around herself.

Avery didn't know what to say. She'd pushed too hard. She glanced briefly at her dad. He made no comment, but his focus was pulled between the rearview mirror and the road ahead. They'd planned to talk about this after work today, but no one could have anticipated being held up all evening due to a crime scene investigation. She should have waited until Tilly was ready to share whatever had happened. She reached into the back seat and squeezed her sister's knee. "Tilly."

The girl shook her head, silent. Her breathing sounded rough, like she might be crying.

"Listen," Avery said, her heart aching for her distraught sister. "I love you. We all do. You're flipping amazing, Tilly, with your elephant-sized heart and your constant positivity. You're impossible not to love. Nothing that's happened, nothing you might have done, can change that."

William chimed in. "Very true."

Tilly sniffled. She didn't move.

Avery let it go. They drove in silence almost the rest of the way home, but it was better somehow, not as heavy now. They were on their way through Lilac Grove, their little town twinkling with white fairy lights in the trees up and down Main Street, when Tilly spoke again.

"Remember you said that."

"What?" Startled, Avery glanced back at Tilly. She'd been lost in thought, as she'd noticed the lights were still on at Mixed Bag, her friend Rachel's vintage secondhand shop. Most of Lilac Grove's stores, especially the little boutique shops along Main Street, closed early on weeknights, but sidewalk sales were starting this week. Rachel was probably busily preparing. Avery tried to keep an eye on the items that came through her friend's store. Now and then she did get a bit of genuine treasure in the form of an antique flatware set or a nice piece of jewelry worth more than she'd realized. Rachel had asked Avery days ago to take a look at a fancy hair adornment she'd stumbled across at an estate sale. Avery would have to stop by tomorrow after her run.

Now Avery replayed in her head what she'd said to her sister, spooked at Tilly's quiet words. How could whatever had driven Tilly to fly home early leave her worried that it'd actually change how her family felt about her? That was crazy.

Tilly sighed. "I can't fix any of it."

William turned onto their road. "That's okay. It's all going to be okay," he said, his tone reassuring. "We'll sit down and figure it all out. You don't have to deal with whatever's happened alone, I promise, Lamb."

A thought occurred to Avery. It couldn't be something as simple as Tilly and Noah calling it quits on their long-distance relationship, could it? They were both so young. As much as the whole family loved Micah's son, Avery didn't think anyone expected them to stay together long-term. She sneaked a sideways look at her sister. "You're sure this has nothing to do with Noah?"

"Stop it, A!" Tilly's outburst broke the quiet calm in the dark car. "Noah's mad at me. Okay? Is that what you want to hear? It doesn't matter what I say; he won't even speak to me. But that is *not* why I pissed you and Dad off by coming home early—jeez, give me a little credit. You think I'd miss classes and spend hundreds of dollars of my babysitting money because of a boy? Do you even know me?"

Avery gritted her teeth so hard she winced as a stab of pain shot across her jaw. Orange sherbet. Oreo. Cookie dough. Cherry chocolate chip. She was several flavors in before she realized she wasn't angry; her cheeks were burning because she was embarrassed. Last year, Dr. Singh had helped her come up with ways to defuse her often intense flares of anger. Reciting as many ice cream flavors as she could think of—with no repeats—had become an effective way of redirecting her attention until she was able to calm down. But it wasn't helping now. Because Tilly's words were spot-on. Avery felt rightfully chastised. William pulled into their long driveway, and she willed him to slow the car's progress toward the house even more. She knew the moment the car was in park, her sister would bolt.

"I'm sorry." She turned and met Tilly's gaze. "I'm really sorry. You're right. I wasn't thinking."

"Whatever." Tilly had a hand on the door handle. The car rolled to a stop in front of the garage, and her sister was gone, fleeing into the house. Through the open front door, an excited Halston bounded up the stairs alongside her. Their family dog was just thrilled his girl was home, no questions asked.

A little before midnight, Avery closed her laptop and turned on the TV. She was on her third time around watching *Sherlock*. Tilly had gotten her hooked. She shifted positions and pulled a throw blanket over her legs. William came in from the adjacent kitchen, taking the other end of the couch and handing her a glass of skim milk.

"Ah," she said, smiling. "Thank you. Perfect."

"Sorry, I don't mean to interrupt your date with Cumberbatch." He tipped his head toward the actor on the screen. "Just wondered if you're leaning a particular way regarding the Pennington assignment."

"I'm torn. I'm already invested and I want to keep going. But I don't want to put any of us in danger."

"Exactly how I feel," he said.

"But I also want to get some concrete answers for Nick. I like him. He's the most down-to-earth member of his family, from what I've seen so far. There's something funny going on there, Dad, I can feel it. What's with the duke's daughter-in-law and her attitude? She's the one who slammed the door on Suzanne as we passed her room that first day we were there. I've had a few more run-ins with her, and she's got to be the most unpleasant person I've met in a long time. Like, to an extreme."

William shrugged. "Not everyone is a ray of sunshine."

"It's more than that. We heard the scream clear as day from inside the house, so I'm sure everyone must have. Why did it take so long for some of the family and staff to even come find out what had happened? The duke and his wife were out there right away, like us. I think the police need to look at whoever was the last person to show up. The person who pushed her would have had to rush down two flights of stairs without being seen and then casually walk outside, right?"

"We can't assume she was pushed. They haven't confirmed that yet. We don't know anything about the girl," he said. "Including her frame of mind or why she was up there in the first place."

"You're right," she said. "I'm just saying, you'd have to go to a lot of effort in order to fall from that roof."

William chuckled. "That's probably true."

Avery went on. "I also wonder if the groundskeeper guy was dating Suzanne. I felt terrible for him. He was beside himself. At least somebody cared that she died. I still can't get over Lord Nico's wife, Annabelle. She actually said Suzanne dying didn't affect them because she was just staff."

His eyes were wide. "Holy Christ. Midge told me about that too. I thought she was exaggerating. She had quite a long conversation with Lady Annabelle. Ask her to fill you in."

"I will," Avery agreed. "I think we'll be okay. We'll make a rule that we never work alone. And we'll keep notes on any other strange occurrences and let that detective know about them. And if any of us starts to feel unsafe, we call the whole thing off, okay?"

"I'm good with that," her dad said. "Wait until morning to get Micah's vote. I'm beat; I'm going to bed. Don't stay up too late, Roo."

She reached over and hugged him before he left. Sometimes she could still hardly believe he was back. She welcomed the use of his pet name for her, a nod to her record-breaking long jump in high school. She was more into running now than leaping, but she hoped he never stopped using the nickname.

With her dad gone, she took over the couch, and she must have fallen asleep; she woke to Sherlock Holmes and Watson bickering loudly. Her phone was buzzing on the coffee table beside her. She grabbed it, seeing it was a text message from this afternoon that had only just now come through, probably due to their patchy service out at the manor. She sat up, rubbing her eyes, and read the message:

*Friday seems too far away. I'll pick you up at six if that works for you. Let me know. Miss you, can't wait to see you.*

Hank had added the heart-eyes emoji at the end, making her smile. They hadn't dated in several months, but when he'd asked her out after bumping into her in town a couple weeks ago, Avery had surprised herself by saying yes. Maybe things would go differently this time around. She'd been the cause of their breakup, but she was doing better now. She started to text him back and then realized it was one in the morning. He was probably still in bed each night by ten. She would have to answer him tomorrow.

# Chapter Four

Tuesday morning, Avery cupped her hands around her face against the glass storefront of Mixed Bag. The shop wouldn't open for an hour yet, but the lights were on. She knocked on the window. In a moment, Rachel came out of the storage room carrying a stack of boxes. Her red hair was wrangled into messy twin buns above her ears. She wore big gold hoop earrings and a patchwork dress with her standard shopkeeper's apron tied around her waist. She rushed over to unlock the door, holding it open for Avery. "Hey, lady! Uh, I was about to hug you, but maybe I won't," Rachel said, grinning. "You're a little sweaty."

Avery laughed. "I don't blame you. That's what happens after six miles; I'm more than a little sweaty. I'm heading home and thought I'd stop by."

"Well," her friend said, standing back with her hands on her generously curved hips. "It looks good on you. You're kind of glowing. Less than two weeks left until the marathon, right? Are you ready?"

"That's the question. I hope so. My dad and I had hoped to do it together last year, but . . . that didn't work out so well. And then even once we had him back, I think he was still shell-shocked—losing my mom, being placed in witness protection, everything. So I'm running for both of us," she finished.

"That's awesome. I'm sure it means a lot to him."

"I think it does. So are you ready for the big sidewalk sale? You look super cute today, by the way," Avery said. "Love the buns!"

Rachel patted her hair. "Thank you! Oh! Do you want to see that hair clip? I almost forgot." She retrieved it from the storage room, rushing back out and placing it in Avery's open palm.

It was vintage, of that Avery was certain. But the fact that it was older than she was didn't mean it was an antique. She turned toward the front window where the sunlight streamed in, peering closely at the clasp and then the outer oval of purplish blue, pink, and green gemstones that surrounded an intricate center pattern with more jewels. The hair adornment was similar in design to ones she'd certified but was likely a well-done piece of costume jewelry. She didn't want to let Rachel down without being certain. "It's lovely. I can't quite place the era or culture." She set the hair clip down and took a few photos with her phone to capture the design so she could research it later. "Let me look into it. I'll bring my kit when I come back. We just started a new job, and I'm not sure yet about the hours, but I'll let you know as soon as I can."

"Perfect, no rush. And make sure you invoice me for your time."

"Um, no. We're not doing that. It's no big deal. Besides, I know for a fact you way undercharged me for that 1920s-era gown I wore to the MOA gala."

Rachel smiled, looking upward dreamily. "That gown. That was one of the most gorgeous vintage pieces to pass through my shop. The cut, the delicate spaghetti straps—that fabric was like liquid silk. You must've been on fire in that dress!"

Avery smiled, remembering. "It did get quite a reaction from my date. And some snark from Tilly."

"Give that girl a hug for me. All right, if I can't pay you, then we've got to have a wine night and catch up."

"Deal. Gotta run!" Avery kissed her on the cheek. She took the last mile home at a slower pace, a cooldown, as she'd already interrupted her run at Mixed Bag. She'd been doing around forty to fifty miles per week for the last two months. Today marked the beginning of her taper. By cutting back on miles in the two weeks before the race, she'd allow for more oxygen-rich muscle recovery, which could improve her marathon finish time by three to six percent. Avery had started running track in school, and then on her own as a way to clear her head, and it still worked. Her time spent outdoors, soles hitting the pavement, the in-and-out *whoosh* of fresh air expanding her chest, her own heartbeat strong and steady in her ears, was as vital to her mental health as the sessions with Dr. Singh.

Her father was waiting with Halston on the front porch as she came up the steps. He handed her a tall, frosty glass. "It's your standard recipe—two scoops of protein powder, skim milk, ice, peanut butter—and I added a banana. You need to replace the potassium you're burning off."

"Thanks!" She took a sip and wrinkled her nose. "I'll never learn to like bananas. Are you ready to go? I just need twenty minutes." She went inside and held the door for him.

"Sounds good. Come on, boy," he called, and the Afghan hound came running from across the yard, shiny black fur rippling. They were fortunate Aunt Midge had decided Halston was happier in the country. Avery couldn't imagine not having him here. And if he hadn't been here last spring, she might very well be dead now—he'd truly saved her life.

"We are going, right? What are we doing with Tilly?" Avery lowered her voice.

"I've been thinking about that," William said. "I checked in with Micah to get his take on postponing the Pennington job. As long as we're working in teams, we should be fine there. But Midge had an appointment she couldn't miss today, and I'm not sure your sister should be home alone."

Tilly poked her head around the wall on the upstairs landing. "Why shouldn't I be alone?"

They stared up at her. "Why are you sneaking around, eavesdropping?" Avery accused.

"I wouldn't have to if people would stop talking about me behind my back," Tilly retorted.

William sighed. "I'm concerned about your frame of mind. You've been less than forthcoming about what happened at school." He paused as if debating. "I got a call from Professor Florescu this morning."

The color drained from Tilly's cheeks. "Oh."

"Mm-hmm." William hadn't taken his gaze from her. "It was a voice mail asking me to contact her. Would you like to clue me in on what she's going to say?"

Tilly opened her mouth, as if about to speak, but then closed it. She looked down and kicked at the carpeting with one toe.

"Whatever it is, I doubt it's as bad as you fear, Lamb."

Tilly turned and fled up the stairs. In the foyer, Avery and her father jumped as the bedroom door slammed shut loudly. She raised her eyebrows at William. "Why is the dean of students calling you all the way from London? You really have no idea?"

"I wish I did." He ran a hand through his thick hair. It was a few shades darker than Tilly's but still blond, almost no gray. "I've got to deal with this. I'm sorry, honey, but would you mind going without me? Micah can be there by ten thirty."

"Should I stay home too?" She'd been racking her brain, but short of Tilly getting kicked out or telling them she was eloping, there was no reason for her secrecy and drama.

"No, don't do that. Go to work." He put a hand on her arm, giving it a light squeeze. "You've done enough impromptu parenting in the last year. I'll handle it. We'll have things all sorted out by the time you get home tonight."

* * *

Avery and Micah spent the first part of the day in Pennington Manor's library. Her father and Sir Robert were right: the nineteenth-century bronze French empire candlesticks listed in the inventory were not in their rightful spot over the fireplace. The pair there now were probably worth about sixty dollars.

Avery turned them upside down, searching for the hallmark. Micah peered over her shoulder. "Find it?"

She shook her head. "Nothing. Not surprising. They're too light." The lack of substantial weight in her hand was one giveaway. These were probably made of brass, a metal much less dense than bronze. "When did France begin requiring the hallmark on metalwork pieces?" she asked.

Micah was their resident historian. "King Philip III decreed that all silver pieces must bear the mark beginning in the thirteenth century. It was extended to gold and other metals in the 1700s. Depending on exact province, the French hallmark from the eighteen and nineteenth centuries would consist of the standard, stamped fleur-de-lis and year of creation. Some makers would add their own designation, but at minimum we'd expect to find the standard mark of the French empire." He picked up the iPad and scrutinized the listing again. "These are described as gilt bronze Napoleonic era items; by then, the hallmark was being widely used."

"So we need to ask Nick about the knockoffs," Avery said, placing the candlesticks back where they were. "I wonder—" She stopped abruptly as her phone buzzed in her pocket. She grabbed it. She'd been thinking about her sister all day, hoping things had gone all right between Tilly and their dad. But her caller ID displayed only *Out of Area*.

"Hello?"

Art's deep voice came through, warming her instantly. "Avery. Tell me you're not at Pennington on the Hudson."

"Um." She put the phone on speaker so Micah could hear. "What would be wrong with me being at Pennington Manor, Art?"

He groaned. "So that is the duke you went to meet the other day. You're there now?"

"I'm here with Micah. We're working. Why, what's wrong? And how did you know?"

"Am I on speaker?" Art asked.

Micah began to step away, but Avery held on to his arm. *Stay*, she mouthed. She hit the button, taking Art off speaker, and put the phone to her ear. "Not anymore. Why are you acting so odd?"

"I have reason to believe you could be in danger," he said. "And I don't know who else is in earshot besides Micah. You shouldn't be there while there's an active murder investigation going on."

She clamped a hand over her mouth, eyes wide. So they were treating Suzanne's death as a murder! She squeezed Micah's arm, and he put his head near hers, listening in.

"We met for October coffee club just now, and one of the guys is a Westchester County detective. He's working a murder angle on a jumper case that he said was at a royal family's mansion on the Hudson. I checked. There's only one."

She frowned, trying to dissect everything he'd said.

"Avery? Did I lose you?" Art asked.

She had to ask. There was no way she couldn't. "You have an October coffee club? What is that, like, a club that meets once a year for coffee?"

"What?" He sounded bewildered. "No, we meet at different places each month for a coffee date. Did you hear the rest of what I said?"

"Yes, but wait. So, you and a bunch of police friends have a club. Where you get together and choose a different coffee house each month for a coffee date and a chat? I love that! How many of you are there? Do you do other things together, like golf or anything?"

"What?" he asked again. "Avery—you're missing my point. You and Micah need to leave. My buddy is still working the evidence, and if the jumper was actually pushed, there could be a killer in that house with you."

She shuddered. "Her name was Suzanne, just so you know. So you don't have to call her *the jumper.*"

"Sorry. Listen, I'm serious. Can you pack it up and take a few days off, until Carter gets the pathology report back?" He wasn't exactly asking her; she could hear it in his strained tone.

"Do you really think that's necessary? Your friend isn't sure yet what happened. And it's not like I'm here alone. Micah's with me. It's super quiet today. So far, we've only seen the caretaker woman. I can't really imagine anyone we've met so far being a murderer." Mega-crab Lady Annabelle popped into her head. Being an angry, classist jerk didn't make someone a murderer, though.

Art exhaled loudly in frustration. His forcefully controlled calm came through in his next words. "Please. I'm asking you to be smart and careful. Fill Micah in, talk to your duke, and get out of there, Avery. I'll be too worried about you if you don't."

She smiled into the phone. "Okay. I promise we'll talk it over." He was silent on his end. Avery knew it wasn't the answer he wanted, but she agreed with her team; they'd be fine working together. She wasn't about to leave unless Micah wanted to. "Thank you for looking out for us."

"Let me know when you're out of there," he said, not giving an inch.

"I'll see you Saturday," she replied, holding her ground.

More silence. Then, "I can't wait to see you." His voice was gentler, the gruff edge gone.

When they'd hung up, she dropped the phone back into her bag and sighed, looking at Micah. "He's concerned," she said. They began carrying their equipment to the other side of the room, where a trio of Renaissance paintings waited for appraisal.

"He sure cares about you," Micah said.

"I know he does. It's just really hard to have a relationship with someone who's so closed off. I needed him to share with me. To let me in. Like that coffee club thing. We dated for two months, and he never mentioned that he has this whole network of colleagues or friends that he meets and bonds with every month. I love knowing that about him."

Micah frowned, deep in thought. "I'm not sure he's entirely to blame for that. It's instilled in boys from a young age that we're supposed to be tough, silent, independent, especially around the opposite sex or those we're attracted to. Then add in being a law enforcement officer, a profession that literally hinges on your detective protecting sensitive information. Keeping things to himself may simply be his default setting."

Avery stared at him. "I never thought of that."

"He was able to clear that hurdle just now," Micah said, "when it meant sharing information in order to keep you safe. Though I'm sure you're right that he has some issues to overcome."

"Well, we all do. I'm not perfect either. I just—I needed more of him. I'm not a suspect or the enemy, and I don't care about stereotypical male archetypes. I don't see how we can be close if he doesn't open up to me."

"Fair enough," Micah said. "I suppose all you can do is tell him that, which you've done."

Avery took another look at the mantel as she grabbed the case for her handheld loupe. "Oh! That's what I was going to say about those candlesticks. My friend Rachel has this jeweled hairpin I'm going to value for her. She happened upon it almost too easily at an estate sale. It might turn out to be nothing. It jogged my memory and made me think of that old practice of wearing a cut-glass diamond ring or a fake fur or—you get the point—out of fear of the real one being lost or stolen. People have been doing that for centuries."

"True," he agreed. "You think your friend's hairpin is a fake version of a more valuable one?"

"Could be. And maybe the duke has some of the manor's more valuable items put away, with dummy items on display instead? That'd explain the candlesticks."

"Ah," Micah said. "Don't you think he'd have remembered, though, and either told us or had the genuine items brought back out? Since we're here to appraise?"

"Yes," Avery admitted. "You're right. Unless . . . well, what if Duchess Mariah or even the duke's mother did it?"

Micah looked skeptical. "And there's a treasure room full of the real heirlooms?"

She pursed her lips. "No. Probably not. We need to talk to Nick about the candlesticks."

They worked in silence for a while. There were no surprises with the trio of paintings. Their authentication and appraisal proved the provenances were up to date and genuine, as was the artwork itself, the set valued at roughly $61,000. Avery and Micah were on their way toward the vestibule so they could work in the parlor next when the doorbell rang.

Mrs. Hoffman appeared in the long hallway ahead of them as if from nowhere. She registered surprise at seeing them a few yards away. "Oh!" She paused, smiling at them. "I was about to come hunt you two down for lunch. You must be starving. One moment, and I'll show you to the dining room." She continued on toward the entryway.

Avery reached the spot where the housekeeper had materialized. She stared wide-eyed at the floral wallpaper, which looked seamless. "Where'd she come from?" she asked Micah, who was standing behind her, a matching dumbfounded look on his face.

She touched the wall, running a hand across the design, and sucked in her breath as her fingers caught on something. She leaned in, peering at it. A small navy-and-rose-toned latch was recessed in the wall, no larger than her thumb, nearly invisible against the matching wallpaper. Avery pressed down on it and put her palm flat on the wall above the ring and pushed.

A hidden door swung easily open, away from them, revealing a staircase. She poked her head inside and saw that the steps went both up and also down to the floor below them. "What in the world?" she whispered. Her heart raced wildly in her chest. This was like something out of the Nancy Drew novels she'd devoured as a young girl. Footsteps echoed from somewhere above, and she stepped back, bumping into Micah and nearly knocking him down. The door snapped noiselessly shut.

"Isn't it neat?" Mrs. Hoffman spoke from the vestibule at the end of the hall. She was watching them, hands on her hips. "Lords Nico and Percy always had so much fun as boys, sneaking through the manor by way of the hidden passages. They do certainly provide nice shortcuts when needed."

"That is so incredibly cool," Avery said, awestruck. "Wow. There are more? How many? Where do they—?" Behind Mrs. Hoffman, Detective Art Smith stepped into view.

He winked at her, the corner of his mouth rising almost imperceptibly. And then Lynn Hoffman turned and looked up at him. "I'm sorry, sir. I got a bit sidetracked." She held out her hand toward Avery and Micah. "You've found your colleagues."

"Thank you, ma'am." He lifted a black case in his hand, addressing Avery. "I brought that equipment you forgot."

"You, uh," Avery said, trying to keep up. "Yes, perfect." She and Micah joined Art and the woman in the entryway. She took the case from him, nearly flinging it across the marble floor because it was so light. He'd brought an empty case as his disguise, pretending to be a coworker in the appraisal business. Art had to have come straight from the Springfield County Sheriff's building—or his coffee club. To protect her.

"Your timing couldn't be better, Mr. Smith," Lynn Hoffman told him. "Lunch is ready now, and there's plenty. Would you all please follow me?"

Avery let the woman get enough ahead of them. She glanced up at Art as they walked. She tried and failed to temper her smile. "Hi."

"Hi there."

"What the heck?" She kept her voice to a whisper. "You're not our colleague. And you look like a detective. I don't know if it's your suit or just you."

He tipped his head closer to hers, and she caught the faintest hint of a clean scent, the soap and shampoo he used. Art never wore cologne but always smelled amazing. "Micah always wears suits. What's wrong with mine?"

She gave him an appraising, head-to-toe look. "Yours screams law enforcement officer with an agenda. Micah's screams middle-aged antiques appraiser with retro taste."

"I heard that," Micah tossed over his shoulder. "I have no wardrobe regrets."

"Avery," Art murmured. "If you're staying, then so am I."

A little shiver spiraled up her spine. "How? You have a job."

"I haven't used a sick day in two years." He held the door for Avery and Micah to enter the dining room first and then followed. "Everything looks delicious. Thank you," he told Mrs. Hoffman.

Their trio was seated at one end of a long, polished table. Lunch consisted of soup and sandwiches, with three types of tiny, individual fruit pies on a large round crystal platter. The moment Mrs. Hoffman left them, Avery spoke.

"Art, you're so sweet to worry, but we're fine here."

"You have no way of knowing that."

"He's not wrong," Micah said, adding his two cents. "Detective, what makes your friend think Suzanne's death wasn't a suicide?"

"I'm not able to discuss the case while Detective Carter is still investigating. But he expects to have some answers soon."

"Does he have any idea who—" At that moment, the doors swung open and Nick entered.

"Good afternoon! I was hoping to catch you," he said, pausing as he noticed the newcomer.

Art stood. "Duke Pennington, I'm Art Smith." Art lowered his voice and stepped a bit closer to Nick as the two men shook hands. "I'm a detective with Springfield County and a friend of Avery's. The detective working your case is a colleague. I hope you won't mind me being here while Detective Carter determines whether your housekeeper's death was accidental or otherwise. It's probably best if the rest of your house assumes I'm with the appraisal company."

Nick's expression registered surprise. "Quite right; that makes sense. You may inadvertently come across something helpful if no one is guarded. I'd appreciate any type of police presence, believe me. I'm quite glad you're here. Let me know if there's anything you require. Detective Carter's team was here into the night yesterday, but I haven't heard yet if they'll be back."

"That'll depend on the findings," Art said. "I'm sure you'll have some answers in a day or two. He mentioned something about a theft, too? You aren't sure if the two things are related?"

"Let's sit. There's no point in letting our soup go cold," the duke said. Mrs. Hoffman came back in, carrying a teapot. Nick waited until she'd arranged it with the cups and sugar cubes on the sideboard and exited before resuming speaking. "A valuable item that's been in my family for generations has gone missing, and I haven't the faintest idea of when it happened. Detective Carter's team went over the locked glass case it was in. I don't think they were able to capture any fingerprints besides mine. I can't fathom how the theft could be related to poor Suzanne's death."

"It may not be," Art agreed.

Avery spoke, spoon poised midair over her bowl. The soup was delicious. "Nick, this may sound like a strange question. You have so many beautiful and valuable pieces in the manor. We've learned in our profession that sometimes people choose to have an authentic-looking copy of a highly valued item made for display while keeping the genuine artifact under lock and key. Is that something you or perhaps your mother might have done in the past?"

"It would have been prudent to have such a practice," he lamented. "I've always felt that we should enjoy and appreciate our collection. My mother was of the same mind. Each item invokes memories and family history. But if I'd been more conservative and kept the most valuable heirlooms out of sight, I'd likely still have the Petrova pocket watch."

"Well, to be fair, the Petrova truly was under lock and key," Avery said. "That should have been enough. The French empire candlesticks on the mantel in your library . . . there's no chance they're in storage or something? Maybe as a precaution?"

The duke met Avery's gaze, his eyes wide. "No. Don't tell me they've disappeared too!"

"I'm sorry. They may have, though it's strange. There are candlesticks there, in their place, but not the ones listed in your inventory. The ones there now are brass rather than gilded bronze, with less metalworking detail and no hallmark. We estimate them to be five to ten years old and valued under a hundred dollars."

"Crimine." The duke put his spoon down and sat back in his chair. "What in God's name is going on here?"

Avery felt awful for him. "I don't know. Do you remember the last time you might have seen those candlesticks up close?"

"I'm in the library almost nightly," Nick said. "Would the change in candlesticks have been noticeable to me, though? I use the wingback chair near the window to read. I don't think we've ever lit a fire in that fireplace. I haven't been near the mantel."

"From across the room in your chair," Micah said, "I doubt I'd be able to see the difference. Not unless I knew to look for it."

Art spoke. "What else is missing? Besides the pocket watch and the candlesticks? Has anyone actually recently viewed or handled each of these pieces that Avery's team is appraising?"

"No," the duke said again. "But we can take care of that right now. This has gone far enough. I'll be flummoxed if I sit idly by while my family's valuable heirlooms are filched right under my nose. We should be able to check on each of the items today, if all we're doing is making certain they're all accounted for. If you have time for that," he added, looking from Avery to Micah.

"Absolutely," Avery said. "Yes. Oh, I hope nothing else is missing, Nick. I'm so sorry."

The duke patted her hand. "No need to be. If you weren't here doing your job, the manor might've been completely cleaned out."

If it hadn't been already. Avery stopped the thought before it turned into words. They'd already authenticated and appraised the Famke statue, the trio of Renaissance paintings, and the items her father and Sir Robert had handled yesterday. She hoped the remainder of the items matched their inventory listing perfectly.

"Duke," Art said. "One thought. I'm trying to figure why our thief went to the trouble of replacing your genuine candlesticks with cheap, similar-looking fakes but didn't make an effort to do the same with your pocket watch. The candlestick swap says the thief hoped the items wouldn't be missed. The pocket watch theft, even with the lazy effort of moving the other items on display about to cover the void, shows a carelessness. Or haste."

Avery watched him think. He truly loved this, puzzling out what might have happened. "So is it an escalation?" she asked. All three men at the table looked at her. She clarified. "In *Sherlock*, the clues get easier to decipher when the criminal becomes careless. Like, a case might start out slow and murky, and then the bad guy takes more and more risks, which eventually gets him caught. Maybe this all started with a relatively low-value item, like your candlesticks, which would have sold for a few thousand, but then progressed to something much bolder—your pocket watch, the last valuation being over a million. And culminating with Suzanne's murder." She frowned. "No, that doesn't make sense."

Art was nodding. "Only the last part doesn't make sense. Everything else you said is spot-on. I'm not convinced the missing items are related to Suzanne's death. But we'll know more soon." Conversation petered out as the group focused on finishing lunch.

Micah pushed his chair back. "Delicious. I've already seen so many unique, valuable antiques in the few rooms I've visited here. I'm dying to know that they're all genuine and safe. Whenever you're all ready," he added.

The duke stood, and Avery and her team followed. "I'd like to start with that painting of King Federico IV in the vestibule, if we could," Avery said. "We covered that piece in grad school. We only ever saw photos. I'd love a closer look." She didn't recall the portrait displaying him with such a prominent brow, but she might simply be misremembering. The duke already appeared stressed. Avery hoped they'd find that the candlesticks and pocket watch were the sum total of stolen pieces and the remainder of Nicholas Pennington's family heirlooms were intact and accounted for.

# Chapter Five

Avery was dismayed to learn she'd been right. The noble-looking man in the painting bore a striking resemblance to King Federico IV, but the tones were off and the brow was markedly different—at least to Avery's eye. Obviously no one in the manor had noticed the replacement. When she found a photo online, she was surprised she hadn't recalled more detail. The real King Federico IV was a fine-boned man with small features. When the artist, Philip St. James, had completed the painting in 1798, he'd received accolades for its uncanny likeness. The major features—the hair, the jewels, and the outfit—were almost identical to those in the online image. But the antique portrait hanging in Pennington Manor vestibule was of a man with a more prominent brow, a long nose, and a wider jawline. Avery didn't need to touch any of her equipment to see this was not King Federico IV.

She turned to Nick. "Does this painting look any different to you than it normally does?"

"I don't think so. To be honest, it's a fixture here—it's been in the same spot for decades. It was a gift from the artist to my mother's family. I'm told it was hung here just before St. James made a visit in the 1800s. You're certain this isn't the genuine King Federico IV piece?"

She showed him the photo online.

"I see," he said. The duke sighed heavily. "I'm stunned that someone would do this. We've always had impeccable staff here."

Avery exchanged a wordless glance with Micah and Art. The idea of the culprit being anyone other than staff seemed foreign but couldn't be ruled out. How did the duke know someone on his personal staff wasn't involved? Or even his family—though she couldn't think of a reason one of the duke's family members would steal items they'd likely end up sharing the profits from anyway. She wasn't about to say any of that aloud.

Duke Pennington checked the iPad screen and began moving toward the hallway to their left. "Let's be on with it. We might as well, ah, what's the phrase? Rip off the Band-Aid?"

Avery fell into step beside him. "Maybe the authorities will be able to recover the items. And your trio of Renaissance paintings in the library was untouched, I'm sure the majority of your collection will turn out to be fine." The words sounded false to her own ears. She was sure of nothing.

"It's not so much the value of the items. Of course, I don't appreciate being taken advantage of, and I know my sons and grandchildren would've enjoyed sharing the profits from whatever we were to liquidate. But it's the history, the sentimental value. My mother and her parents and even my great-grandparents all contributed to the items on display here. Many were generous gifts from dignitaries and allies of Valle Charme. It's quite disheartening." He turned and held the door open to the regal theater they'd passed on their first day here. "Well. Welcome to Pennington Cinema."

"What a fantastic idea," Avery said. "I love this. Has the manor always had its own theater, or did you renovate and add it?" The space was done in rich red and gold tones, with six tiered rows of seating and a full-size screen flanked by lush red curtains. The ornate wall sconce lighting, muted ceiling artwork in the style of Michelangelo, and an old-fashioned looking concession stand all made her feel as if she'd stepped into another world.

"The theater was added during the 1952 renovation." A voice came from behind them, and Avery spun around. The duke's assistant, Mathew, had noiselessly followed them in.

"Oh! I wonder, was that when the hidden staircases were added as well?"

Mathew registered surprise. "I'm not certain. Your Grace?" He directed the question to Duke Pennington.

"My great-great-great-grandfather had those incorporated into the blueprints when the manor was built in 1817. At the time, he was estranged from his parents, having set sail for the Americas against his father's wishes. It wasn't until much later that my family began summering here on holiday."

"Travel by ship was no picnic back then," Micah said. "Your ancestor must have been quite determined."

Nick nodded. "He was said to be so. He eventually reconciled with the family after his father passed. You know, I've never gotten a straight answer to the question of why he built the manor with the secret passages. Mathew, will you join us? We're itemizing the collection based on inventory. There's been a disturbing development—" He fell silent as Art interrupted him.

"Would you look at that! You even have an old-fashioned street vendor popcorn cart!" Art pointed to the vintage wheeled cart in the concession area.

Avery stared at him, wide-eyed. Did he realize he'd rudely interrupted the duke?

Mathew stepped closer to Duke Pennington. He kept his voice low, but Avery was mere feet away and heard every word. "We've got a problem with Percy."

Nick frowned at his assistant. "What is it this time? When will he grow up, for God's sake?"

When Mathew didn't reply, Avery turned her head just enough to get a glimpse of them in her peripheral vision. Mathew was staring right at her. She cleared her throat and casually moved farther away. She caught only fragments of what was said next.

". . . resisting arrest . . . released if . . ."

Oblivious, Micah spoke beside her. "I've never seen one of those in person before. I wonder what it's worth." He started to move toward the popcorn cart but stopped when he saw Avery wasn't following. "Want to check it out?"

She groaned inwardly. He'd talked over the rest of Nick and Mathew's discussion. "I think they go for around five hundred dollars," she told Micah, not budging.

"Apologies, friends," Duke Pennington said. "I have some business to attend to. Mathew, would you please let Roderick know we're going out?" Nick faced Avery's trio again. "I hope it's still possible for you to do the walk-through without me?"

"No problem," Micah replied.

Art glanced beyond Nick at the door Mathew had just exited through. He spoke quietly. "Duke. Er, Your Grace."

"Nick."

"Ah. All right. Nick, I can't stress this enough. I'd like any details about your case—missing items, fake replacements, anything regarding the death of Suzanne Vick, and the fact that I'm not an appraiser—to all stay strictly between the people in this room. Detective Carter and I getting to the bottom of what's happened depends upon that."

The duke returned Art's gaze, his expression solemn. "I understand. I don't—I'm sure none of my family or personal staff are involved, but I do agree with you. People talk. Oh." His eyes grew wider as Art's words sunk in. "I see. I was about to mention to my assistant what we've discovered today. I promise I won't, to anyone. Mum's the word."

"Thanks." His phone buzzed, and he stepped away to answer.

"We'll get through as many of the items as possible today," Avery said. "I hope everything's all right." Her mind was racing with possibilities about Percy. She followed Micah to the concession area.

He was examining one of several fine porcelain serving bowls that were apparently being used for popcorn during movie nights. He turned the bottom of the bowl toward her. "Look. I don't believe it's on the inventory, but these are genuine Willoughby Wades. The logo's done with embossed gold."

"Nice." Avery stood back, staring at the framed black-and-white movie poster in the center of the wall adjacent to display counter. The portrait lighting around the poster hinted at its prestige. "Micah, look at this. *The Arrest of a Pickpocket*," she read.

He read aloud from the brass plate beneath it: "*As Britain's first film and the world's first crime movie,* The Arrest of a Pickpocket *signifies the advent of cinema in 1895.*" He looked at Avery and then back at the poster.

"Amazing," she said. "Impressive."

"Ironic," Micah added.

She raised an eyebrow at him. "That's for sure." She slid a finger along the bottom of the frame. "I hate to say this, but I don't have the first clue whether this is authentic or not."

"We may have to come back to this one. I guess I never knew what the first movie was, crime or otherwise."

Art's call ended, and he joined them. "That was Carter. The medical examiner found fibers underneath the victim's fingernails." He bent down and opened the drawer on the popcorn vendor's cart. "Don't suppose there's a chance of getting some popcorn."

"I doubt it." Avery frowned at him. "You're hungry now? What does that mean, that Suzanne had fibers under her nails?"

He straightened up. "It could mean that she was with someone on the roof and she put up a fight before she was thrown off. Or it could mean nothing. As the housekeeper, I'm sure she spent good portions of her day scrubbing and cleaning. Fibers could have gotten there any number of ways."

"That's it? That's all they know? There's got to be more."

"Oh, there will be," Art said. "The ME is still in the postmortem. He's sent the fibers for analysis. That'll provide a better idea of what happened. Detective Carter's just keeping me updated."

By late afternoon, they'd made it up to the third floor and the duke still hadn't returned. Avery'd been keeping an ear out as they moved from room to room. Percy was only three years older than Tilly. For his sake and for Nick's, she hoped he was okay and she'd misconstrued what she'd heard. It was a good thing they were doing only superficial assessments, because she was far too distracted to focus very well.

"Avery?" To her left, Micah jarred her from her thoughts.

"What? Yes, sorry."

"I was saying that we only have four more rooms, but it's getting late. Should we call it a day and finish when we come back?"

She checked the time. "Maybe we can get through them."

Micah looked dismayed. It was odd for him to want to leave early; Avery normally had to force him to quit. Then it hit her. His commute home to the city must be close to two hours.

"You know," she said, "you're right, let's pack up. I wish I'd thought to mention this earlier, Micah, but you know you're always welcome to stay in Lilac Grove with us. Especially while we're working on this case. Duke Pennington actually offered our team rooms here for the duration. Dad and I were considering it, though in light of what's happened, we thought it wouldn't be advisable." She directed the last bit at Art.

"You thought correctly," Art said. "I'm glad you're being cautious."

Avery smiled. "Pretty sure you'd have thrown a fit if I said we were spending the night."

Micah snickered. "I can't picture the detective here throwing a tantrum."

"Thank you. I don't throw fits."

Micah spoke to Avery. "I'm going to head back this time. Noah's home for a few days. But I may take you up on your offer and stay with you at some point during the assignment. It'd save me quite a drive."

She nodded. "Give Noah a hug from me." Micah's wife Cicely had passed away two and a half years ago. Since then, he'd lived alone in his Harlem brownstone except when his twenty-year-old son Noah was home from Lehigh University. Avery had grown up babysitting Noah and Tilly whenever their parents were out together. Tilly had finally acted on her longtime crush on Noah this past summer, and the two had been inseparable until she left for London. Normally, Avery would've invited Micah and his son over for dinner, knowing Noah was in town, but she refrained. She had no idea what was going on in Tilly's life, which was a first, and not a good feeling.

They were on their way out when the sound of shattering glass came from upstairs. Their trio froze, looking upward.

"Enough! You're out of control," a man's angry voice shouted. "We're not going over it again."

A quieter woman's voice followed. Avery craned to hear, even taking a few hesitant steps toward the stairway, and then the sound of a door slamming hard resonated through the vestibule.

Lord Nico strode purposefully into sight above them, halting abruptly. He scowled. He descended the steps, and by the time he joined them in the entryway area, his features were rearranged into a mildly exasperated expression. An equestrian helmet hung from one hand. "Jet lag," he said simply. "It's a killer. I travel quite a bit, but my wife isn't used to the time difference. I'm sure she'll feel more like herself soon."

Avery nodded. "Jet lag can be terrible. I remember my aunt telling me and my sister that we needed an attitude adjustment once when she took us to Japan." She paused. "Um. Not that Lady Annabelle needs an attitude adjustment! That's not what I meant."

Lord Nico grinned. "Of course not. No worries. Are you heading out?"

"Yes, we'll be back on Thursday. Your father has it on his schedule," Micah said.

"Have a nice evening," Avery added. Outside, she raised her eyebrows at Micah and Art.

"Lord Nico's wife has a bit of a temper," Micah observed.

"She was mad enough to throw something at him—something substantial, by the sound of it," Art said.

"Maybe they're having marriage trouble," Avery suggested, keeping her tone quiet.

"I wouldn't necessarily assume that," Art said. "Marriage is messy. That could've been over something trivial, if you factor in the jet lag."

Micah nodded. "True. Cicely and I had our share of stupid fights and always moved past them."

"It happens," Art agreed. He was nodding as if he understood what Micah was saying. More than that—as if he could relate. Avery scrutinized his face, her curiosity over Lord Nico's spat with Lady Annabelle waning. Art had never been married. At least, not as far as Avery knew. But his comment about marriage being messy—was that simply an observation from his profession? Or something else?

"Oh no." Art looked at Avery. "I had a friend drop me here earlier, since I wasn't with my car. Do you mind if I grab a ride home with you?"

"You're on my way," she said. "I don't mind at all." An hour alone in the car with Art was no hardship. On the heels of that came a stab of guilt as she thought of seeing Hank on Friday—but why should she feel guilty? She hadn't meant to schedule dates with two ex-boyfriends on the same weekend. Maybe it'd push her to figure out what she really wanted. At twenty-six, she'd been a serial monogamist ever since she started dating. That must be it—the source of her discomfort with seeing Hank Friday and Art Saturday. It wasn't typical for her.

She and Art set out for Lilac Grove in a heavy silence, charged with all that had happened, and hadn't happened, between them. Minutes crept by as she phrased and rephrased in her head what to say to him. She didn't want to set them up to fail before they'd begun. She wasn't good at deception. She had to tell him, and probably Hank as well. But how to tell Art that she had a date the night before theirs to try to learn whether there was anything left between her and the man she'd dated off and on since college?

"It's so crazy that someone is swapping out fakes for genuine antiques and pieces of art at the manor," she said, needing to break the silence.

"We've got to assume it's related to the pocket watch disappearing. The lack of a replacement for that is throwing me, though," he said.

"Maybe whoever's doing it had planned to come back and leave a replica before it was found missing?"

He shook his head. "Then why take it? Why not stay under the radar and wait until the fake was ready?"

Avery frowned. "Maybe they got sloppy?"

"Humph. With the highest-value item that was stolen? Why? There has to be a better reason."

She sneaked a peek at him beside her. His long legs fit awkwardly in front of him even with the seat moved all the way back. Art's brow was drawn down and his jaw was set as he stared straight ahead, deep in thought. He was a serious person. Even his sense of humor was dry and deadpan, easy to miss if you didn't know him.

"If the thief is one of the Pennington Manor household staff, they'd have been nervous with the whole family suddenly arriving, right?" Avery asked. "What if it was an ongoing kind of thing, but they panicked and had to speed up the process once they knew the Penningtons were coming?"

He stared at her.

"Or," she went on, "the pocket watch disappearing is totally unrelated to whatever was happening with the rest of the items. Maybe it was taken by someone in the newly arrived entourage from Valle Charme, the family or their personal staff. Someone who knew the value of the watch and took it before it could be appraised and possibly sold. They'd have had no way of knowing there was another kind of theft going on in the house. And then there's Suzanne, who was either murdered or took her own life or fell. How does she factor in?" She could feel his gaze, still leveled at her.

"I'm sorry I screwed things up with us," he said, his deep voice quiet.

She glanced at him, surprised. "It wasn't only you."

"It was mostly me, Avery."

She didn't argue. She pressed her lips together, watching him in her peripheral vision while keeping an eye on the road.

"There's too much you don't know," he said.

Good Lord. So he was finally coming to terms with the fact that he really had given her very little to go on in trying to get to know him. They'd met first at the museum, and then again in the middle of the night on her front lawn when Halston saved her life and she learned Art was one of the detectives who'd worked on her parents' case. He'd told her early on that he'd been put on leave from the NYPD after making a critical mistake. And then rather than going back to work, he'd left the city entirely and secured a job in sleepy Springfield County. She knew he'd chosen the upstate New York town of Lilac Grove because it was close to his three sisters. But Avery knew none of what had led to his suspension or how it had led to a change in career and location. She didn't want every messy, painful detail. But without knowing at least some of his past, how was she supposed to forge a relationship with him into the future? For a smart man, he was surprisingly dense at times.

"Go ahead, say it," Art told her.

"What?"

"I know you were right. I guess I knew it when we stopped seeing each other. Some things are hard for me to talk about. But I will, if it means . . ."

Avery met his eyes, and her heart flipped over, a fluttery feeling zinging around her chest and stomach. The intensity in his gaze was breathtaking. She forced her attention back to the road.

"If it means there's a chance of you wanting to be with me again," he finished.

"I never stopped," she said.

Art slipped his pinkie finger through hers, leaving them casually linked on the console between them. "I miss you."

Warm tingles spiraled from her fingers through her hand and up her arm from that tiny point of contact. He wasn't helping to calm her racing heartbeat. "I miss you too, Art."

"I don't know where to start," he said. "You probably should kn—"

Avery interrupted him. She had to. Too much time had passed before they'd really started talking, and now they were almost to his house. "I have to tell you something."

"All right."

Right now, she wished like crazy that she'd kept in better touch with her friends in Philly. She had no one here besides her family and Rachel, no other girlfriends to bounce things off of or tell her when she was making a mistake. Was it a mistake to tell Art? Should she keep it to herself and hope he never found out? She turned onto his street.

"Hey. What is it? You can tell me anything," he said.

"I have a date on Friday," she blurted. "I'm sorry. I mean, I'm sorry I didn't tell you earlier. It's . . . I, uh. It's something I have to do. I can't cancel."

He looked at her, poker-faced. "Sounds like you're doing it under duress."

She laughed in spite of herself. "No, I'm not. It's my ex-boyfriend from last year. Really, from the last handful of years, off and on." She put the car in park now that they were in Art's driveway. "You probably remember—the night my house got broken into and Halston got hurt, I had to have Hank go to the vet clinic for him while I was in the ER."

"Oh." Art unbuckled, quiet for a moment. "Your dog was incredibly brave that night. So. Hank. Are you off or on right now? We can forget Saturday if you want."

"No!" Avery faced him. "I don't want to forget it. I just . . . it was my fault things ended badly with him. I think I just need to see him so we can talk and get some closure. I think that's what'll happen."

"But you aren't sure." He made it a statement rather than a question.

She sighed heavily. The weight of her attraction to Art set against six years of history with Hank was crushing. "I'm not sure," she said softly.

He was still. She'd noticed that about him early on. He didn't fidget, tap his foot, bounce his knee. He was very self-contained. "Well. Then you owe it to yourself to find out." Their fingers were still touching. He moved to get out, and she tightened her finger around his.

"Art. I—"

He encircled her forearm with one large, warm hand, leaned in, and kissed her on the temple. "It's okay. I promise."

Avery's eyes stung as she watched him go in through the side door of his garage. She drove the two miles home half wishing she hadn't told him and half relieved she had. She didn't know how she'd expected him to respond. His calm, confident reaction only confused her more.

She pulled into the lilac-lined driveway, thankful to have Tilly to focus on for a bit instead of stolen antiques and dating angst. By now, William would've gotten to the bottom of whatever had happened in London. But the house was empty, with only an enthusiastic Halston there to greet her. When she'd finished giving him the hugs and pats he needed, she found a note from her dad on the kitchen counter.

*Tilly had a tooth emergency, had to run her to Dogwood Heights for the after-hours dentist. Back soon, Dad*

# Chapter Six

Avery had eaten a chicken breast and rice and was sitting on the porch with Halston when Tilly and their dad returned. She rushed down the steps to help. Her sister had an ice pack on one side of her face and was as limp as a noodle when William helped her out of the car.

"What happened? Are you all right?" She put her arm around Tilly, supporting her.

Tilly looked up at her and mumbled something unintelligible around the gauze in her mouth.

"She had an impacted wisdom tooth pressing on her sinuses. She's going to be groggy for a while," William said.

She was pathetic. Avery tried to help her up to her room but ended up settling her in on the couch when she cried that she didn't want to be alone. Medicated, iced, and snuggled under a fluffy blanket, Tilly reached out and grabbed Avery's arm as she was about to step away.

"I'm just going to get the remote so we can watch *Friends*," Avery told her. "I'm not leaving."

Her little sister nodded. With her puffy cheeks, red-rimmed eyes, and mussed hair, she looked nine instead of nineteen. Avery joined her on the couch, lifting Tilly's feet and resting them on her lap when she sat down. She put their favorite show on, glancing up at William as he crossed in front of them to his chair. He sighed audibly and took off his glasses, rubbing his eyes.

Avery leaned on the armrest, keeping her voice to a whisper. "When did this happen?"

"The dentist said it's probably been infected for a while. She had to have been in pain. We were talking through all that happened at school, and she grabbed her cheek and started crying."

"Ugh." She shook her head. "Poor Tilly." Her sister was already asleep beside her, snoring softly around the gauze.

"It's been a long day. We spoke with the dean. The short version is that Tilly's been suspended for plagiarism."

Avery sucked in her breath, staring at her dad. "Oh no."

He nodded. "There's more. But I've already called your Dr. Singh. She scheduled an appointment for Tilly to come in and talk, and she was able to give me some good general advice. Tilly should tell you herself what happened. The more she talks about it, the easier it'll become for her to own what she did. Or something like that. I like her—Dr. Singh. You did well choosing a therapist to help get the two of you through losing Mom and me." He leaned forward, peering around Avery at his youngest daughter. "I'm glad she's asleep. She's got to be exhausted."

"You must be as well," she said, frowning at her dad. "I can stay down here with her. Maybe you should go to bed."

"I'm fine. My world's in this room, you know."

\* \* \*

Wednesday wasn't spent at Pennington Manor. Avery stayed home with Tilly while William went in to the Manhattan office to work on a few outstanding assignments that were in progress when Duke Pennington hired them. Sir Robert was holding down the fort at Antiquities and Artifacts Appraised when the team was at the manor, as his area of expertise was finance and marketing. And since he'd won them the contract with Barnaby's Auction House, they'd been fairly nonstop.

Tilly was half chipmunk when she finally woke up close to noon on Wednesday. Avery brought her a new ice pack. She slipped it gently underneath the stretchy fabric she'd wrapped under Tilly's chin and tied on top of her head, settling the ice against her swollen cheek. "Looks like you're storing nuts for the winter," she said, handing her two pain pills and a milkshake.

Tilly giggled and then winced. "Ow. Don't make me laugh. Or talk." She swallowed the pills.

"I had all four wisdom teeth out at once when I was nineteen. Must be the age for them to act up," Avery said. "I know it hurts. I also remember being able to talk."

Tilly pulled her blanket up to her neck and closed her eyes. "I'm tired."

"You just slept fourteen hours straight. Spill. What happened at school?"

"My roommate hates me. All of my friends there hate me now."

"What?" Avery asked. "Why?"

Her little sister groaned and sat up, throwing the blanket off. She faced Avery, keeping the ice pack in place. "I don't want you to hate me too. You're so perfect—you'd never do anything as stupid or—"

"Oh sheesh." She scooted over and gave Tilly's shoulder a squeeze. "You're ridiculous. I'm nowhere near perfect. I mess up all the time. We all do. Nobody's perfect."

Tilly narrowed her eyes. "I don't know. You have to promise not to be mad."

"I can't promise that. I promise I won't stay mad—is that good enough? I promise you'll still be my favorite pain-in-the-butt sister." She expected that to elicit another laugh, but it didn't.

Instead, Tilly looked down. She picked at a loose fiber in the blanket. "It was hard. Like, way harder than I expected. I'm not stupid." She raised her gaze briefly to Avery's. "I'm not. I really tried. But I've never learned any of the stuff they expected us to know for my algebra class, and physics was just—ugh. I don't get it. I went to the professor's office hours and used the free tutor, but it didn't help. Why do I need that stuff if all I want to do is sing?"

Avery was quiet, listening. She waited.

"My roommate Isla told me her boyfriend writes papers for people and she took me to meet him, and Theo said he does it all the time and I wouldn't get caught and nobody really cares anyway as long as it's decent and turned in on time, so I paid him to do my physics paper that was due right before exams, and Professor Bunil made me meet with him and the TA because they didn't think I'd done the paper." She fell silent. She pulled at the loose threads, winding them around her fingers, and took a deep breath. "Which I guess makes sense, because my marks were failing until I turned in that fricking paper."

"Oh wow."

"I know," Tilly said. "I'm sorry. I apologized to Dad too, but probably not enough. I never meant to let you guys down. I suck."

"No, you don't," Avery said. She captured her sister's hand, holding it. "You're tearing a hole in my favorite blanket."

"Oh."

"Listen. You left and went to college in another country, after the most painful year of our lives. College is hard even under good circumstances. Do you get why what you did is such a big deal to the school—to any school? Would you ever do it again?"

"Never! Oh my God, never." She clutched her cheek, cringing. "I would undo it if I could. It makes me feel so horrible and gross inside. I can't go back there. Theo got suspended too, like me, but I think for longer, and he's there on scholarship, so now they might take it away and he'll have to leave! Isla isn't speaking to me and she told all our friends what happened and they're, like, actively trying to get me kicked out of school, A. Not even kidding. Jaime and Nicola lit candles in my room when I was in class and called the peer leader, so I got written up for breaking the no-open-flame rule. And then Isla lied and made a report that I had a boy spend the night!"

"And you didn't," Avery said, confirming.

"No! Why would I? I'm with Noah. Or . . . I was with him. I think we're broken up now. I don't even know anymore. Isla and Nicola changed our Wi-Fi password and wouldn't give it to me, so I missed my three-month dating anniversary with him—I couldn't call him or get online or anything. When I went down to the common room to try, they locked me out of our room and I had to sleep in the hallway, and the peer leader found me and wrote me up again. She accused me of being drunk! I've never even had more than a taste, A, except for when we were with Auntie Midge in Rome. Then when I finally got through to Noah the next day, he thought I'd forgotten our anniversary. He was so upset, I had to tell him about the paper so he'd understand, and now he hates me too like everyone else."

Avery's heart ached for her distraught sister. She finally understood why Tilly had acted the way she had. "Hey," she said, squeezing Tilly's hand. "Noah could never hate you. I am positive of that. He's liked you since you were three. And as for the rest of it, I mean, jeez. I wish you'd reached out to me when you knew you were failing. Or at any point, Tilly, for real. I'd have found a way to help."

"You can't fix this. Those girls were so awful to me. I can't go back. Dad told the dean yesterday that we were going to take some time and find the best solution, but the school will never forgive me. I'm always going to be a cheater to them." She drew a hitching breath as tears started falling. "I'm a huge screw-up!"

Avery put her arms around the girl and hugged her. She didn't speak at first. Platitudes wouldn't help, and she didn't want to dismiss the gravity of what Tilly had done. She carefully smoothed her sister's hair off her face. "Tilly. It's a mess. I can't argue with that. But you are not a screw-up. You're still you. You made some bad decisions, and I think you've already been paying the price."

Tilly nodded. She swiped at her eyes, trying to get her crying under control. Halston got up from his spot in the sun on the dining room floor and came over, putting his head in Tilly's lap.

"Dad says you're going to talk to Dr. Singh," Avery said. "I'm sure that'll help a little. I do have one suggestion."

"Okay." The word came out split in the middle around a sob.

"Listen. Things will eventually be okay. You won't always feel this way." Avery frowned, waiting for her sister to calm a little. Her breathing finally evened out. "Here's what I think. You'll be home for almost two more weeks, no matter what happens. Let's decide not to decide anything for at least a few days. Maybe we can start talking about a plan this weekend. But not sooner. I don't think it's smart to make a decision about your future when you feel like this."

"I'm still gonna feel this way this weekend. I would be disgusted if someone I knew bought a research paper instead of doing it themselves. I *bought* a paper, A. I'm not that kind of person—I didn't think I was, anyway."

"You don't have to be. You're deciding right now not to be that kind of person. Everyone makes mistakes, right? We all do things sometimes that we aren't proud of. Maybe what counts most is whether we learn and try to do better."

Tilly laid her head on Halston's and hugged him. "My buddy. At least Halston still loves me."

Avery smiled. "We all still love you, goof. You cheated. Which is very bad, obviously. But it's not like you killed someone."

Tilly sighed. "I'm starving. We don't have any pudding, do we?"

Avery blinked at her, Tilly's words not fully registering. What she'd said to her sister had knocked loose an idea about Suzanne the housekeeper's death. *It's not like you killed someone.* Maybe the key to discovering what had happened was to focus not on why, but who. Who in Pennington Manor would have had access to the housekeeper to throw her from the roof? Art had said Detective Carter didn't have a definitive answer yet about the cause of death, but why would Suzanne have had fibers under her fingernails if not due to a tussle with someone? Avery needed to call Art. They had to focus on who—

"Avery Addison Ayers." Tilly put her face close to Avery's, bringing her back to the living room and her little sister's puffy, ice-packed cheek. "Are you in there?"

"Sorry. I had a—it was an idea about the assignment we're working on for the duke. Pudding, right? I'll make you some. I think we have chocolate or butterscotch," she said.

Tilly followed her into the kitchen and sat at the counter while Avery worked at the stove top. "Did they find out what happened to the lady who fell off the roof?"

"They don't know yet," Avery said. "I think it'll take a few days."

"You should ask Art to help. He'd be able to figure it out. Plus then you wouldn't be in danger when you're working at the mansion."

She raised her eyebrows at Tilly. "I'm not in danger; don't worry. Art actually showed up yesterday. He's friends with the detective working on the case."

"Ha! I told you he was still into you."

"That's not why he's pitching in." It sort of was, but she didn't want to create false hope. Tilly had given her the cold shoulder for days after she broke up with Art this summer. "He's helping out a friend, that's all."

"Hello!" Aunt Midge's singsong voice floated to them from the foyer. She appeared in the kitchen doorway, arms full of bags and boxes and a *Get Well* balloon floating at the end of a ribbon tied around a purple teddy bear. "How's the patient? This little guy is for you. And I brought sustenance from town. Clam chowder and baked perch from O'Shannahan and chocolate mousse and cannolis from the White Box. Obviously, you'll have the chowder and mousse," she said to Tilly. She deposited everything on the counter.

Tilly threw her arms around Midge. "Thank you, Auntie."

Avery poured the pudding from the saucepan into a bowl and put it in the fridge. Tilly could have it later. "You're the best, Auntie." She planted a kiss on her cheek and began unpacking items. It all smelled delicious.

"How are you feeling?" Midge asked Tilly as they dug in.

She was taking baby-sized spoonfuls of the soup. "Not too bad. The ice helps more than the pills they gave me."

"Avery felt the same way with hers. I'm staying over tonight. I miss you girls, and I do miss my Halston," she said, glancing down. The Afghan hound was sitting at attention, well mannered and not begging but ready to catch stray morsels.

"Yay! We miss you too," Tilly said. She pushed the soup aside and switched to the mousse. "Better," she murmured.

"Tell me," Midge turned to Avery, "how is Nicholas holding up? I have a message in to him, inviting him and Duchess Mariah to dinner. I'm sure they could use a diversion. They must be reeling, having to contend with stolen heirlooms and a suspicious death."

"The duke seemed to be weathering everything all right until yesterday afternoon," Avery said. "Something happened with Percy. I only overheard a snippet, and I don't want to leap to any crazy conclusions."

"Hmm." Midge popped a bite of fish in her mouth, nodding.

Avery'd hoped Midge might offer some information. After all, she'd known the duke forever. But Midge remained mum, busy devouring the onion rings on her plate.

"The duke's assistant came to get him while he was showing us around. Mathew told him there was a problem with Percy. The bits I heard were concerning; it sounded like he'd been arrested. Nick wasn't happy; he had Mathew go get the driver."

The older woman registered a distinct lack of surprise. She simply gave a brief nod and dabbed at the corners of her mouth.

"Auntie, should we be worried? Do you know something about Percy? Is it related to what's going on in that house?"

"Oh no." Midge finally spoke. "Percy's a sweet boy. Though I believe you absolutely should be concerned about your safety at the manor, but only in regard to the stolen items and whatever might have happened to that poor woman who plummeted from the parapets. Percy is harmless, if somewhat challenging."

"Challenging how?" Avery asked, leaning forward.

Midge set her fork down. She pursed her lips, meeting Avery's gaze but clearly deep in thought. "You must keep this in mind. No family is perfect. If they seem it, they've just learned to hide their problems well. I'll offer you the benefit of the knowledge I've gained in my long friendship with Duke Pennington, but you must promise me you won't talk out of school."

Tilly giggled. "What does that even mean? Nobody says that anymore, Auntie."

Avery shot her a look. "You feel better, huh?"

"Cheeky," Midge said. "Is it ever wise to allow rudeness to dictate our behavior, Matilda Marie?"

"No, ma'am." Tilly looked down. She continued spooning mousse from her sundae glass.

"As I thought. Now, Duke Pennington's sons are separated by nine years. They are as unique from each other as you two. I'm not sure you're aware, but Lord Percy is only twenty-two. And according to Nicholas, he has no interest in his expected role in Valle Charme. I did think he'd grown up a bit since last year's debacle . . . but perhaps not."

"Oooh, what did he do last year?" Tilly asked.

"Lord Percy borrowed a friend's yacht from a marina in Marseille. Without asking permission."

"Whoa," Avery said.

"But," Tilly said, "it was a friend's boat. I mean, how much trouble could that have caused? Did he bring it back?"

Midge shook her head. "Apparently, by the time it was discovered stolen, nearly two weeks had gone by. Lord Percy and two cohorts were eventually apprehended near Athens. When authorities recovered the sixty-foot yacht, it was in need of repair, and apparently there were cases of illegally smuggled cigars on board."

"Oh wow," Avery breathed. "That's hard to imagine. What on earth was he thinking? He was so friendly and charming when we met him."

"Oh yes, quite! He certainly has a magnetic personality," Midge said. "Nicholas said the boys had planned to find buyers for the cigars in Greece, though heaven only knows why Lord Percy was involved in that at all. He told his father they'd done it on a whim; I'm not sure how much forethought went into any of it. From Nicholas's explanation, the whole escapade sounded along the lines of a very high end, extended joyride. Percy is fortunate to be a Pennington. He was fined and shipped off to a country-club-style correctional facility for a few weeks while his father made sure the incident was kept quiet. It did get back to the collegiate polo team; he was suspended for the season. I'm certain he'd have been removed completely if not for his father. My dear friend has a blind spot where his younger son is concerned." She sighed, her eyebrows furrowed in concern.

"What about Lord Nico? I take it he's more serious and reliable than his brother? At least, that was the impression we got."

"Oh yes, in matters of business, Lord Nico is impeccable," Aunt Midge said. "Nicholas would be lost without him. He had his wild days as well, but he settled down and got married, and then those two darling girls arrived. We need more tea." She rose to refill the pot.

"Auntie, what do you think of Lord Nico's wife, Lady Annabelle?" Avery carried their empty plates into the kitchen, following her.

"Ah." Midge paused, teakettle in one hand. "Well. I really don't know Lady Annabelle. We'd never met prior to the other day."

Avery picked up the distinct vibe that Aunt Midge was uncomfortable dishing about her friend's family. "Oh." She really wanted to know if there was some odd dynamic between Lord Nico and Annabelle, but she hated to push.

"I did chat a bit with her, after you'd gone back to the car. Often, our own insecurities and lack of self-confidence may lead us to cultivate a prickly exterior. I try to remember this when encountering someone who seems difficult or abrasive."

"That makes a lot of sense." Avery frowned, musing, "I can't figure what on earth someone like Lady Annabelle has to feel insecure about. You always make me think, Auntie."

"Good! Never a bad thing." Her aunt turned to Tilly, who was sneaking oyster crackers to the dog lying at her feet. Midge raised an eyebrow at her. "Halston's had quite enough.

And you, darling girl, would benefit from a bit of sunshine and fresh air. It's beautiful out. Let's move to the porch."

"You two go ahead," Avery said. "I need a run, as long as you don't mind." She couldn't allow herself to slack, not with the marathon eleven days away. She cleared the dishes and then went down the hall to the home office to make a quick call before changing into her running gear. In the doorway, force of habit pulled her gaze to the rug they'd used to cover the dark spot in the hardwood floor last spring. Blood was one of those stains you could never fully get rid of. Her father had been distraught learning about that night, so the rug had served its purpose. Avery didn't mind the stain. That was the night she'd learned she could do things she didn't even know she was capable of—like the upcoming marathon. She wasn't the fastest runner anymore, and it didn't matter. She just wanted to know she'd done it, for herself and for her dad.

She crossed to her desk opposite her father's in the office. The Lilac Grove home office was cozier than their setup in the Manhattan shop—a plush sofa against the wall, a thick oval rug in the center of the polished floor, and twin windows behind the desks looking out over the lilac-filled yard. She occupied her mother Anne's desk in both offices. She'd kept her mother's colorful floral trinket boxes along the edge of her desk, using them to organize office supplies and notes to herself here and in Manhattan. She dialed Art.

"Miss me already?" Art's voice came on the line.

"Of course. I had a thought about the housekeeper's death I wanted to run by you."

"You said you wouldn't be back in the Hudson Valley until Thursday. You're not there now, are you?"

"Nope, I've been babysitting Tilly all day—she had to get a bad wisdom tooth pulled last night. Listen, I've been thinking about the weird things happening at the manor. I know Midge is worried about the duke, and I've been trying to come up with a reason someone would bother to replace stolen items with fakes, and what on earth the housekeeper could've done for someone to want to push her off the roof."

"Avery, I—"

"No, wait," she said. "Maybe you could pass this on to your friend, Detective Carter. When we heard Suzanne's scream, Micah and Dad and I ran outside right away. It was loud. I know you don't know yet whether it was an accident or not, but if it wasn't, I think you have to focus not on why, but who. Does Carter know who ran out there right away and who took a while to come out? Did anyone fill him in on that?"

"I'm not sure," Art replied. "Listen, could you stop by my office tomorrow morning? I don't want to discuss details at the manor, but the autopsy is finished and the pathology report is back. Suzanne Vick was forcefully pushed off the roof."

# Chapter Seven

Avery's alarm rang at six in the morning. She crawled out of bed, limbs heavy, body protesting, but mind already gearing up to run. After pulling on running clothes and her pink-and-black Brooks Ghost shoes and letting Halston out, she slogged through the first mile into town, veering left off Main Street and checking her pedometer. She'd been pushing herself with high-mileage runs earlier this year, until she'd connected with the Swifties, a small upstate New York runners club. She always preferred running alone, with her dad as the one exception as a partner, but the Swifties had surprised her as an invaluable resource. She went to the online meetings and had also mined their Swifties advice board for marathon preparation tips. She'd learned that three or four very long runs each week wouldn't prepare her as well as five moderate-distance ones and one long endurance run, usually on weekends. Now she covered her twelve miles throughout Lilac Grove only on Sundays. Until she'd tapered down this week, all of her other runs had been a much nicer six miles. Today's route took her along the lake west of town, through the old farming community, and then back up Main Street in Lilac Grove.

She hit her two-mile mark, and it wasn't getting any easier. The first few were always the hardest. When she'd moved home last year, in the wake of losing her parents and taking on the business along with shared care of Tilly, Avery had been a mess. She'd been heartsick and angry, and it had spilled over into her newly rekindled relationship with Hank and even into how she'd treated Tilly. Then she'd found Dr. Singh. One of the psychologist's suggestions was that Avery should start running again. She'd always loved it, and before the accident, she and her dad had been throwing around the idea of trying to do the New York City Marathon. At first, she'd told Dr. Singh no. It would only be one more reminder of her dad being gone. She'd resisted until the day she'd lashed out at Tilly so badly that her little sister had screamed that she hated her and she should just go back to Philly. Their parents had been gone a month. By then, Aunt Midge had moved in. Avery could've left—Tilly, the business, New York. She started running instead.

It hadn't fixed everything at once, but it was a start. Now, halfway through the third mile, she tried to rationalize cutting it short for today. She was tired and stressed, and the idea of a nice cold protein shake on the front porch sounded like heaven. She gritted her teeth and picked up speed, ignoring the complaints from her shins and that pain in her side. She couldn't quit. The marathon was ten days away. Jesus. How was she going to force her body into another handful of miles when right now she just wanted to cover the last stretch of road home and collapse?

Avery scrunched up her face and blew her breath out forcefully with a grunt and kept going, eyes on the horizon. And then she felt it. The pinch in her side was gone. Her shins were fine—were her shins even there anymore? Her thumping heart settling back into her chest where it belonged instead of her temples, her breathing came easier, the pavement was smoother, the whole day was sunnier. This was easy, effortless, like running on air. Aside from the running-as-therapy thing, this was why she ran. The high. She finished her third mile and breezed through her fourth, sure she could go another thousand. She slowed as she passed Mixed Bag in town again, darting a glance through the front window in case Rachel was up, but the shop was still dark. All of Main Street was still closed; it wasn't even eight yet.

She'd started so early, she had time for that shake on the front porch before jumping in the shower. She washed and blew out her long, brown hair so it fell in a sleek curtain to the middle of her back and chose a cute, crisp, white blouse with a black satin tie around the waist to pair with cropped black pants. She met her dad in the kitchen and filled her travel mug, and they were on their way to the Springfield County Sheriff's Department in Dogwood Heights before Tilly and Midge woke.

The desk sergeant peered at them over her blue-rimmed glasses. The brass plate on the middle-aged woman's desk read *Sergeant Lynn Tunney*, though Avery already knew her name from the last time she'd been here. She braced herself for another bout with the sergeant's chilly attitude and gave her a big, friendly smile.

"Good morning, Sergeant Tunney! You probably don't remember me—"

"I do, Ms. Ayers." The sergeant blinked slowly, her expression unchanged. "How may I help you?"

"Oh! We're here to see Detective Smith. This is my father, William."

Tunney gave William a curt nod. She picked up the phone and spoke into it, and a moment later Art appeared from around the corner behind Sergeant Tunney. "Hey." He held up a hand. "Buzz them through, Lynn. We'll talk in my office."

Avery started in his direction but paused, seeing her father still hovering near the double glass doors they'd just come in through. "Dad?"

He cleared his throat. "I'll wait outside. You can fill me in on the way."

She studied him, confused. "It won't take long, Dad. Come on."

William didn't take his hand from the metal railing on the door.

Art spoke. "Hold on." He moved closer, eyeing Avery's father. "Let me grab something, and I'll come out to you. I'll meet you outside. No worries."

Avery glanced back at her dad. Without another word, William pushed back outside through the doors, darting quickly to the right and out of sight.

"Thank you." Avery tossed the response to Art over her shoulder and hurried outside to her father. She found him already at the end of the sidewalk leading to the parking lot, bent over with his hands on his knees, his eyes closed. She gently touched his back. "Dad? What's wrong?"

He shook his head but didn't answer. She kept her hand on his back, unmoving. William sucked in air and blew it out through pursed lips, in and out, over and over.

"Should I call an ambulance? Or your doctor? What's going on? Tell me how you feel. Does anything hurt?" Her pulse raced along with her mind. He was healthy, as far as she knew. She couldn't help him if she didn't know what was happening. She dialed 911 and let her thumb hover over the send button, at a loss. If he didn't start talking in the next minute, she would call.

He slowly straightened up. The doors to the precinct building swished open and closed as Art exited the building. He reached them, frowning in concern at William. "All right, man? Here, let's go sit down." He led them to a nearby picnic table in the shade in what must be an outdoor lunch break area.

William ran a hand through his hair, and Avery saw now that it was damp. Her father's normally pinkish complexion held a clammy pallor, a faint sheen of sweat across his forehead. "I'm sorry. That was unexpected. Felt like I was having a heart attack for a moment there."

"You what?" Avery exclaimed. "How do you know you aren't?" She grabbed his wrist and searched for his pulse, scrutinizing him.

Her dad gave her a small smile. "I don't think that's how you check for a heart attack, honey. I'll be okay."

"What happened? Does your chest hurt? Or your left arm, or—" She tapped her phone and typed in *heart attack symptoms.* "Do you have pressure at all? Heartburn? Pain in your jaw?" They'd gotten him back only four months ago. She'd be damned if she was going to let anything take him away again.

"Avery. I'm better now. This . . . it's not the first time it's happened. It's, um . . . I'm not sure, but I think this is what a panic attack must feel like."

"A panic attack? From what?"

"They don't have to be from anything," Art said quietly. He passed William a bottled water. "They can come on without any kind of trigger. Though in your dad's case, it's a pretty good bet that being here brought it on."

"I think so," he agreed.

"For months," Art said to Avery, "the only people your dad had contact with were doctors, nurses, and law enforcement. From the moment he was well enough to leave the hospital and be placed into protective custody, he saw the inside of too many FBI field offices and sheriff's departments, mine included. How much have you shared with your family?" he asked William.

"I don't like talking about it."

"Nothing." Avery supplied the truth. She squeezed her dad's hand. She'd tried getting him to talk about it at first, but it upset him every time she brought it up. She'd stopped trying after the first few weeks.

William took another deep breath and blew it out. "Detective. Avery. We didn't come here to rehash the past year. I'm really all right. You said you wanted to talk with us before we got to the manor?"

Avery felt Art looking at her. When she met his gaze, the concern in his expression mirrored her own. She gave him a brief nod, saying without words that she'd take care of her dad. Maybe right now after a panic attack wasn't the time, but they were definitely going to talk about this.

Art rested the manila file folder on his knees. "I'm going to be accompanying you to Pennington Manor until this case is solved—not on sick days or vacation time but as part of Detective Carter's team. Carter's taking point, obviously—it's his county, his case—but we're hoping my presence as your colleague will serve a dual purpose, as I mentioned. We may be privy to information Carter wouldn't: snippets of conversation, personal relationships and tensions, that sort of thing. You'll need to keep me in the loop so I can plan my schedule accordingly now that we're certain the vic—Suzanne—was murdered. We'll also need an itemization of every antique and heirloom that appears to have gone missing."

Avery hadn't even realized how uneasy she'd been feeling about heading back to Pennington Manor after all the strange occurrences there until she registered the immense relief of knowing Art was officially on the case. She'd learned while working on the dragon medallion case with him that he was excellent at his job—and pretty great at helping keep her safe in the process. "We'll get you the list today. We're almost finished with the preliminary assessment. Art, can I ask how you were able to prove she was pushed? What's in the file?"

"The Westchester County coroner's report. The were some odd findings," he said, flipping through a few of the papers and finding the one he wanted. "Pathology identified trace amounts of wine on her lips, and those fibers under her finger-nails came back as an uncommon poly-rayon-silk blend. No DNA was found—no skin or hair. But the definitive proof is some bruising that became visible during the postmortem. There's a set on each of her arms. Coroner says they're from trauma that had to have occurred a maximum of two hours before her death."

Avery's eyes were wide. "Oh my God. How awful!"

"How can they be sure the bruising was from a struggle as opposed to anything else in the few hours leading up to her death?" William asked.

Art pulled another paper from the file and turned it face-down, his palm on top of it. "It's one of those things that's hard to explain unless you're in law enforcement. I can show you. But it's not necessary; there's no doubt the coroner is right."

"I want to see," Avery said, eyeing the paper.

Art's gaze rose to William as the man stood. He took a few steps away from them and pulled out his phone. "I'm going to make sure Midge knows to make sure Tilly takes her antibiotic today." He strolled slowly toward the shade of the next big maple tree in the lunch area as he put the phone to his ear.

Avery scooted a little closer to Art, lowering her voice. "I think he's okay. I forget sometimes about all he went through. I've never seen him like that."

"It's normal. This kind of thing gets better. It'd be a good idea, though, to get him talking a little somehow. He may not want to burden you or Tilly or his sister with it, though. I've seen it before." Art was focused on William, who had his back to them several yards away.

"So maybe that's why I'm just now finding out he's having trouble dealing? But keeping us at arm's length isn't going to help."

Art met Avery's eyes. "Get him to talk to you, however you can. If he doesn't, this trauma will seep into every part of your lives as a family."

She frowned. "Wow. You really have had to see other people go through this kind of thing." His forehead was lined with worry. "I'll work on it. Thank you for the advice."

Art pushed the facedown paper over to her and took his hand away. "Take a look if you want to. The photos of the bruising were taken by the medical examiner."

Avery flipped the paper over and sucked in her breath. Two side-by-side photos depicted the backs of Suzanne's pale arms, shown at an angle to capture the lateral sides of both. On each arm was a set of four elongated, deep-purple bruises. Each bruise comprised two to three faintly connected ovals. Avery finally spoke, her tone stunned. "Oh."

"These are the pads of the fingers, obviously," Art pointed. "There are other photos that show the thumb imprint on the inner arm, but these tell us a pretty clear story."

Avery crossed her arms in front her chest, wrapping her fingers around her upper arms. She shuddered. "Poor Suzanne."

"Yes," he agreed. He took the photo away, sliding it back into the folder. "A good amount of pressure would have been needed to make those bruises. She wouldn't have been able to break free."

Avery couldn't tear her gaze away from the file folder. What other horrors were in there? What else had Art seen in his career? "Is there any way to narrow down the suspects with what you have now? The fibers and this bruising? Oh, and you said there was wine on her lips. What does that mean?"

"Hypothetically, it could mean she was secretly drinking on the job, but I'd say that's not the most likely scenario. Carter's thinking the killer might have tried to make it seem like she had a drunken fall from the roof."

Avery frowned. "Hmm. That wouldn't work, though. Doesn't the autopsy include lab work and stomach contents? If she was drunk, you'd know, right?"

Art raised his eyebrows. "Very true. So what's your take?"

"She was lured up to the roof by someone. Under the guise of having a romantic drink together—or more. So we catch the guy she was having an affair with, and we've caught our killer."

"Not necessarily," Art said. "We don't *know* there was an actual affair, or that it'd be with a man. And it could have been a setup. She could've been summoned up to the roof by anyone. You can't assume the person doing the luring was really who Suzanne thought it was."

"Ah. You mean, for instance, if the object of Suzanne's affections was married," Avery said, catching on. "A significant other could've learned about the affair and tricked Suzanne into coming up to the roof alone, thinking she was meeting her lover, but instead she'd have been confronted by the spouse." She couldn't help thinking of Lady Annabelle's extreme reaction to seeing Suzanne pass by her room that first day. She had a feeling Art might consider the dirty look and slammed door trivial, but . . . "Okay, maybe this is nothing, but the first day we were there, Lady Annabelle gave Suzanne a look that could kill when we walked by her."

He raised one eyebrow, skeptical. "Suzanne got a dirty look from Lady Annabelle? And then what?"

"Lady Annabelle slammed her bedroom door."

His expression didn't change. "All right. That could have been over anything. Literally. Overstarched sheets or just a general dislike."

She nodded. "True." She groaned inwardly—she'd known better than to throw something so flimsy out to him.

"But let's think about this. The duke and his son Nico are the only men in the manor with wives. Oh, and there's the caretakers, Lynn and Ira Hoffman. Detective Carter's background check showed the rest as single—all of the manor staff and the entourage from Valle Charme that traveled with the family, and Lord Percy, of course."

"But if Suzanne's death was a crime of passion, then the stolen artifacts are probably not connected. Right?" Avery asked.

Art sighed. "I don't know. We're getting into a lot of speculation."

"I see that," Avery agreed. "Maybe it'll help if we're little flies on the wall today and try to pay attention to any tidbits of conversation that could mean something."

"Exactly," Art said. He rose as William rejoined them. They headed toward the parking lot.

"You can just ride with us," William offered.

Art didn't respond right away. Avery kept her gaze focused forward; she could feel him looking at her. She was conflicted and didn't want to sway him one way or the other. She yearned to be around him as much as possible, but she was trying to keep an open mind about Hank. Less than a week ago, Art hadn't been in the picture, and she'd been excited at the prospect of a date with her ex.

Art finally spoke. "Thanks. But I think I'll just drive myself."

\* \* \*

By noon, the team had completed the remainder of the third-floor items, finishing in the fourth spacious guest suite the manor housed. Micah clicked his pen and clipped it back onto the pocket protector he was never without. "I think that's everything," he said to Avery, William, and Art.

"Awesome," Avery said. "We'll go back down to the lab and finalize the preliminary assessment list. I'm excited to start the appraisals. I was thinking, maybe we could start in the—" She heard footsteps on the stairs and cut herself off, poking her head out of the doorway. "Oh! Nick."

Duke Pennington tapped the screen on his iPad and handed it to her. "My assistant, Mathew, reminded me to have you take a quick look at the spa. Mother has a few items in there. It was one of her favorite places in the house."

"Really? A spa, like a hot tub room?" Avery asked.

"Not exactly," the duke said. "It's a pool and sauna. I'll show you. Apologies for all the stairs," he added, throwing a glance back at the group following him down the hallway toward the staircase. "I pushed Mother to add an elevator for years, but she insisted it'd mar the aesthetics here, or something along those lines."

"She sounds like a smart woman," Micah said. "The architecture and structural layout in the manor is quite consistent with the era your home was built, from the parapets to your stately entrance area. It'd be a shame to interfere with that."

Nick smiled. "You sound like her. It's a nice thought in theory, until you've got to trudge up and down these steps several times a day."

"I'll side with you, Lord Pennington," Art spoke up. He chuckled. "My bad knee can understand the appeal of an elevator."

Avery shot him a curious look. How did a thirty-three-year-old have a bad knee? High school football, maybe? Add Art's knee issue to the growing list of things she didn't know about him.

When they reached the main floor, Nick took them down the only hallway they hadn't explored yet. After a long stretch, the duke turned into an alcove, and Avery came around the corner to see a recessed door with frosted glass. The smell of chlorine floated in the air.

"This blasted keypad," Nick murmured, standing back and glaring at the keypad above the locked door handle. "We had it installed so the girls can't stumble in unsupervised. I never remember the code, but everyone has it. One moment; I'll call the staff." He pulled out his phone.

Avery leaned against the floral-wallpaper-covered walls. This area was done in lighter shades than the corridor off the reception room. Her dad elbowed her.

"Hey." He spoke under his breath. "Is this what you were telling me about the other day?" He tapped the wall, and she followed his gaze.

Below her dad's hand was a small indentation in the blush-and-gold tones of the paper. Avery pressed her fingers into the indent, confirming the tiny lever was present, the same as on the other door. "Yes," she hissed, her eyes wide.

"Here we are!" Twenty feet away in the alcove, Nick now had the door open, revealing a gorgeous in-ground pool. He ushered them inside. The pool deck was an expanse of black-and-tan marble, the domed ceiling made up of dozens of glass panes. In the Olympic-sized pool, perfectly still water revealed a navy-blue geometric pattern set within the pale-blue under-water tile. Lush green ferns hung at intervals around the enor-mous space. A stainless-steel refrigerator with a glass door, holding all manner of juices and other drinks, stood between two large white shelving units filled with various-sized towels. On the opposite wall was a red cedar door bearing a gold plate with the label *Sauna*.

"This is just . . ." Avery stared at Duke Pennington. "Beau-tiful. You must want to spend all of your time here."

"I should," he admitted. "I don't take advantage of the pool nearly often enough. I hear my granddaughters adore it, though, so it's going to good use. You'll notice, at the far end, the pair of marble statues Mathew reminded me about."

Avery and her team followed him across the deck. She resisted the urge to dip her fingertips into the water—was it functional and cold or tepid and soothing? As they walked, she spotted the leavings of the duke's granddaughters—a white cabinet with one door standing open had bright pink and green water noodles sticking out among other colorful toys inside. She'd kill to have a pool like this in her house, especially during marathon preparations. Not that this pool would fit anywhere in her house!

Nick stopped at the large window that made up the entire wall on the far end of the space. A pair of three-foot-high marble statues on white marble pillars flanked the window, which overlooked the rolling hills and trees at the rear of the Pennington property.

Art moved closer, tipping his head as he assessed the first statue. "It's one of the Greek goddesses, right? I've forgotten my mythology. But I think I know this one," he said, crossing in front of the window to the other figure. "What better god to have in your pool area than Poseidon?"

"The goddess is Aphrodite," Nick supplied.

"Micah." Avery said his name as she stood staring, first at Aphrodite and then at Poseidon.

"I know." He was beside her, frowning.

"What is it?" Nick asked. "Please don't tell me these are imitations."

"We know these statues," Avery said. "Micah and I authenticated and appraised this duo four or five months ago when the Museum of Antiquities acquired them."

# Chapter Eight

"Is Sir Rob—er, Robert—still in the office?" Avery asked of no one in particular. Her mind was racing.

"He's at Barnaby's today," William replied.

"We'll have to reach out to Goldie," Micah said. "She can put us in touch with Nate or the new liaison so we can learn more about the acquisition of Christo's *Ara Eros*."

"And we'll trace it backward from there. We should send Goldie the list of swapped-out items and have her check inventory for the rest too," Avery added.

"This makes seven." Nick spoke quietly. "With the Petrova pocket watch, the King Federico IV painting, the candlesticks, my mother's tea set, the diamond brooch that belonged to my aunt, our Thomas Tompion clock, and now the god and goddess pair, seven heirlooms have been stolen."

"And all but one of those had similar-appearing replacements left in their place," Art added. "I'm almost positive your pocket watch was taken impulsively, coinciding with your family's arrival."

The duke sank into a nearby chair, one of several in the area with small white café tables. "The tragedy is that we're focusing on these missing items rather than the loss of poor Suzanne. Her death far outweighs the theft."

"It absolutely does," Art agreed. "Suzanne's murder is why I'm here. But we have to consider that finding out what's happening to your valuables will lead us to the killer. It's unlikely that we're dealing with two unrelated crimes."

Nick was pensive, frowning at Art. "I understand that logic." His gaze shifted to Micah and then Avery. "You're speaking of MOA, aren't you? Are you certain my god and goddess are at the museum—this isn't them? Who is Goldie?"

"Yes," Micah said. "I'm sure the statues we worked with were yours. These aren't quite up to snuff. To begin with, they're missing any kind of a patina—a hallmark sign of aging in marble and most other materials used for sculpting. Historically, skilled forgers have techniques for faking a stone patina, so the absence of it points to an amateur creating these replacement pieces. William is our resident geochemical expert; he can probably explain it better."

William took the baton. "We'd normally need to study the composition of the material used in creating the sculpture to determine its makeup, using total organic carbon analysis and spectrometry. You know, just to determine chemical elements, compounds, and isotopes. But Micah's right—there's no need here. These are poor copies." He scraped a thumbnail against Poseidon's leg. "The real *Ara Eros* set is made of pure-white Carrara marble, the same type of Italian marble

Michelangelo preferred. If I had to guess, I'd say this material is some kind of resin with an overlay."

"On top of the lack of effort put into making the dummy statues," Avery said, "the Aphrodite is known to have a crack along her shoulder, where her arm is extended, from here to here." She traced a line along the back of the shoulder to the elbow. The group moved in closer to see. "Marble tends to crack along mineralized veins, and even when it's repaired, the cracks will sometimes persist or lengthen. This poor girl's got too many giveaways. There's not a mark on her shoulder or anywhere else."

"Damn." Avery turned to find Art staring at her. He shook his head. "I had no idea appraising antiques involved so much science."

Avery laughed. "It's a good thing it does. It's one of my favorite parts of the job." She caught Nick's drawn expression and quickly sobered. "Anyway. I'd have to go through our files to know when exactly Micah and I worked the *Ara Eros* assignment, but I know it was earlier this year. Goldie Brennan is the curator at MOA, Nick; we'll get her involved."

"I know your MOA. Fine museum. It seems as if I may need to visit again to retrieve what's mine."

"I'd advise against that," Art said. "Let me and Detective Carter handle it. We'll get the pair back unharmed. And your team here will submit the list of missing items to the curator."

Avery spoke. "I'll be surprised, though, if anything else turns up at MOA. Wouldn't a smart thief split up the stolen items?"

"Definitely. But maybe we'll be lucky and they'll have put the same amount of effort into selling the items as they did in faking them," Art said.

"We do have connections across the country," William said. "Art and antiques dealers and a few other museums. We'll reach out. Maybe we'll get lucky and find more pieces."

"And if we do, it shouldn't be hard to trace a stolen item in reverse, from the new owner to the acquisitions liaison to the dealer who submitted it, back to whoever offered it up for sale," Avery said. "Find the thief, find the killer."

Art cleared his throat. "I, uh, didn't exactly say that. But you've got the process figured out—you two recognizing the god and goddess is a nice break in the case."

Avery elbowed her partner beside her. Micah chuckled. "We can't really take any credit for that. You don't forget a piece after you've put it through the gauntlet making sure it's real."

Nick stood. "I appreciate all you're doing here. I'm afraid I'm off; I have an appointment. I'll have Mrs. Hoffman put something together for lunch—she'll call you when it's ready. It'll bolster you if you plan to continue working this afternoon."

"We do. Thank you," Avery said. She wanted to make as much progress in appraising as they could today. A trip to the Manhattan office and MOA would take most of tomorrow.

As the duke led the way back through the long hallway, Avery slowed her pace, falling behind. Nick seemed in a hurry, and William, Micah, and Art were immersed in a discussion about craft beer. When the men had almost reached the vestibule, Avery turned and ran silently back to the hidden latch in the wall across from the pool entrance. She slid her hand over the wall—where the hell was the thing? They might notice she was gone at any moment. Ah. She pressed her finger against the latch and pushed down. A door she hadn't seen a few seconds ago within the floral print gave way under her hand.

Avery ducked quickly inside, closing it behind her. Even though this was the main floor, the staircase led both up and down, the same as the other one. She hadn't thought past doubling back and getting into this passageway. Should she go up? Or down? Making the logical decision, she sprinted up the steps, her long legs clearing two at a time. She reached the second-floor landing and whipped her head around, peering down the stairs. She'd heard something, but now it was as silent as before. She kept going to the third floor, finding that, while the second floor held an exit door that looked like the one she'd come in through, there was no exit here. She took the last flight up, excited to reach the roof, mind racing. Suzanne or her potential lover could've used either of the two passageways she'd found so far to get to the roof, without anyone knowing. Except for the killer.

The fourth flight of stairs ended at a door. She held her breath, turned the doorknob, and pushed—too hard. It opened easily, spilling her onto the asphalt of the roof. She stood up, about to exit fully onto the roof, but hesitated. What if she got locked out? The door wasn't locked, but would it stay that way? She twisted the doorknob back and forth. There was no manual lock, only a keyhole on either side. She went back inside, pulling it closed behind her but wishing she'd taken the chance and gone out onto the roof. As she descended, she realized it didn't matter. She didn't need to get through that door to comprehend the implications of what she'd found.

She rounded the last bend in the first flight of stairs and ran smack into a man, his hands coming up to grip her arms and triggering an image of Suzanne's circle of finger-shaped bruises on both arms. A scream was halfway out of her throat before she abruptly clamped her mouth closed against it. She stared into Art Smith's hazel eyes.

"Oh Jesus!" Avery whisper-yelled at him. "You almost scared me to death."

He raised an eyebrow at her. "Interesting wording."

"What are you doing? You didn't need to follow me." Good Lord, he smelled like an evergreen had just bathed in clean, slightly spicy aftershave. She took a deep breath, trying not to be obvious.

"Avery." There it was. She still had no clue what it was about the way he said her name, just her name, the one word, that turned her knees to Jell-o. No one said her name like that. She didn't even care if he was about to scold her. "Next time you take off looking for trouble, at least bring me with you."

She flushed warm, and her idiotic heart revved and somersaulted before settling back in its rightful place. "I'm not looking for trouble. Aren't you curious about these secret passages?"

He dropped his hands, as if suddenly aware he was still holding on to her. "Sure I am."

121

"I have a theory," Avery said. "Come on." She got the hidden door open and poked her nose around the corner, seeing no one.

"They're back in the lab putting a call in to Goldie Brennan," Art said. "I told them I'd go see if you got lost in this maze of a house."

She looked up at him. "That's a great idea. Getting lost, I mean. That's what happened." She pulled the door shut until she heard the latch click. "So that staircase goes all the way to roof. But the access door was locked. I bet everyone in the manor has a key. The family for sure, and probably most of the staff." She slowed as they reached an actual, visible door along the hallway.

"Makes sense," he said. "Hey!"

Avery pushed open the door and stuck her head in. "Oh! It's a bedroom."

Art kept his tone low. "What are you doing?"

"Just looking. It's fine; no one's even around." She hoped.

"All right. Let's go."

She quietly closed the door and kept walking. "I'm sure you've already thought of this, but listen," she said, matching his hushed tone. "I was thinking that whoever rushed outside when Suzanne screamed had to be innocent, and the stragglers who came out last were the likeliest suspects. Right? But," she rushed on, not giving him a chance to reply, "the hidden staircases change everything."

"Possibly," he said.

Avery found the next door unlocked like the first. "Huh. Another bedroom. This—" She leaned farther into the room.

"These rooms must belong to the staff. I wonder if they're all bedrooms?" She closed the door and stared down the hallway. There were three remaining.

"I'm sure you'll find out," Art murmured beside her. His phone buzzed, and he checked it. He typed something in before dropping it back in his pocket.

The next door Avery tried opened into a large maintenance closet that was the size of her bedroom. She stepped inside, taking in the shelving units that lined the walls, filled with cleaning supplies, towels, tools, and equipment.

Art stepped in behind her and closed the door. "Look." He pointed to the opposite wall.

"That's it!" she exclaimed. "I know it is, I can feel it." She crossed to a second door that was partially obscured behind a sheet of drywall propped against the wall. She nudged it sideways with her hip, sliding it out of the way, and pushed against the heavy steel door. It swung open onto the stamped concrete that encircled the manor, revealing a view of the nearby lily pond and the stables across the green pasture.

"Unbelievable."

Avery turned to face Art. "Not really. You can tell from inside that this is the wing closest to where Suzanne fell—was pushed," she corrected. "Lord Nico came through this door right after I got out there. Nick and his wife were already outside near Suzanne, over there," she said pointing.

"Right, and you said the gardener was kind of hunched over the body, crying, right? And then who else came out?"

Avery searched her memory. "The younger man from the stables came over—Bryan Wolf. And then Aunt Midge pulled up and I got distracted. I think when I looked back over there, Nick's driver and assistant were joining the group around Suzanne, and then Lord Percy came out the front door along with Lady Annabelle." She gasped and smacked Art lightly with the back of one hand. "Wait. Where was the girls' nanny? What's her name—Gretel? Gretchen. Oh! And Mr. Hoffman—was he out there? Wouldn't they have heard the scream? I know Mrs. Hoffman is innocent for sure; she was talking with us when it happened."

"We need to get back," Art said. He held the door for her. "Mrs. Hoffman's probably wondering where we are."

She walked back through the room, thoughts spinning. She exited through the second door into the hallway, glancing back at Art as she went. "We can narrow it down to—"

Avery fell suddenly silent, spotting Lord Percy twenty feet away, heading down the hall in swim trunks. His phone was to his ear, his head down as he walked, listening. "I know. Those two ponies have been with me the longest, I'm not about to—" He interrupted himself as he glanced up and spotted them. "Soon. That's all I know."

Art smoothly saved them both, slipping his arm around her waist and pulling her close. He put his lips near her ear. "Go with it." The abrupt shift, Art's warmth against her skin, his breath on her neck, instantly brought back their time together this summer and sent shivers zinging up her spine. She struggled to catch her breath, turning her head just enough to meet Lord Percy's gaze and then drop her own, her cheeks burning. Art's quick actions had left her having to feign nothing.

Art nodded at Lord Percy. "Good afternoon, sir. We, uh. Well, I guess we got lost."

Lord Percy gave the two of them an appraising glance, and then his face broke into a knowing grin. "No worries here. It happens."

Avery took a step to get Art moving. He did, keeping his arm around her waist. Lord Percy continued on his way toward the pool. The moment they'd passed each other, Avery spoke to Art in a stage whisper. "I've told you before, not while we're working!"

One corner of Art's mouth rose in a crooked grin. He dipped his head toward hers, matching her tone. "It's not my fault. You know all this science stuff turns me on."

She widened her eyes at him, mouthing, *Oh my God!*

The digital tones of the keypad outside the pool area drifted to them, and then the click and snap of the door. Lord Percy was gone.

Avery waited until they were in the reception room before stopping and facing him. "I can't believe you."

Art had the good sense to look surprised. "Would you rather still be there, explaining why we were really in that closet? And why you came out talking loudly about narrowing down suspects?"

"I did not! I mean, I guess I did. I was just excited. I should've stopped to make sure it was all clear first," she admitted.

"So, you're welcome."

"Pfft," she scoffed. "That was super cheesy, by the way. 'Science turns me on.' Not sure he bought that."

Art shrugged. "I don't think it matters. He was convinced the moment he saw you blush."

Micah appeared in the doorway from their lab. "I thought I heard you in here. We got ahold of Goldie. She asked if we could come by tomorrow morning."

"Yes," Avery said, relieved to have an excuse to tear herself away from Art's disconcerting focus. "Absolutely. Meet by the elevators?"

"I'll bring the coffee," he said.

The crackle of a radio came from the hallway, and Mrs. Hoffman's husband came through the door. "Excuse me, folks. The missus sent me to let you know lunch is ready."

On the way down the long hallway, Avery fell into step with him. "You and your wife have been with the Penningtons for generations. That's true dedication. You must really care about them." She was fishing and she didn't have a clear idea of what for, but this was the first time she'd seen the man since that first day when he'd been carrying in luggage.

"Like they're family. Duke Pennington has always been good to us."

"Does he get to come here frequently? I know he'd said his mother spent quite a bit of time at the manor, but the duke seems so busy. Or at least he did when we had lunch with him in London."

"We don't see much of him, but Lords Nico and Percy come and stay pretty often. I think they have some type of business dealings to tend to. Well, that'd be more Lord Nico's department, I guess."

"Really? Not both of them?"

Ira Hoffman glanced in both directions as they crossed the vestibule before answering. "You know how it is. Lord Percy is young, that's all. I can't figure what they'll do after the place is sold. Stay in hotels, I suppose."

Avery tried for a natural tone. "What'll you and Mrs. Hoffman do? Maybe it'll be nice, not being tied to the manor after all these years?"

He frowned at her. "I'm forty-four years old. A long way from retirement. What would you do if you had to start over in your forties? I can't say anything about this will be nice."

Avery's eyes went wide. She lowered her volume. They were almost to the dining room. "I'm so sorry." She took a chance and pushed a little further. "I suppose the sentiment is the same among all the staff here."

The caretaker pulled at his neatly trimmed beard, clearly weighing what to say. "It'll be an adjustment. It's the Penningtons' home, not ours, we all know that. You caught me in a bit of poor temper, Miss. I was just out at the stables helping old Jerry Wolf load up a horse. He wasn't happy with the buyer. But they all have to go." He shook his head as if trying to shake off the sour mood. He stood to the side as they reached the dining room, letting her go ahead. "It'll work out."

Avery hung back, waving her team in. She faced Ira Hoffman, somber. "I'm sure it will. I'm sorry if I was a little nosy. I'm so impressed with the way you all keep this place running so smoothly. Even now, without a housekeeper—I'm still shocked about poor Suzanne." She'd pushed as far as she could; she knew that. She drifted slowly through the doorway, hoping he'd comment.

His wife came up behind him, carrying a tray with condiments. "We all are." She stepped closer to Avery. "The dust bunnies are my responsibility for now. I haven't asked Duke Pennington if he'll fill the position. Might be better to leave it vacant—the manor housekeeper job is cursed."

"Really? What—oh!" A giggling Lucy and Ava, the duke's granddaughters, raced between them into the room, jarring Lynn Hoffman's tray. Avery put a hand out and steadied it before the contents could slide off.

"Girls!" Their nanny was close behind, breathing hard, brown curls escaping from the long, bright-pink ribbon she wore as a headband to match cute pink cropped pants. She was a tiny thing, the top of her head even with Avery's chin. "Goodness. Sorry for the disturbance, Mrs. Hoffman. I've chased them all the way from the gardens. I don't know where they get their energy!"

Mrs. Hoffman patted the young woman's arm. "No need for apologies, Miss Gretchen. They'll sleep well tonight!"

Gretchen nodded once and hurried over to the girls. "Ava, Lucy, full halt this second or no swimming today! Let's go wash our hands. Your mother's taking her lunch with you soon." She ushered them out the opposite side of the dining room, a hand on each girl's shoulder.

Avery, Art, Micah, and William had just finished Mrs. Hoffman's fabulous fettucine alfredo when Lady Annabelle arrived in the dining room with Lucy and Ava. She was once again dressed elegantly, head to toe in black right down to her heels. She stopped short just inside the doorway and scanned Avery's group. A look of disdain crossed her fine-boned, delicate features. Avery stood. "We were just leaving. The room's yours, Lady Annabelle."

The woman blinked at her. "Yes. Girls," she said, without looking at them. An entirely different Ava and Lucy than the ones who'd rushed through a half hour before silently took their seats.

"Have a nice afternoon," Avery called as they exited, passing Mrs. Hoffman coming in with a newly replenished tray.

"Brrr. Chilly," Avery commented when they were a few yards from the dining room.

"Freezing is more like it," Art said. "That woman's odd."

The afternoon flew by with Avery, Micah, and William all working on appraisals for separate pieces. Art moved from room to room, using the fact that they were split up into two or three rooms most of the day to his advantage. As they were packing up, he rejoined Avery in the movie theater.

"Remind me to tell you what I overheard between the brothers," he said quietly.

Avery widened her eyes. "Ooh, tell me."

He shook his head. "Later."

Outside in the circle drive, when Micah had departed and William had climbed behind the wheel, ready to leave, Avery paused at the passenger side. "Hey," she said, stopping Art before he opened his truck door. "What did you overhear?" The curiosity was killing her.

"Not here. I'll call you." She followed his exaggerated head tilt and saw Ira Hoffman a short distance away, pruning the rosebushes and scowling, a cigarette hanging from his lips. She doubted he'd even notice them talking.

"All right. Don't forget," she said. She wished he'd just driven with them. She turned to get in, and a flash of bright pink caught her eye. Across the green lawn, Gretchen stepped into Lord Nico's arms in the stable doorway. They disappeared inside.

# Chapter Nine

F riday morning at the Museum of Antiquities, Avery met Micah at the entrance. He handed one of his three coffees to her.

"Thank you! One for Goldie too—smart man," she said.

"I checked to see if I should get one for your dad, but he said you dropped him at the shop. He didn't want to say hello to Goldie?"

Avery shook her head. "No. I think he's struggling. He's still not quite himself since he's been back. He wanted to stay home, but I twisted his arm."

Micah frowned. "He's been through a lot. I doubt it'd be good for him to sit at home. It seems difficult for him to be in certain spaces . . . here, the shop, places he and your mother spent so many hours working closely together."

"I see that. It's hard for me too sometimes . . . you know that. Even sitting at her desk sometimes makes me feel choked up. With my dad, it seems like he hasn't really dealt with losing her at all. Maybe he was able to avoid the reality of it that year he was away from us."

"Right. It's hard to ignore it, though, when everything he does now used to be something they did together."

Avery was silent, Micah's words sinking in. All the pain she and Tilly and Aunt Midge had gone through in those first few months was still there, but it wasn't quite so sharp now. Her dad was probably still in that beginning stage, learning to breathe and work and function without his wife of thirty years.

She met Micah's eyes. He was speaking from experience. His wife, Cicely, had been gone over two years. Avery slipped her hand through his elbow, giving him a squeeze. "He has us. We'll help him get through it."

"He's in good hands with Sir Robert this morning. He'll talk William's ear off. How is Tilly doing?" Micah asked, concern in his tone. "Did you find out what brought her home a week early?" They turned down the hallway that led to the curator's office.

"We did. It's . . ." Ugh. Micah was a father figure to them, even more so since they'd thought they'd lost William. She didn't want to betray Tilly, despite the fact that her sister had screwed up in a big way. "Today's the first day she's home alone. We've been taking turns with Aunt Midge, keeping an eye on her, especially with her bad tooth on top of everything else. Her first couple months at the conservatory haven't gone well. I should probably have her tell you about it. Has Noah said anything at all about what happened?"

"Nothing. Which is unusual for him. I can't even tell you how often your sister's name has come up in the last few months since they started dating," he said, chuckling. "But lately he's been surprisingly close-lipped. Did they have some kind of falling out?"

"I guess you could say that. I kind of think they just need to talk. They were so sweet together."

Micah gave her a sideways glance as they arrived at Goldie's office. "As were you and the detective. I don't know what happened with you two, but I don't get the idea that he's a bad person. Sometimes people deserve a second chance."

She pursed her lips. He was right, but she could also apply that to her date with Hank tonight.

Goldie Brennan waved them in. "Avery, Micah. It's so lovely to see you." She took the coffee Micah offered. "Perfect timing. I was about to go for a refill." Goldie removed her glasses, perching them atop her shiny silver bob. At seventy-five, she'd been MOA's chief curator for over two decades.

"I'm sorry we had to break the news to you yesterday about the *Ara Eros* being a stolen antiquity," Avery said. "We were shocked to find the copy at Pennington Manor. I swear we did our due diligence, Goldie. When we certified the statues, there was no doubt they were authentic, and the last provenance listed online was—"

Goldie put a hand up, shaking her head. "No. Now listen to me. Your company has provided the most accurate, meticulous work on every assignment you've done for MOA. The Emperor's Twins was an anomaly. Your parents had that managed until it was taken out of their hands. I have no issue with your work."

Avery relaxed, but still had to explain. "We appreciate that. I just need you to know, though, that we did verify the hard-copy provenance was genuine. I mean, we really thought it was. It passed every marker, so even though the online records show the last record of ownership dated in the 1800s, we did trust the recent change in hands noted on the hard copy. We know sales don't always get logged the way they should."

"It's also worth mentioning," Micah added, "that an Albert Beauchamp is listed as the owner in the 1800s. The name Pennington has never been attached to the piece. I like to think Avery or I would've realized right away that we'd worked with a piece belonging to the duke had that name been on the provenance."

"Who is Albert Beauchamp?" Goldie asked.

Avery took the question. "There are dozens from that era in Europe. We know now that our Albert Beauchamp was King Albert III of Valle Charme, Nicholas Pennington's great-great-grandfather."

"Quite a noteworthy piece, then! Even given the small kingdom of Valle Charme. I confess I hadn't heard of it, but the island is gorgeous. I've already spoken to our risk management department. There's a procedure for instances like this. We'll make sure the piece is returned to Duke Nicholas Pennington immediately. The authorities will have to track down how the *Ara Eros* found its way into MOA's submissions."

"What about the purchase cost? Will you be able to recoup that from the antiques dealer?" Micah asked.

"And who *was* the dealer or collector? I think that's the million-dollar question," Avery said.

Goldie handed a file across the desk. "The *Ara Eros* was Nate's first independent acquisition. I haven't seen him yet this morning, but I have a message in to him. He'll be able to tell us if there was anything odd about the deal. The dealer is listed in the purchase agreement."

Avery perused the contract. Nate Brennan was Goldie's grandson. She'd had a few issues with him at first, mainly his cocky, arrogant attitude. He was her age and had stepped into his assistant acquisitions liaison role, and a seat on the board, with no qualifications simply because he'd been cut off from the family money and needed a job. He'd spent several months learning his role under the wing of Francesca Giolitti, lead acquisitions liaison and the woman responsible for Sir Robert's broken heart.

A shiver crept up Avery's spine when she checked the date at the top of document. She looked up at Goldie. "This contract is dated a week after Francesca disappeared. Was she involved in this acquisition? You're sure this was all Nate?"

Goldie nodded. "I'm certain. It came up after she was gone, so he wouldn't have had an opportunity to consult with her." She paused, gaze moving from Avery to Micah. "You're wondering how I can be so sure."

Avery fought to rearrange her expression. She'd never had a good poker face, and she knew Goldie's blind spot was Nate Brennan. "I'm sorry. But yes. I can't help thinking she had a hand in this."

Goldie folded her hands on her desk. "Nate insisted on having a sit-down with me before the purchase was finalized, specifically because it was his first solo acquisition. He knew we'd make the deal, but he wanted me to glance over everything and make sure he hadn't missed anything. Francesca wasn't working here when the *Ara Eros* acquisition was finalized."

"Ah. All right. I had to ask. So, this dealer listed: Raul Cordoba. Do you know him? Have you had other submissions from him?"

Goldie turned toward her computer screen and put her glasses back on, tapping on the keys. "We have. A handful in the last several years. Let's see . . ." She frowned, reading. "Mostly lower-value pieces, though we did get *Fated Union* from him, one of the more famous paintings recovered from the *Titanic*. That was certified authentic by your mother and Micah six years ago."

"Oh wow." Avery's eyes widened.

"I remember that piece," Micah said. "It was an easy assignment. The pigment, canvas, and technique all matched the artist and era, and there was no change in ownership since the original purchase."

"Sounds like it was all legit. Weird that a reputable dealer MOA has history with would submit a valuable stolen artifact. Maybe he didn't know it was stolen." Avery leaned forward, placing the contract on Goldie's desk. "Is it possible for you to give us Raul Cordoba's contact information? I know you're not supposed to, but it will be faster than tracking it down ourselves. I don't know what exactly is going on at Pennington Manor, Goldie, but one person's been killed already. The faster we help clear this up, the better."

The older woman returned her attention to her computer and jotted down contact details on a purple sticky note. "I've also forwarded your list of other stolen artifacts to risk management. I don't show that we've acquired any of those items. But we can coordinate with our partners in other locations and let you know if there are any flags."

"That'd be amazing. Thank you so much for your help."

Micah stood as Avery did. "We hope to be finished with the Pennington Manor job by next Friday," he said. "We've got your Turkish tapestry set assignment scheduled for the following week, but if one of us has time sooner, we'll be in."

Goldie stood too and shook both their hands. "I'm not worried. Give your father my best, Avery, will you? I hope he knows how much I value his and your dear mother's work."

"I'll make sure to mention that to him," Avery assured her.

Avery left her car in the parking garage at MOA, and she and Micah walked the six blocks to their shop, since parking was scarce near their building and Micah had taken the subway in from his Hamilton Heights neighborhood in Harlem. Fifteen minutes later they approached the door sandwiched between the Manhattan branch of Shinola, a chic watchmaking company out of Detroit, and one of the city's many coffee shops. Deep-gold Old English lettering in a curved arc on their glass door read **ANTIQUITIES & ARTIFACTS APPRAISED, est. 2008**, with the phone number and APPOINTMENTS ONLY in smaller lettering underneath.

Avery stopped abruptly on her way through the door. Tilly looked up from their father's desk, laptop open in front of her as if she worked here. Sir Robert was speaking with a client in the reception area, a small but well-appointed space with a vintage brown leather Chesterfield sofa and coffee table on a red-and-gold Oriental rug. William was nowhere to be seen.

Avery stopped in front of Tilly. "You surprised me! How did you get here? Are you okay?"

"I'm good. I got a ride in with Mindy."

"Oh. You could have come with me."

"It was kind of a snap decision." Tilly stood and gave Micah a quick hug. "Love your bow tie."

Micah touched the russet-orange-and-brown plaid tie, nicely coordinated with his brown suit coat and oxfords. "You're too sweet. Noah's going to be upset he missed you in the city. Have you let him know you're here? I'm sure he'd jump on a train."

Avery caught the pained look that crossed her sister's face, which also was a little fancier than usual today. Tilly rarely wore makeup. But now her already long, dark eyelashes were accentuated with mascara, and there were faint black smudges under her eyes. Like she'd been crying. Tilly looked down. "No, I, uh, didn't tell him I'd be here. Do you think he's at home?"

"I know he is. He came home for the weekend, but he's got a big paper due. He was working on it when I left this morning." He moved to his desk.

"Oh." Tilly sat back down, swiveling the chair one way and then the other. She left it at that. Avery met Micah's gaze over her sister's head. There was nothing she could do—Tilly had to work this out with Noah herself.

"Hey, have you seen Dad?" Avery asked. She leaned down nonchalantly, trying to get a peek at what her sister was working on.

Tilly closed the laptop. "Nope. Sir Robert said he had a headache and left."

"Huh." She grabbed a water bottle and took her seat. Her desk and Micah's faced each other. It always seemed to help when they were brainstorming ideas or figuring out schedules and assignments. There was no mistaking which desk was whose. The edges of Avery's were lined with small, floral boxes that held everything from paper clips to hand lotion. On her desktop were her laptop, notepad, pen, and charging station. Across from her, Micah's desktop wasn't visible. He had his own filing system and claimed to know where everything was, but Avery had no idea how.

"Should we try to see Raul Cordoba today?" she asked Micah when she'd powered on her laptop. She sneaked another look at her little sister. She needed to find out if Tilly truly was okay before they ran off again.

He held up the sticky note from Goldie. "He's located in Brooklyn. I just called and got his voice mail. It says he's out of town until Monday."

Avery groaned. "I wanted to try to get somewhere with this today. We'll have to go Monday morning. Maybe we'll be lucky and get to him before the MOA risk management people or the authorities do. It'd help to see his genuine reaction when he learns he sold the museum a stolen artifact worth a million and a half."

Sir Robert joined them, the bell on the door jingling as his client left. "Was Goldie upset? Your father filled me in on the *Ara Eros* debacle."

"She handled the news graciously," Avery said. "She didn't seem too ruffled."

"That's what insurance is for. They'll mitigate the loss one way or another. Who was the dealer?"

"Raul Cordoba. Does the name sound familiar?"

"Of course. I see him now and then at Barnaby's," Sir Robert replied. "But he's a straight shooter. He'd never have submitted to MOA if he'd known the items were stolen."

"That was Goldie's feeling too," Avery said. "Micah and I wanted to bring you up to date on what's happening at the manor—I wish my dad hadn't left. Should we do that now, or do you want to tell us about the new intake?" She eyed the grandmother clock in Sir Robert's arms.

"This will wait. Let me go put it in the back, and then I want in on your update."

"Did Art ever call to tell you what it was that he overheard?" Micah asked.

"No." She'd waited all night, hoping he'd call, but he never had. She wasn't about to chase him down. He'd never seemed like a game player to her, but the more she was around him, the less she felt she knew about him.

"Then call him," Micah said.

"Who?" Sir Robert returned from their lab at the back of the shop. He grabbed a package of chocolate candies from the stash at the coffee station and slid his chair over to Avery's and Micah's desks.

"Detective Art," Micah said. "He caught some conversation yesterday between Duke Pennington's sons, but he couldn't share while we were there."

"Ooh, call him." Sir Robert popped a chocolate in his mouth. Avery estimated he'd gained a good ten or fifteen pounds since losing Francesca; he'd never have been caught dead eating candy while they were dating. But he was finally starting to perk up. The first few weeks without her, he'd been miserable to be around.

"Guys." Avery looked sternly from Sir Robert to Micah. "I'm trying to maintain some boundaries here. We don't need the one extra snippet of information that Art has right this second."

"Plus she has a date with Hank tonight," Tilly murmured, not glancing up from the laptop she was typing on.

"What? Since when?" Micah asked. "Why didn't you say so?"

Avery laughed. "I don't know—because I didn't think my dating life was that interesting to everyone. It's not a big deal."

"I disagree. You told us that he broke up with you because you kept picking fights with him," Sir Robert said.

"He did. But I'm not the same person now. He understands that I was trying to deal with losing both my parents."

"What made you decide to ask him out again? You two have tried and failed more than once, haven't you?" Micah asked.

"Oh my God. I obviously tell you all too much. He asked me out. We had a good thing for a long time before it fell apart. So yes, that's tonight, and it's honestly been rough spending time with Art this week knowing we didn't work out and I have a date with Hank. I just want to do my job."

Sir Robert held the candy out to her. "You need these more than I do."

"Oh no. No way, no sugar, not a week before the race. Let's focus. Did you have a chance yet to see if any of those missing items from the manor are logged as exhibits elsewhere? Maybe Detroit or Chicago or even the antiquities museum in LA?" she asked him.

"I have not," he said, his tone defensive. "I had to deal with Mr. Oswald and his antique revolver first thing this morning, and then as you saw, I was tied up with Mrs. Kim."

"We'll work on it together," Micah said, ever the peacemaker. "I can start with Chicago."

Avery nodded. "All right. I'll check into Detroit and that other Michigan museum in Lansing."

"Dad could've helped. Since when does he get headaches?" Tilly grumbled.

The three of them turned to stare at her.

"What? I'm just saying. Whatever. Can I print from here?"

"Sure," Avery said. "Just choose print on whatever you're working on and then find ours—it should come up as a Canon GL and some numbers. I'll show you." She stood, but Tilly did too, one hand at the top of the now open laptop screen.

"I've got it. I don't need any help." She bent down and tapped a few more keys.

"Sheesh. Fine. Then you'd better go turn on the printer too." Avery watched Tilly covertly as she printed whatever it was she working on, took it off the tray, and slid it into a large manila envelope.

Tilly picked up her purse. "I'll be back."

Avery and Micah frowned at each other. Avery followed her sister outside. "Hey. Hold on."

"Dude, seriously. I've lived overseas for two whole months on my own. I think I can find the subway." Tilly kept walking.

"Tilly, stop." Avery jogged over to her, touching her shoulder.

Tilly finally stopped and spun around. "Oh my God, stop hovering! I've got this." She challenged Avery with her blue, wide-eyed stare.

"You've got what? What's going on with you? Why were you crying—yes, I can see that you were crying. What's in the envelope?"

"I'm an actual grown-up, A. I don't need any help." Tilly's jaw jutted forward stubbornly.

"Age doesn't make you a grown-up. How you handle responsibility does. And for the record, I'm an *actual* grown-up, and even I need help sometimes. Where are you going?" Avery held Tilly's gaze. "Hey. It's me. I always have your back, you know that. No judgment."

The girl drew in a huge breath, pulling her shoulders up, and exhaled heavily. "I went to Harlem to see Noah this morning. He was home—you heard Micah. He didn't answer his phone or the doorbell. He really hates me."

Avery sucked air through her teeth. "Oh."

"I know, right?"

"No," Avery said, shaking her head. "He can't possibly hate you. He was asleep or had music on or something. I can't think he'd intentionally avoid you, Tilly."

"Well, he did. So I guess that's my answer. It doesn't matter how many times I try to tell him I know I screwed up, he's made up his mind."

"I don't believe that. Let's go try again. Or do you want Micah to get ahold of him and see if we can stop by?"

"No!" Tilly's eyes widened even further in horror. "Just forget it. And this"—she raised the envelope in her hand—"is something I have to do alone. I'm being responsible, I promise. Let me try."

"Okay." Avery stepped back. Her sister looked shocked.

"Okay," Tilly said.

"I hope it goes well. Whatever it is." Avery turned and headed back to the shop, forcing her feet to move and sending as many positive vibes straight at Tilly as she could summon.

"Thank you!"

Avery turned back, one hand on the doorknob. She smiled at her sister and gave her a little wave. Tilly was certainly trying hard to do something, though she couldn't imagine what.

They'd been silently working at their desks for a couple hours, researching the stolen items, when Sir Robert raised both fists in the air victoriously. "I've got the brooch!"

"No way! Where is it?"

He read from the screen. "It's part of the *Royal Heirlooms in Nineteenth Century France* exhibit at the Roquefort Museum in Palo Alto, California."

Avery came to look over his shoulder. "Wow. Somehow I didn't think it'd get all the way across the country. Cool exhibit, though."

"I may have a lead on the King Federico IV painting too," Micah said. "Not sure yet."

"I'm going to have to call Art, aren't I?" Avery knew it was a redundant question.

Micah spoke. "We can't keep this information to ourselves. We either need to call Detective Carter, if you still have his card, or Art."

She sighed. "He's going to be hurt if I go around him to the other detective. Dammit." She pulled out her phone and took the coward's way out. She texted him instead of calling.

*Sorry to bother you, but we have leads on at least one of the stolen items from the manor and maybe more. If you're busy, we can notify Detective Carter.*

She hit send, then instantly regretted her little passive-aggressive dig at the end; it wasn't like her. She'd wanted to say, *Why didn't you call me like you said you would?* But that sounded way too possessive and needy.

Her phone rang in her hand, startling her. It was Art.

"Where are you?" he asked.

"I'm not at the manor, don't worry. I promised I'd keep you updated on when we're going. We're at the Manhattan shop."

"Oh! That's perfect. I'll come to you. I'm a few miles away."

"Um." Avery glanced at the clock on the reception area wall. Hank was picking her up in Lilac Grove in exactly three hours. "All right. But I'm leaving soon."

"On my way," Art said, and the line went dead.

Ten minutes later a NYPD squad car pulled up out front and dropped Art off, then pulled away from the curb and squealed away, lights on and sirens screaming. He was dressed in his usual today, a dark suit, a change from the more casual style she'd quickly gotten used to when he was posing as their colleague at the manor. He stood in the reception area as if waiting for an invitation to come back to where their desks were. Avery went over to him.

"Nice ride."

"He got a call as we were pulling up. Listen, I know you have plans tonight. I'm not staying. We should be able to go over this pretty quickly."

She frowned at him. "It's fine, I have time. It's nice of you to worry about making me late, though." It wasn't nice at all! Why was he being so accommodating? If Art was about to go on a date tonight with another woman, she imagined she'd be flustered or irritated or jealous. Maybe he wasn't into her the way she'd hoped. "Follow me. We'll tell you what we've found."

They filled Art in on the whereabouts of the diamond brooch that had belonged to Nick's great-aunt. Micah had also now confirmed that the King Federico IV portrait was accounted for. It had been acquired by the Chicago Antiquities Museum from a dealer six months ago.

"We've reached out to the curators at both places, Chicago and Palo Alto, in hopes they'll give us the names of the submitting collectors or dealers. But we figured this is something you'd want to let Detective Carter in on," Avery explained.

"This is great work," Art said. "I'm impressed. Carter spoke with Goldie Brennan at MOA a little while too."

"There's something else. I was going to mention it when you called about whatever it was you overheard, but . . ."

He looked sheepish. "I meant to call. I had a sort of emergency I had to take care of."

She raised an eyebrow at him, but he didn't add more. "As I was leaving yesterday," she said, "I saw the girls' nanny, Gretchen. She was going into the stables."

"Nick's probably given the staff permission to use the pool and ride the horses, the same as he did with us," Art said.

"Sure, but she wasn't there for the horses. She was meeting Lord Nico. I saw them together. Like, *together* together."

"Whoa." Micah spoke beside her. "I didn't see that coming."

"That's something," Art said. "Because I had reason to wonder if Nico had something going on with Suzanne. I was in the sitting area on the second floor, by that big sculpture with the dog. Sound carries really well up there from the foyer. Nico was chewing Percy out for making their father come bail him out of jail."

Avery gasped. "I knew it! I thought something like that had happened. What was he arrested for?"

"Detective Carter's finding out—we have to go through the proper channels, and he's lead on this. But listen. Percy got defensive and called Nico trash for cheating on his wife."

"Gretchen the nanny," Avery said. "Told you."

"Right, apparently so. I was wrong to assume it was Suzanne. There's more. Nico hit back—literally—I could hear some kind of scuffle. I turned my camera on and held my phone out by the railing, but I couldn't get the right angle to see anything. Next thing I heard was Nico saying that their father wouldn't even be selling the place if Percy wasn't such a screw-up."

"Oh wow," Avery said. "So it sounds like neither of Nick's sons wants the manor to be sold. Percy is in trouble with the law, and Nico's sleeping with the nanny. His wife is a crabby, miserable person, but maybe I at least understand why now. She probably knows he's up to something. But what does all this have to do with someone wanting Suzanne dead?"

"I don't know yet. There are too many missing pieces," Art said. "When did you say that Brooklyn antiquities dealer is back in town?"

"Monday. We'll have one more piece first thing Monday morning if Raul Cordoba will tell us who he got the *Ara Eros* from," Avery said.

# Chapter Ten

Avery offered to drive to Harlem Friday afternoon before heading home so Tilly could try once more to talk with Noah. Tilly turned her down. Her mood was better, but she didn't say a word about her mysterious errand. She spent the drive home talking about weekend plans with her friends Eve, Mindy, and Chase. Given the way her friendships in London had gone up in flames, Avery was relieved Tilly still had her close-knit Lilac Grove friend group.

Home by five PM, Avery found William in his easy chair watching television through his eyelids. Everything about his behavior lately was off. Normally the TV didn't get turned on until late in the evening, if at all. She switched it off, thinking that might wake him, but it didn't. She made Tilly promise to make sure he ate something for dinner and sprinted upstairs to get ready for her date.

Before moving home last year, Avery had been in what her friends called a dating drought. The long-distance thing hadn't worked well between her and Hank. Even though they'd dated since college, it had been a mutual split a few months after her career took her to Philadelphia. In her two-plus years in Philly, she briefly dated two men—the barista from her building, which ended badly and caused her a lack of good coffee, and a coworker who'd turned out to be a bigger jerk than the barista. She and Hank had picked things back up again when Avery moved home last year—he'd always been the sweetest boyfriend, something she'd learned to appreciate even more after Philly. Most of their second time around was Hank repeatedly throwing her a life preserver and Avery batting it away and continuing to drown herself and take him with her. The night it ended, she said some terrible things to him that she'd never be able to take back. Their second breakup had been inevitable from the moment he'd kissed her on the swings at Lilac Grove Park after the funeral.

Now, with their third "first date" looming in a few minutes, Avery sat on the porch in dark denim jeans and the new yellow blouse she'd bought because it was Hank's favorite color, wondering if this was a mistake. Maybe they were crazy to try again. He was either the most misguided or most understanding man she knew. He pulled into the drive, and Halston leapt up beside her and was running over to him before he could even get out of his car. The dog loved Hank. Though, to be fair, Halston loved everyone.

She met him at the bottom of the porch steps. "Hi."

"Hey, Avery," he said. He leaned in tentatively, and she hugged him. He was exactly her height, solid, muscled but not obnoxiously so. He smelled of the same cologne he'd been using since college.

She stood back a little, meeting his blue eyes, and then she lightly touched his sandy-blond hair. "You let it grow." It had been military short when she and Aunt Midge ran into him at Old Smoke.

He smiled. "It's not Kenneth Branagh length yet, though."

"Aunt Midge comparing your waves to Kenneth Branagh's was a high compliment, trust me. You do have beautiful hair."

"Uh, thanks. I guess."

"Never say a man's anything is beautiful," Avery said, making an imaginary check mark in the air. "See, I've already stuck my foot in my mouth not two minutes in. I saved us both from having to worry about doing it later."

"Well. You look beautiful. As always." Halston pawed at Hank, and he gave him more head scratches. "I thought we'd have dinner at O'Shannahan, unless you have somewhere else in mind?"

She grabbed her purse. "Sure! I could go for some salmon." O'Shannahan in town had the best seafood in the county. It was an old favorite of theirs.

Hank ordered the same thing he ordered every time they'd been here: fish and chips with a Chardonnay. Avery had salmon and brown rice with asparagus. She squelched the urge to order a cold beer and got iced water instead. One of the first things she was going to have when she could eat what she wanted to after the marathon was an ice-cold beer and a greasy burger. For now, salmon and water served their purpose.

"Everything okay?" Hank asked.

They'd covered her job, his job; they'd caught up on each other's families; Avery had congratulated Hank on becoming an uncle for the second time; and in between were periods of silence she didn't know how to fill. She chased the rice around her plate with a bite of fish on her fork, glancing up at him. "Sure. Why?"

He shrugged. "You make a face every time you sip your water."

She hadn't bothered to explain her drink choice. Avery chuckled. "That's because it's not what I really wanted. I'm prepping for the marathon next weekend. Beer and wine are off the menu."

"That's awesome! I didn't know you were still doing that."

She raised her eyebrows at him. "After all the volunteer hours it took to get in, there's no way I'd drop out. I'm a little nervous. I've never done a full twenty-six miles. The most I've run at once is eighteen, and I've only done that twice."

He nodded. "I'm not nervous for you. You've always been able to do whatever you put your mind to."

She met his gaze. "That is one of the best things anyone's ever said to me, Hank."

He shrugged. "I didn't say it to be nice. It's true." He put his fork down and sat back. "I miss talking to you."

Avery's throat felt suddenly thick. She swallowed hard. "I miss us too. I miss complaining to you after a bad day or calling to tell you about a super cool artifact I'm working on."

"You were my best friend," Hank said, his tone quiet.

She reached across the table and squeezed his hand. "You were mine." She studied their linked hands. Being with him was like putting on a favorite, comfy old sweater. There might be newer ones in the closet, but none fit the way this one did.

*But.* She turned their hands over, so the back of hers was resting on the table now. There was absolutely no spark. She'd much rather sit here and talk with him than go back to his place with him.

He stroked her hand with his thumb. "Avery. This isn't going to work with us, is it?"

An overwhelming sadness pressed down on her, startling in its abruptness. "I don't think so. But . . . does it mean there's no friendship either?" She hesitated. "I understand if we can't be friends." The sharp edges of those words hurt as she said them.

"Maybe we're ready to just be friends after all these years," Hank said. "I don't know."

She leaned in closer. "Hank, those things I said to you the last time, I wish I could take them back. That was much more about me than you. I'm so sorry I hurt you."

"I know you are. It's okay. We're okay."

She smiled, and one tear slipped down her cheek. She swiped it away. "I'm still a mess sometimes," she said, rolling her eyes.

"Nah. You're not. Hey, it's the end of an era, right?" He smiled back at her. "Third time isn't always the charm."

She nodded. "We aren't right for each other anymore. Maybe we've grown up a little."

"Since we were twenty-one? God, I hope so." He let go of her hand. "I am a little short on friends, though."

She had a feeling she might always love Hank. "I'm shorter. I have exactly one friend, Rachel at Mixed Bag, unless my little sister counts." She cringed, realizing she still owed

Rachel a dinner invitation and the appraisal of the hair adorn-ment. Maybe Micah and Sir Robert counted as friends too, but they were also colleagues.

"Tilly's a force of nature," Hank said, laughing. "She counts. Rachel's cool too. So, two friends? You're right, you're even more pathetic than I am. I've got, like, five guys, at least. Seven if golfing's involved."

When he dropped her off after dinner, Avery hugged him more tightly than she had the first time. "I hope you know how much I appreciate you."

She watched his taillights disappear, feeling like a weight had been lifted off her chest. She didn't know what had com-pelled him to ask her out tonight. Probably the same thing that had made her accept. Maybe they'd both needed a better ending to their five-year history.

* * *

Avery was cooling down from her morning run Saturday when her dad came out on the porch with her phone. "Your detec-tive has called three times, and I think he's texting you now."

She took the phone, scanning the messages. "He wants to know when we're coming to the manor today. Oh! He says Detective Carter will be there interviewing the rest of the family and staff. Art wants to be on-site in case anything comes up." She went inside, holding the door for her dad. "I can be ready to go in half an hour, if that works for you."

William stopped at the foot of the stairs, looking up at her. "You don't need me. I feel like cleaning up the garage and futzing around the house today."

She frowned. "No, Dad, I do need you. You know this antiques stuff like the back of your hand."

"Right, but that's not what today's about." He tipped his head, scrutinizing her. "I know you made Tilly drag me off the recliner and take Halston for a walk last night."

Avery trotted back down the steps to the foyer, facing him. "I'm worried about you."

William sighed. He sat down on the bench in the foyer. He patted the seat, looking up at Avery. She joined him. "I don't want you to worry. I think I'm just trying to figure out how to live in our new normal. Without your mom."

"I get that."

"Since I've been slowly getting more involved in projects at work, it's like I'm losing her all over again. We were always together," he said, his voice quiet. "Always. Here at home, at the shop, on assignments. She would've loved Pennington Manor— can you imagine?" His smile was the saddest Avery'd ever seen.

"I've thought of that too—a real-life castle for her to explore. She'd have asked Nick a zillion questions," she said. "She'd have demanded an in-depth tour the very first day, ground floor to parapet and stables included. We'd probably have had to drag her away when the job was over." She matched her dad's smile.

"I miss her. I see wisps of her everywhere. I haven't said much because I don't need you worrying." He leaned forward, resting his elbows on his knees. "Being at the sheriff's office the other day was awful. Being at the shop is difficult. Hell, being here is hard. Being surrounded with our team on assignment is brutal. She should be with us."

155

"I know," Avery whispered. She put a hand gently on his back.

"The first thing they told me when I woke up after the accident was that she was dead. And then they said if I went home, it could get you and Tilly killed. The day of our funeral, I was on a medevac flight to an Ohio safe house. By the time I could stand on my own, a month had passed and all they'd tell me was that Midge was with you two."

Avery hugged him. They had never discussed his time away from them. She'd tried, but he'd steadfastly refused. She'd finally given up, thinking he must know what was best. But he needed to talk about it; she saw that now.

He cleared his throat after a time, and she loosened her hold on him. "Listen. I'll be okay," he said. "I just need some time."

"We have plenty of that," she said. "Maybe I should stay home today with you. I don't mind."

"I'm all right, Roo. I promise. I've got this guy to keep me company." He reached over and patted Halston, and the dog put his head in William's lap. "And your sister can help me clean out the garage, if she ever decides to wake up."

Avery frowned at him, considering. "I guess I'll go. If you're sure."

He stood, and she did too. "Positive."

She turned to head back upstairs and stopped, looking over her shoulder. "I almost forgot to tell you. Aunt Midge is coming for dinner tomorrow, if you're up for it. I told her to bring Wilder too. We've been missing him."

Her dad's face lit up, warming Avery. "Wonderful. Then Tilly and I will clean up the patio instead. Maybe we'll have dessert on the patio. Might be the last time for a while—there's a cold front moving in next week, maybe an early snow. I hope it breaks before your run."

"Snow? No thank you! Not yet. It's only October twenty-ninth!"

"We had snow on Halloween when you were seven," William said. "You wouldn't wear anything that'd cover your costume. You made your mother stuff your winter coat under the Cinderella gown."

She laughed. "Unbelievable that you remember that."

He smiled. "I remember all of it."

Avery called Art as she was pulling out of the driveway.

"About time," he said when he answered.

"I was running. Listen, I just left the house, but my dad and Micah are out. It's just me today." Micah had sounded disappointed he'd miss a day at the manor, but he and Noah had preexisting plans. "Are you already there?"

"No. Want to pick me up on your way through town? I had a complication slow me down—I'm not being evasive; it's just easier to show you when you get here."

\* \* \*

Art opened the door before she had a chance to knock. "Do you know anything about cats?"

Avery's eyes widened. "Uh-oh. Why?"

"Follow me."

The first time Avery had gotten to see the inside of Art's house was on their third date last June. She'd been pleasantly surprised to find that the detective kept a tidy house. It wasn't white glove ready or so meticulous as to be uninviting, but it was obvious that he put time and effort into having a nice home. She'd learned during their two months together that he stayed organized using a whiteboard calendar in his mudroom—updated often, listing appointments and time slots with notes like *trash day* and *mortgage due.* He synced his cell phone every night with the virtual assistant speaker on his kitchen counter, his tablet, and his home laptop, and each morning the speaker announced his schedule for the day. She'd admired his organization so much that she'd tried to adopt a few of the same habits herself.

Now she followed him through to the kitchen and gasped. A large playpen sat in the middle of the floor. On a worn old quilt in the pen were a scruffy-looking calico and seven kittens. "Oh! My God! You're a cat dad!" She reached in, letting the mother cat sniff her hand. She looked up at Art, unable to stop grinning. "They're so adorable!"

He looked less thrilled than she felt. "I am not a cat dad—I don't even like cats. Do you want them?"

She straightened up from petting as many of them as she could reach. "What?"

"The mother cat showed up on my porch last night, making a lot of noise. So I gave her some scraps of turkey. She's pathetic." He gestured at the cat. "I had to. But this morning she was back, and she had four babies with her."

"Seven," Avery corrected.

"No, four. She went and got the other three, one at a time, while I tried to shoo them all away. She piled them all on my damn porch mat! What the heck is wrong with her?"

Avery almost grabbed him and hugged him. Her arms ached with the need, as if he were the magnet and she were the paper clip—completely inappropriate, considering they were broken up. She balled up her fists at her sides. "Nothing at all is wrong with her. She's a new mother and needed a safe place to keep her kittens. She can tell you're a safe place." She met his gaze and had to look quickly away.

"What am I supposed to do with them? I only brought them inside because it's going to rain later."

"Leave them in here for now. They look pretty comfy to me."

"Leave them in the house? The whole time we're gone today?" The look of horror on his face cracked Avery up. She couldn't help it.

"They're just cats, Art. What do you think they're going to do?"

"I don't know," he admitted. "You think it's fine to leave them? Should I put food in there with them? What do they eat?"

"You only need to feed the mom for now. These little ones are probably only a few weeks old. Maybe some more of that turkey you gave her last night? We'll pick up some cat food on the way back."

Avery watched him cut the meat carefully into tiny pieces and put it on a plate near the mother cat, then add a small bowl of water. He grabbed his keys and wallet but hovered near the playpen, not willing to leave yet. "Is that too much water? What if one of the babies spills it or drowns in it? I can't leave the water in there." He bent to remove it, and Avery stopped him with a hand on his arm.

"It's good. It's barely any water. I think they'll all be fine, Art. Better than fine. You're giving them a warm, dry, caring place to stay." She chanced another glance at him, this time holding his gaze. "Cat dad."

"All right, all right. You're a comedian," he said. "Let's go. Leave your car here; I'll drive. They're all going back outside when I get home."

"Sure," she agreed, resolving to change his mind before that happened. Once they were on the highway, she asked, "So, what are you going to name them?"

He shot a skeptical look at her. "Nothing. They're not staying. I have no idea how to take care of eight cats."

"It's not that hard. I'd help you find homes for some of the kittens. Hey, why do you have a playpen?" She wondered if his three sisters had kids—she'd never met his family.

He was quiet. She waited, but when he didn't answer, she spoke again.

"Never mind. It's none of my business. I shouldn't have asked." The high she'd been on after seeing Art and the cat family plummeted. This was exactly the way it had been the entire time they'd been together. There were so many tightly locked little rooms inside this man that he wasn't willing to open for her.

Art stared straight ahead, the muscle in his jaw pulsing, a scowl setting in. "No. Ask. It's good. You're good for me, Avery." His scowl deepened, but he pushed forward. "I was married before. We were going to have kids."

"You—you were married?"

"Yes. And my wife was pregnant." He barreled forward. "It was a girl. She had a miscarriage, but by then we'd already had a baby shower and collected so much stuff. She took most of it after the divorce. I don't know why the playpen ended up here with the move. I wasn't in a good headspace when I left Manhattan. I had forgotten about it until the cats came."

Avery's mind was reeling. It was a lot, so much to process at once. He'd been married? And—had gone through a miscarriage with his wife. His ex-wife. Jesus. How had she dated him for two whole months and he'd never once thought to mention any of this? How long had he been married? Was it losing the baby that had led to the divorce? She glanced up at him as he cleared his throat.

He rubbed the back of his neck. "I should have told you I was married."

"Art," she said softly. "I'm so sorry. That must have been awful." She pressed her lips together. What else could she say? No wonder he hadn't wanted to open that wound. She couldn't imagine how he must feel—being married, expecting a baby, and then losing everything. She'd known something had happened when he was with the NYPD. He'd told her once that he'd made a mistake that nearly got his partner killed and he'd never gone back after his suspension ended. She knew nothing else about it. Avery was starting to doubt she'd ever really be able to know him.

"It was awful. It was a long time ago. If I shared more, maybe it wouldn't seem like you're walking through a minefield every time you ask me an innocent question."

She gave him a small smile. "Very true," she said. They drove the last half hour in silence. Art's posture had relaxed, and Avery let the hum of the road and the rolling storm clouds in the distance take her mind off the manor, Tilly, her dad, even the soon-to-be-homeless cats. She was surprised when Art's truck rolled through the gates of Pennington Manor and down the long, winding driveway; it seemed like only a few minutes had passed.

"He's out there again," Avery said, leaning forward and pointing toward the stable. Nick's eldest son was in the paddock with a majestic-looking brown stallion and one of the Wolfs. The father and son groomsmen looked too much alike from a distance to discern a difference.

Art slowed to a crawl, following her gaze. "I thought most of the horses were Lord Percy's, for polo, right? I know we've seen him out there too, but Lord Nico sure visits the stables a lot. See the nanny anywhere?"

She'd already scanned the area, narrowing her eyes trying to see through the open door into the dark barn. There was no sign of Gretchen today. "Not this time." The other groomsman came out, leading a slow-moving, stout black mare, definitely not one of the polo ponies. Duke Pennington was with him. "Maybe Nico and his father are going out for a ride."

Art parked on the circle drive beside Detective Carter's black unmarked car and a Westchester County Sheriff's Department cruiser. As Avery and Art walked toward the front door, Nick's wife, the Duchess Mariah, spoke animatedly with two people setting up camera equipment on the lush green lawn. She pointed toward the expanse of rosebushes that framed the front entrance.

"You're going to have to come back. I understand my husband scheduled you for today, but we couldn't have predicted—"

The woman—in a navy-blue suit and white blouse with a wide, flouncy tie at the throat—was quieter than the duchess. Avery had to strain to hear her. ". . . there'll be a cancellation fee . . ."

Mathew came through the front door just then and hurried over to Duchess Mariah. "May I be of assistance, please?" He shook hands with the man and woman, who, Avery now saw, wore name badges for their real estate company.

Mariah turned to him. "I won't allow the real estate photos to show this kind of neglect! I've been trying to tell them that our groundskeeper's been out all week. He's unreachable. The photos must be rescheduled."

Mathew nodded, addressing the real estate photographers. "Of course. We'll have to postpone your photography until our groundsman returns or we have a replacement. We'll pay the cancellation fee, and we'll be happy to reimburse any additional costs due to the inconvenience."

Avery waited until she and Art were safely alone in the temporary lab. "We saw Mr. Hoffman trimming the rosebushes Thursday when we were leaving, remember? So that's why. I figured he was just helping out the groundskeeper—Gregory something; we met him when he helped carry our lab equipment in for us last Monday."

Art pulled out his laptop and waited for it to boot up. He tapped a few keys. "Good memory. The groundskeeper is

Gregory Lightfoot. He's one of the only staff who doesn't live at the manor."

"And he's unreachable. That's kind of crazy; why wouldn't they have found a way to check on him, if he's suddenly just not coming in to work? Especially after seeing the way he was the day Suzanne died."

"What do you mean?"

"I think he must have been dating her. Either that or else they were good friends. When we heard her scream and ran outside, he was huddled over her body, crying and wailing. The whole thing was awful and upsetting, obviously, but he was beside himself. It was so sad."

"Interesting," Art said. "So he probably hasn't been to work because he's grieving."

She nodded. And then a terrible thought popped into her head. "I hope that's the only reason he hasn't been in. I hope whoever murdered Suzanne didn't go after him next."

# Chapter Eleven

"Detective Carter needs to know this," Art said. "I don't know how Gregory Lightfoot's demeanor was by the time the first responders arrived. And I doubt anybody's thought to mention to him that Lightfoot's been MIA all week."

"Right." Avery was stacking items on the end of their long table that she'd need for today's work. "Do you want to go find him?"

"Not yet . . ." He had his cell phone out and was texting. He finished and dropped it back in his pocket. "I filled him in. He's in the library. I'm going to float from wherever you are to the general vicinity of the library. But first . . ." He scanned the case in her hand and then the other items in the room.

She tipped her head, studying him. "I wish I could read your mind." She narrowed her eyes. "I feel like it's a lot of numbers and weird symbols on a blackboard in there, lines connecting equations, that kind of thing," she teased.

"You're overestimating me," he said, straight-faced. "I'm wishing I'd eaten more for breakfast."

She scoffed. "I doubt that's what's going on in there."

"Can you set me up with a few pieces of your equipment in a case? I realized the other day that the small magnifying thing I borrowed from you was probably not a great cover. I need to seem like I'm actually appraising things."

"Good thought," Avery said. "You need more than a loupe." She moved between Micah's workstation, her dad's, and her own, collecting a larger loupe magnifier, a handheld dichroscope, a set of calipers, a notebook, pens, and a tangle of cords for good measure. She fit them all into a hard-sided carrying case like her own and handed it to him.

"Nice. I'm official." He hefted the case in one hand. "Heavy."

"Don't break anything."

He raised his eyebrows. "I promise I'll be careful. Ready?" He held the door open for her.

Crossing the large vestibule, Avery halted, backing up— she'd caught movement outside. "Wait," she whispered. She pointed. Through the tall windows on either side of the entrance, the family's sleek red Tesla rolled to a stop on the circle drive.

Art's eyes widened. "Sweet car!"

As they watched, the falcon-wing rear doors opened upward, and a pair of trouser-clad legs emerged. The rest of Percy Pennington lurched forward and he stood, taking a few steps toward the manor. His white button-down hung open, his tie undone and hanging against his bare chest. He was jerked back almost comically by his jacket sleeve, which seemed to be hooked on something. Percy spun in a surprisingly graceful circle, arms spread wide, shedding the jacket as he turned. His movements were fluid and loose, and Avery needed only a quick glance at his face to see he was drunk. It was noon, and he was likely still three sheets to the wind from wherever he'd been the night before.

"Oh boy," Avery murmured.

"I'm getting the feeling he's a bit of a black sheep," Art observed.

Freed from the constraints of his jacket, which now trailed halfway out of the car onto the driveway, Percy bent down and knocked repeatedly on the passenger-side front window until it went down. Avery moved closer, peering to see who was in the car, but she couldn't tell. Percy gestured as he spoke, then turned and made his way toward the front door. The falcon-wing door began to close and then stopped. The family's driver got out and walked around, scooping the discarded jacket back into the car, and then closed the door. Roderick quickly caught up with Percy, offering him an arm to steady his gait.

Lord Percy pushed him away. Roderick stood where he was and waited until Percy had made it up onto the wide, stone entryway before he got back in the car. Avery rushed over to the staircase, yanking Art with her, so it wouldn't seem like they were spying. She needn't have hurried. Percy fumbled with his keys in the lock for a minute. And then a few minutes.

Avery moved toward the door. "We should let him in, right?" She didn't wait for Art to answer. She opened the enormous, heavy front door to a surprised Percy, his out-stretched hand pointing a key at her.

"Antique girl! You're the *best*," he said, putting his face much too close to Avery's. She was assaulted with a cloud of booze. It was on his breath and virtually leaking from his pores. "Thank you. I always knew they'd change the locks on me some day. Tall man!" Percy spotted Art and waved, laughing. "I remember you. You two getting into trouble again? Hush, shh, keep it down," he slurred, quieting his boisterous voice. He stumbled toward the stairs.

Avery exchanged looks with Art. As comical as Lord Percy seemed, there was nothing funny about a grown man coming home drunk in the middle of the day. And right after being arrested earlier this week. She felt sorry for him. "Lord Percy, do you need any help? I could . . . should I get someone? Mrs. Hoffman or your brother, or—" She knew the instant she'd mentioned Nico that it was a mistake. Of course it was, given the argument Art had overheard.

Lord Percy drew back from her, his eyes wide, horrified. "Why would you do that to me? Terrible idea. I never should've trusted him. I'm not the problem. *He's* the problem. Nico the narc. I just need a little more time!" He'd gotten loud again and quickly put a finger to his lips. "Shh. If he'd kept his promise, this place would be mine. None of them would be here. You two wouldn't be here. You look cross. What are you cross about?" Percy was leaning limply against the stairway railing, looking up at Art now.

"Come on, we'll help get you upstairs," Art said. He held out a hand out.

Percy rolled his head to the left, toward Avery. He spoke in an exaggerated whisper. "I think I'm in trouble. Your husband's a stern mister, antique girl. We'd better go."

Avery pressed her lips together, determined not to laugh. He did look stern, easily mistaken for irritation. She'd had the same first impression of him before she knew him. She met Art's gaze and was surprised to see uncharacteristic color creeping into his cheeks. "Yes," she said. "Let's go."

Percy straightened up with some effort, and Art steadied him as he slowly climbed the steps, Avery on his other side. Lord Percy's head swiveled from Art to Avery. "You're both so lovely. Thank you. I'm quite all right."

Mrs. Hoffman spoke from the second-floor landing, hands on her hips, watching their ascent. "Oh dear. Lord Percy. What were you thinking?" She shook her head, face washed in disappointment. When they'd reached the top step, she slipped a firm hand through Percy's bent elbow. "This isn't the way, young man. It won't help your case with your father," she said quietly.

Avery exchanged a concerned glance with Art.

Mrs. Hoffman guided Percy down the hallway in the opposite direction of Nico and Annabelle's suite. Avery and Art were turning back when Mrs. Hoffman called to them. "Ms. Ayers, Mr. Smith. I'm sorry you had to see this. It's a difficult time right now. Please don't say anything to anyone, not even within the manor—it's a matter for the family to handle."

Avery nodded. "Of course." What did she mean, a difficult time? Was she referring to Lord Percy's trouble earlier in

the week? Or his father selling the house? And his ponies—
maybe that was part of it. Lord Percy was certainly distraught,
judging by his slurred comments. It almost sounded like he'd
planned to stay at the manor. But the Penningtons' primary
estate was in Valle Charme. She looked up at Art. "I wish
we'd had more time with him—what was that all about?" she
asked, keeping her voice low.

Art shook his head. "No idea, but it's something to look
into."

Voices carried from downstairs; Detective Carter was
thanking someone for their time. They headed back downstairs, turning away from the library, where Carter and his
partner were conducting follow-up interviews of the manor's
occupants. Avery had a plan. It was close to lunchtime when
she went through the double doors into the manor's bright,
updated kitchen. The room was even more spacious than it had
looked from her passing glances. A long butcher-block-topped
island ran down the center of the room. Two industrial-size
ovens and a restaurant-size range took up one wall, with deep,
side-by-side sinks on the opposite side.

At a small, round kitchen table in front of the window at
the far end were Nick's assistant and Mr. Hoffman, drinking
coffee and talking. Avery raised a hand in greeting. "Hi there.
I don't want to interrupt, just working."

"The coffee's hot," Mathew said.

"And Mrs. Hoffman will be making sandwiches soon, if
you're hungry," Ira Hoffman added.

"Thanks!" Avery fished around in her case until she found
her earbuds. She opened the music app on her phone and

chose the pop-rock playlist Tilly had made for her, hitting play. Music blared from her phone. "Oops!" she blurted, trying her best to look mortified. "So sorry! Let me just . . . here we go. Sorry." She popped the earbuds loosely into her ears, rerouting the music. She stood back and admired the one item in the room on their appraisal list: a French antique tiger oak Louis XV sideboard. It was one of the most strikingly beautiful pieces she'd seen so far in her career. Crafted in the early 1880s, with a marble server top, the sideboard was well maintained and polished despite its obvious functional use, even now. From the layout of the kitchen and the empty bread basket on the marble surface of the sideboard, she was sure it was used as a holding area for food and beverages in the process of being brought out to the dining room.

When she bent to set her case down, she covertly swiped the music app closed, killing the playlist. Now anyone in the kitchen would assume she was tuned out to any conversation, though she could hear perfectly well around the tiny earbuds. As dazzled as she was by the Louis XV sideboard, she wasn't only here for the antiquity. Kitchens were always the best place to catch up on the latest goings-on, her own kitchen included. She was betting on it being the same here at the manor. Avery opened her case and began going through the motions of measuring, examining specifics in the wood grain and glass, and documenting on her laptop. She took her time, purposely moving much more slowly than she normally did, which wasn't hard, as she wasn't paying much attention to the job.

"Again?" Mathew asked at the kitchen nook.

"That's what Roderick said," Ira Hoffman replied, matching Mathew's quiet tone. "The lad's out of control. Lynn's always had a soft spot for him, but for Pete's sake, even she's getting to the end of her rope."

"Understandable. He's got no regard for the family. You don't even want to know what it took to keep the press in the dark about his arrest. We've got to get him out of the States; he's running wild here. He'll come around once this place is sold and he's back home," Mathew said.

Hoffman grunted and made loud sipping noises, not answering at first. "I'm still not convinced it's the right thing to do. His Grace is going to regret it."

The chair slid back as Mathew stood. "It's been a long time coming. Poor luck, though, for you and Mrs. Hoffman. All right then. I'll be back for a refill later."

Ira Hoffman wasn't alone long after Mathew had gone. Lynn Hoffman hurried in and stopped short, staring down at Avery, who was now sitting on the floor and using calipers to measure the hinge on one of the doors.

"Hello again! Oh, you can't hear me." Mrs. Hoffman waved a hand near Avery, gesturing to her ears.

She removed one earbud and smiled up at the woman. "Hi, Mrs. Hoffman."

"My oh my," Lynn Hoffman said. "That's quite a detailed process, isn't it? I had no idea. Fascinating." She moved to the sink to fill a teapot, and Avery put the silent earbud back in. Lynn addressed her husband. "I just passed Mathew; you didn't say anything about Lord Percy, did you?"

"Uh. Not much. Why?"

The woman shook her head. "They already think poorly of him; it'll only make things worse. Gads. Why doesn't that boy's mother do something to help him? First the fight last week, and now this. Sometimes I don't understand rich people," she said, the bitterness in her tone reflecting the scowl Avery spied in her peripheral vision.

"But you do understand the duchess," her husband protested. "We both do. Every day I see the same empty bottles from her chambers you do. I know you don't like to think of her that way, dear, but it's a disease. Lord Percy could be headed down the same road, and she might not see it." He stood beside his wife at the butcher block, helping her assemble the sandwiches she was working on. Avery sucked in her breath, concerned now about Duchess Pennington. Did she have an alcohol problem?

"Ira, I haven't seen the boy drunk like that since the accident with his pony last year. Poor old Butterscotch. And poor Lord Percy. It took him weeks to get over losing that horse. Don't you think," she asked, turning to glare at her husband, "if he was already like his mother, we'd have seen some sign of it before now? No." Lynn Hoffman shook her head vehemently, answering her own question. "He's acting out, the same as when he was a child."

Mr. Hoffman grunted ambiguously. "Well. Either way, none of this behavior is going to convince His Grace to postpone the sale."

"Of course not. But I'm not going to stand idly by while Lord Percy continues on this path. I'm not sure His Grace really knows how upset he is. We have to do something," Lynn

Hoffman said, her tone anguished. "We should sit down with His Grace and Lord Percy and talk this through, before the boy gets worse. Do you want to find him floating in the lily pond one day like poor Tia?" Her voice cracked at the end, and she drew in a shaking breath.

Avery had stopped evaluating the sideboard altogether. She tapped keys on her laptop, the power off and the screen black, and covertly watched the Hoffmans, riveted.

Ira Hoffman hugged his wife. Lynn set the paring knife down and hugged him back. "I'm sorry," she sniffled.

"It's all right, dear." He patted her back. "I know you love him like he's our own. I do too. He's not going to end up like Tia."

"The more His Grace treats Lord Percy like an errant child, the more reckless the boy becomes. He did have a plan. I'm not sure he was given enough time to make it work."

"All right now, it's not our place to second-guess His Grace's parenting," Ira said firmly, his volume dropping.

Mrs. Hoffman's brows went up. "Oh no. I'd never suggest that. But . . . can't we try to help a little?"

Mr. Hoffman nodded. "Okay. You've always been the brains between us. If you think we should sit down and talk to His Grace about the lad, then we will. What's he going to do, fire us?"

Lynn Hoffman chuckled. "Right. We have nothing to lose."

Avery admired the way they worked as a team. She supposed they'd have to, living and working together. Sort of like her own parents. No wonder her dad was so lost.

Roderick burst through the door in a huff and stomped to the coffeemaker on the counter. "How many jobs can one man do at once?" He grabbed a mug and poured himself a steaming cup of coffee, nodding at the Hoffmans and then spotting Avery. "Hello."

She could feel him looking at her, but she kept her head down, feigning total absorption in her work. She needed to look for any identifying marks underneath the cabinet anyway, so she lay down on her side and shined her flashlight underneath, scanning the wood.

"She can't hear you," Mrs. Hoffman said, tapping her own ear. "They're still working on the appraisals. It's quite an undertaking."

She saw in her side view that the driver had moved to stand by Ira. He reached for a sandwich wedge. "I've already been out all night. I need some sleep. But we're leaving in a moment for Duchess Pennington's salon appointment, after which Lady Annabelle insists I take Gretchen and the children for ice cream, and Lord Nico has a meeting in Manhattan after that. When the devil does His Grace think I've got time to garden? Anyone heard from Lightfoot?"

Ira Hoffman slapped the driver on the back. "You're preaching to the choir, buddy." Avery suppressed a giggle. She wasn't sure whether it was the back slap or the *buddy* or the combination of both. Even in his exasperated state, Roderick struck her as refined and dignified as the Penningtons. Probably a result of being with them constantly, whether here or at Valle Charme. Ira continued. "They made me try my hand at the rosebushes, and it was a massacre. Not my skill set. I have no clue how to do Greg's job."

"He'll be back Monday," Lynn Hoffman said. "The funeral is at one o'clock tomorrow. I emailed everyone a few days ago so we could plan on going."

"Oh. Did you talk to him?" Mr. Hoffman asked.

"Not since Thursday, but he had to help with the funeral arrangements. We are all going, I hope? Does anyone even check their email? Greg was worried his family would blame him, but he was only trying to help by getting her the job."

"That'd be cruel, to blame him," Roderick said. "He had no way of knowing what'd happen to her. One o'clock tomorrow? Where is—er. I'll check my email," he said, his tone sheepish.

The elder groomsman poked his head in through the kitchen doors. "Sorry to interrupt. That detective says you're next, Mrs. Hoffman. He sent me to find you."

Avery remeasured the leg height on the sideboard and turned on the laptop for real now, as she was getting surrounded by Pennington employees. It wouldn't do to have any of these people see her working on a black screen.

"He needs me this second?" Mrs. Hoffman nearly shrieked. She looked at her husband and then back at the disembodied head of the groomsman between the doors. "I can't—I'm—can you go tell him I'm in the middle of making lunch?"

Jerry Wolf's brow scrunched up with worry. He stepped fully into the room. "I don't, um. You want me to go—" He turned and looked back over his shoulder briefly. "You really can't talk with him now?"

Ira Hoffman frowned at him. "It's all right, man." He gave his wife's shoulder a squeeze. "I'll go. I haven't had a turn yet. I'd offer to finish making lunch, but no one would want to eat it," he joked.

"Oh good," Jerry said. Avery heard relief in the grooms-man's tone, though she wasn't sure why. Detective Carter hadn't seemed a bit intimidating when she'd met him last Monday. "I've gotta get back out there; we sent His Grace off on the trails, and he'll be back soon. Do you mind if I take a couple, Missus? I know Bryan'll be hungry too." He eyed the growing stack of sandwiches. Mrs. Hoffman packed some up for him.

Avery stalled, hoping that Jerry Wolf being so frazzled or Ira taking Mrs. Hoffman's place might spark more conversa-tion, but the crowd in the kitchen dissipated, Ira going to speak with Detective Carter, Jerry taking the sandwiches and heading outside, and Roderick putting his chauffeur cap back on and leaving too. Only Mrs. Hoffman was left. Avery took out her earbuds and began packing up her case. She hoped she could remember everything she wanted to fill Art in on.

Lynn Hoffman handed her a plate of little sandwich wedges. "For you and your partner. Are you all finished with that?" She tipped her head toward the sideboard.

"Yes, it's quite a beautiful, functional antique. It's nice to see a piece like this being used as it was intended," Avery said. "It's what it was made for."

"Well, I don't know anything about antiques, but it's a pretty sideboard. We try and make sure to take care of it. I hope you weren't too distracted," the older woman added. "The kitchen's never a quiet space."

Avery chuckled. This kitchen had been exactly as she'd hoped. "It isn't in my house either. No worries, I wasn't distracted at all. I was wrapped up in this playlist my sister made for me." She waggled her phone, which now had the earbuds stacked on top of it.

She found Art in the third-floor reading nook, looking through the wrong end of the loupe at an antique vase. This space was similar to the one on the second-floor landing below but lined with bookshelves and comfy seating. Voices drifted from one of the rooms down the hall. He motioned her over, grabbing two of the sandwich wedges and devouring them. "Starving," he said. "Thank you."

She sat beside him on the gold-and-hunter-green velvet chaise longue. "Hear anything good?" she whispered.

"Not much." He matched her tone. "Do you want these?" He pointed to the other two wedges on the plate.

"Nope. I had a protein bar from my purse."

"Of course." He ate a third sandwich in two bites and took the last one. "Did *you* hear anything good?"

"Tons. Well, maybe tons. Or possibly a lot of nothing. How's your friend doing downstairs? Can you text him?"

"I have been." He glanced down the hall and put his head closer to hers. "Do you need me to tell him something?"

"Ask him who Tia is. And tell him that he made the groomsman Jerry Wolf super nervous. And ask him if he's talked to Greg Lightfoot, the groundskeeper. I was right, he was close to Suzanne . . . boyfriend, husband, brother, something."

Art stared at her. "I'm not even surprised. That's too much to tex—" He put a hand up, stopping abruptly as a commotion rose from down the hall.

"How?" Mathew came running toward them, phone to his ear. "Where the hell is His Grace?" He pulled the phone away from his ear, giving it a look that could kill, then shouted into it. "Get out there and find him, for God's sake!" He darted to the window to their right and pressed a hand to the glass, head moving frantically as he searched for something.

Avery and Art stood and looked too, seeing only the rolling green property with the stable and paddock in the distance and the forest beyond. She started to speak, to offer whatever kind of help might be needed, but Mathew sprinted away, flying down the stairs. Avery narrowed her eyes, scrutinizing the view from the window. One of the Wolfs was now on a horse, galloping into the woods. She turned a fearful gaze on Art. "Something's happened to the duke."

# Chapter Twelve

S he and Art made their way across the lawn to the paddock, joining Mr. Hoffman and Jerry Wolf and Mathew. All eyes were on the trailhead past the barn.

"His Grace was on a trail ride, and his horse came back without him," Ira Hoffman told them.

"Oh my God! What can we do? Was he an experienced rider?"

"Depends on what you call experienced," the groomsman said. "He and his son had planned on riding together, but Lord Nico had to take a phone call. His Grace has been out riding alone before, but not often. My son's out searching for him."

"I can't just stand here and wait," Mathew said. "Put a saddle on that one, would you, Wolf? I'm going to look too. Bryan might not find him; the more eyes out there, the better."

Jerry Wolf hesitated, a hand on the back of the horse beside him. "You ride, Mr. Nolan?"

Mathew looked insulted. "I'm sure I can figure it out."

A muscle pulsed in Jerry Wolf's jaw. "I'm not putting you in a saddle so you can fall off too. I'll go." He led the horse back toward the barn but had gotten only a few feet when the radio at his hip crackled. He grabbed it, speaking into it. "Say again?"

"Found him. Get an ambulance; he's unconscious." The words coming through the speaker were fringed with static but clear enough to trigger panic in Avery. Jesus. She'd never imagined Duke Pennington was the target in whatever was going on here. Until now, they'd been dealing with some stolen valuables and a housekeeper who was either an innocent victim or possibly involved in the thefts, but why on earth would anyone want to kill the duke? Lord Nico and the groomsmen had sent him out on a ride and—what? Had he really fallen off his horse? Was he unconscious, or . . . Avery's mind shoved the other possibility away; it was too awful. And on the heels of that, she thought of Aunt Midge. She'd be beside herself if something had happened to her dear friend.

Time both slowed down and sped up in the moments that followed. Mathew called an ambulance for the second time in a week. Mr. Hoffman went to wait for them in the circle drive. Jerry Wolf barked into the radio that help was coming and Bryan shouldn't try to move the duke. He saddled the mare and took off into the woods to locate them.

Mathew motioned to Avery while on hold with dispatch. "We need to get His Grace's wife and sons out here. I don't know how bad this is." He spoke into the phone. "Yes, that's right, we'll have the gates open for them. Yes, I'll wait." He returned his attention to Avery. She was startled to see tears in the man's eyes. He was consistently cool and collected, but he obviously genuinely cared about Nick. "I need to stay here until they bring him out."

"I'll get them." She had to do something, and it seemed no one but paramedics could help the duke now.

They met Detective Carter halfway across the lawn. Avery left Art to update his colleague and raced toward the house. She nearly knocked Lord Nico down as she burst through the door—he'd been on his way out.

"Mrs. Hoffman said there's been a riding accident?"

"Yes. Your father was—um. I'm not sure what happened, but Mathew is out there now with the Wolfs, and he's called 911."

Lord Nico was already on his way down the front steps. She nearly asked him where his brother was but thought she already knew. He was likely still in bed, considering the shape he'd arrived home in. Should she go search upstairs until she found his room and wake him? Especially considering this might involve one of his ponies? Ugh. Where was Mrs. Hoffman? Avery checked down each hallway off the vestibule and spotted no one. When the kitchen was empty too, she steeled her resolve and went upstairs. She turned the corner and was relieved to find the woman ushering a bleary-eyed Lord Percy out of his room. The sound of sirens in the distance drifted to them, and Lord Percy straightened up.

"I'm all right." He extracted his arm from the woman's grasp, patting her hand. "Thank you, Mrs. Hoffman."

"Ms. Ayers," she said, shooting a worried glance at him but rushing toward Avery. "Have you seen the duchess? I've got to find her."

The conversation from the kitchen came back to her. Hadn't the duchess had a hair appointment? "I think Roderick took her to the salon," Avery said. "I'm not sure, though."

The woman smacked her own forehead. "Of course. I saw it on my calendar this morning. Goodness, I hope His Grace is all right. I'll let you boys decide when to call your mother," she said to Lord Percy. "Perhaps it's not too bad."

Avery accompanied them outside, Lord Percy fretting the entire way, his complexion pale. "Which horse was my father on?" he asked. When Mrs. Hoffman shrugged helplessly, he groaned. "It better have been Blackberry. The Wolfs know she's the gentlest. Father doesn't ride enough to handle any of the others well. God, this could be bad," he muttered, increasing his pace. He looked fully sober now.

Avery opened her mouth to say they'd seen the duke with a stout black mare this morning, but the sound of sirens filled the air as they reached the paddock. She stood with Art, watching as an ambulance and another squad car pulled into the circle drive near where Ira Hoffman stood. Ira waved them forward, and they veered off onto the grass, coming to a stop in front of the paddock. Three paramedics carrying a long orange back board and an enormous red duffel jogged over to the trailhead where Detective Carter stood, waiting with Jerry Wolf to take them to Duke Pennington.

Avery and Art waited in silence with the rest of the bystanders. When the paramedics hadn't emerged yet after what felt like too long, she finally asked him, "How bad is it?"

His gaze slid to the right, to where Mr. and Mrs. Hoffman leaned against the fence with Mathew a few yards down.

"Walk with me," he murmured. He moved away from the corral and the gathered family and staff. When they were out of earshot, he spoke. "Jerry Wolf came back and said it looked as if the horse threw Nick. He was found lying near the trail, still unconscious. Listen, we're going to need to take off soon. It'll look strange that we're hanging around, and I don't want my cover blown just yet."

"Do you think it was an accident?" Her mind was replaying the scene with Lord Nico and the duke from this morning when they'd arrived. "I mean, is it normal for a horse to throw its owner? Was Nick on the little black mare we saw him with in the paddock?"

"No, Wolf said the duke took the stallion even though he cautioned him not to. That stallion is known to be young and a little wild, according to the stable guys. Lord Nico brushed it off, telling Wolf his father was capable of choosing his own horse." He frowned at Avery. "If he's not an experienced rider, you'd think his son—hell, his stablemen too—would have made sure he was on a safe horse. But this is all conjecture; it doesn't—look. They've got him," Art said.

Nick was strapped to the back board, two paramedics on one side and a third plus Detective Carter on the other. They set him gently on the gurney the two police officers had brought to the edge of the trail and rolled him to the ambulance. Avery drifted closer, craning to see him. She hoped not to have to break terrible news to Aunt Midge tomorrow over dinner. She gasped as Nick stirred, trying to sit up. "He's awake." She basked in the momentary relief. At least he'd regained consciousness.

He was surrounded now by Lords Nico and Percy and Mathew, the others hovering close. Avery glanced at Art. "I think this is our cue. I'm just the niece of a friend of the family who was hired to do a job. We should go."

In Art's truck on the way home, Avery took a deep breath in and blew it out slowly. "Wow. What in the world is going on at Pennington Manor? I'm glad to be out of there, at least until Monday. Did you get a chance to ask Detective Carter any of my questions?"

"He's going to get back to me. He was able to answer one, though. You were half right about Suzanne and Gregory Lightfoot, the groundskeeper. They weren't dating; they're related."

"I knew it. That's why he was worried his family would be upset with him, with Suzanne ending up dead after he got her job. Was she his sister or something?"

"Cousin. Carter said she was hired last year after the former housekeeper left."

Avery's mind was spinning. "Huh. I guess my imagination was working overtime, thinking the killer had gotten to him too. Mrs. Hoffman heard from him the day before yesterday with funeral plans. He's coming back to work on Monday."

"Yeah, that's what he told Carter today over the phone. He's the only person that hasn't been interviewed yet, other than the brief statements everyone gave the day of Suzanne's death. Carter is going to let Lightfoot deal with the funeral tomorrow and catch up with him on Monday."

"Knowing now that he was Suzanne's cousin and that he got her the job," Avery said, "Roderick and Mr. Hoffman were jerks talking about him today. They were both complaining that they can't do his job on top of theirs and he'd better hurry and come back to work."

Art's eyebrows went up. "Nice compassion there. You really were the fly on the wall today, weren't you?"

She explained her method to him, earbuds included. "I think I was kind of invisible to them. I mean, I'm technically staff, like them, plus I'm only temporary. And they thought I was totally tuned out."

One corner of Art's mouth rose and he glanced at her. "Like a pro. When you retire from studying molecular structure and hallmark stamps and mineral deposits on hundred-year-old teapots and medallions, you can start your second career as a private eye. What'd you catch about Lord Percy? Anything? Or are they used to him coming home like that?"

Avery wasn't surprised that Art actually got the nuances of her job. He was all about the details. "The whole Lord Percy situation is confusing and sort of heartbreaking. Lynn and Ira Hoffman seem to feel he's struggling with something, some plan he had that didn't happen, and now he's acting out. They said something about a fight last week, which must be what his arrest was for. And they made a reference to Duchess Mariah, his mother; I think she has a drinking problem. Art, there's some weird dynamic between the brothers. With what you overheard from your perch on the second floor and then all the talk today, and the way Lord Percy reacted when I offered to fetch his brother or someone to help him, I really feel something's not right there."

"What are you thinking?" he asked.

"Well, Mathew made it sound like all will be well once the manor sells and they've gotten Lord Percy home to Valle Charme and under control. Which jibes with what we heard from Percy today, right? He said this place was going to be his and none of us would be here . . . but he shouldn't have trusted Nico."

"Nico the narc," Art said. "I remember that. It sounds like Nico treats Percy like a screw-up younger brother. And maybe Duke Pennington is feeling that way about him as well, based on Mrs. Hoffman's observations. The dynamic isn't good, you're right. But you know, in royal families, the eldest son holds all the responsibility and reward of carrying on the family name."

"Even now, in modern times?"

"I think that's still a constant. Lord Percy probably has very little culpability, knowing he's second in line for everything."

Avery was quiet, letting that sink in. When she spoke, she was disheartened at her own words. "I hate to say it, but that for sure gives him motive, doesn't it? At least for the theft. If he has to fight for every scrap he's given, maybe he's decided to take what he feels he deserves. As for whether he could have killed Suzanne . . ." She paused, working through it in her head. "I mean, we know Nico's a cad. Maybe the nanny isn't his only dalliance. If Lord Nico was sleeping with Suzanne too, who knows if Percy might've used that as another way to get back at his brother."

Now Art was quiet for a moment, digesting her theory. "Lord Percy was one of the last ones out of the manor when Suzanne hit the ground. Okay, hold on. Let's break that down. I've got notes, but I'm pretty sure I remember. We've got the duke and his wife outside by the body almost immediately. They were already there when you and Micah came running out."

"Yes. And we know Mrs. Hoffman didn't kill anyone; she was talking to us when we heard Suzanne's scream."

"There was someone else—the groomsman came over from the stables. The younger Wolf, Bryan. And Lord Nico was there pretty quickly too, right?" Art asked.

"Lord Nico came out that door on the side of the manor, near where Suzanne landed. I've been thinking about that. He totally could've used the hidden staircase to race down the two flights and show up outside, right after shoving her off the roof. We could time it, if we could ever get access without someone around," Avery said.

"It probably takes less than a minute to run down two flights of stairs from the roof," Art said. "So we can't rule him out. As for a motive, Lord Nico could've been sleeping with Suzanne but wanted to end it."

"Or she wanted to end it," Avery said, playing devil's advocate. "Or she could've threatened to tell his wife."

"Or Lady Annabelle could've learned about the affair and killed Suzanne herself."

"Alleged affair." Avery snickered. "So basically, we're saying it could be anyone except Bryan Wolf and Nick and his wife."

"Yes and no," Art said. "Lord Nico had no reason I can think of for stealing the pocket watch. Same with Lady Annabelle. We established Lord Percy's motive, and all of the manor employees would probably have reason to want a piece of the Pennington fortune before the place sold. I'm sure Suzanne and her cousin Greg Lightfoot did, as well as the Wolfs. And the Wolfs didn't want to have to sell the horses and move any more than Percy himself did. A scandal might've convinced the duke not to sell."

"Same with the Hoffmans. They didn't want to move. Oh! Ira Hoffman made a comment that Duke Pennington was going to regret the decision to sell. It's a little out of context— he was talking about the Percy situation—but where was he when Suzanne was pushed?"

"Carter covered that with him, as he and Gretchen the nanny were the only ones not accounted for. Lynn Hoffman says she rushed to look out the window after you and Micah ran outside, and Ira Hoffman was working on a pipe under the kitchen sink when Suzanne screamed. He says he stayed inside with his wife, as she was distraught. Gretchen told Carter she was with the girls, and Lady Annabelle backed that up."

"I was so disappointed to see Gretchen with Lord Nico. She's so sweet with those little girls. I hate thinking of her running around behind Lady Annabelle's back."

Art took the exit for Lilac Grove, slowing as they neared town.

"We're back earlier than I thought we'd be," Avery remarked. It was half past four.

"About our date tonight," Art said. "I have a small problem."

"You do?" Avery'd been looking forward to some one-on-one time with him that had nothing to do with crime.

"Well. That's not true. I've got eight small problems."

She laughed. "The kittens! You need cat food," she said suddenly, pointing. They were almost past Grove Grocery. He turned in, and they grabbed a few supplies before heading to his house. "Can I come in for a minute and see them?" Avery asked.

"You can come in for more than a minute." He pulled into his driveway alongside her car. On the porch, key in the lock, he hesitated and glanced at her. "So they've had a chance to warm up and stay dry and eat; if I put them back outside, they'll be fine, right? The mother cat will still take care of them? They aren't like birds or other wild animals where once you've touched them, the parent will abandon them?"

"That's a myth, actually," Avery said. "And even if it wasn't, no, the mama cat isn't going to abandon them." She made a sad face at him. "I should have lied to you. Yes. Yes, your fear is correct. The mama cat will abandon them if you turn them loose. You touched them, so they're yours now, Art."

His expression shifted, his eyes dropping for the briefest moment to her lips. He was inches away. He'd been close enough to kiss most of the day. Avery forgot to breathe. Art abruptly turned back to unlock the front door. She followed him inside, telling her racing heart to chill out.

In the kitchen, the overwhelming sweetness inside the playpen hit her full force as she peered over the edge. They were fast asleep in a pile, the mama cat curved around them. One orange rebel was sprawled across her, rising and falling with the larger cat's rhythmic breathing. The food was gone and the blankets were mussed, but other than that, they looked to have spent their day sleeping. "I can't stand it," she whispered. "They're so cute!"

He nodded, leaning down to pet the orange kitten with one finger. He straightened up, sighing. "What am I supposed to do with them?"

She liked this side of Art. He usually knew exactly what to do. She opened a can of the cat food and put it in the pen with fresh water. She sat down on the floor and flipped the latch on the playpen. It was a plastic eight-panel fence that could form a square or octagon. She pushed on the section near her, widening the gap, and looked up at him. "Sit."

He did, kicking one long leg out to the side and wincing as he did.

"What happened to your knee? I heard you say you have a bad knee—I didn't know that."

He registered surprise. "It's fine. Stairs aggravate it. I crashed a motorcycle years ago, when I was nineteen. It usually doesn't bother me, but sometimes it acts up."

"A motorcycle? Really?"

"I sold it. My sisters wouldn't give me any peace until I did."

She laughed softly. "I like your sisters, and I don't even know them." That pang pinched at her again.

"That's my fault," he said.

She put a hand out, palm up, to the tiger-striped kitten who'd climbed out of the pile and was drunkenly moving toward her. "Hi there," she said. "You're so tiny."

The sound of thunder carried to them from somewhere in the distance. The sky had gotten dark in the short time since they'd come inside. Avery jumped at a much louder roll-clap of thunder, followed immediately by lightning. The rain began as a sudden torrent, no drizzle or scattered drops first.

"Whoa," Art said. Two more kittens broke free of their slumber cluster and bumped against Art's knee, their quiet mews pathetic and endearing. He scooped them both up. "I guess it's a good thing they're inside."

"You don't have to keep them. If you want, we can take them to the Begonia Bend animal shelter. I'll go with you. Um. But I know they close early on weekends."

"I didn't say I don't want them. I've never thought about getting one."

"Ours was twenty when she died," Avery said. "I was in high school. My parents got her before they were married. They're not hard to care for. But some people just don't like cats, and that's okay."

Art turned to face her, holding the two kittens to his chest. "I didn't say I don't like them. How could I not?" One of the kittens sniffed his five-o'clock-shadow-covered chin and then rubbed her head under it, and he laughed.

Avery faced him, her knees touching his. "Maybe keep them overnight, since it's storming, and then decide what to do. Tomorrow, you can put them all back outside with the mama, or we can take them to the shelter, or if you wanted to keep one or two, I could help find homes for the rest." She was trying to imagine eventually bringing one home herself. She wasn't sure they had time for one.

Art placed one large, warm hand on Avery's knee. "All right. I'll think about it. Thank you." He set the kittens down, and they stumbled toward the others that were waking now. "For dinner, I thought we'd go to that new Italian place, Fratelli's, in Rosewood. Unless somewhere else sounds good?"

She gazed out through the door wall to Art's patio. It was dark as night and only five o'clock. The trees in his backyard swayed wildly through rain so heavy, it was coming down sideways. She'd planned to wear her wispy pink chiffon blouse with the short, flouncy black skirt Aunt Midge had given her for her birthday in September. The skirt was an unlikely item in her closet, one of only a couple other skirts and dresses. But Auntie had planted her wisdom along with the gift, advising, "It's a unique thrill to dip a toe outside our comfort zone now and then, my dear." Wearing a skirt might be routine for some, but Avery was most comfortable in her Lycra leggings and running shoes. She'd tried on her outfit the night Art asked her out and had been looking forward to "dressing up" ever since.

Now, with the thunder and patter of rain and tiny furry kittens crawling over her and Art's hand on her knee, she was loath to end it. "Maybe we could have a rain check for Fratelli's?" She looked at him hopefully. "I—"

"Sure." Art dropped his hand and stood up. "You might want to let the rain slow down before you go, though." His tone was cool.

Avery got quickly to her feet. "I don't want to leave."

He stared at her in confusion.

"I meant, could we postpone going out to dinner? This is nice. Being here with you, in your space, just us."

"Oh," he said. He looked down, laughing softly. "I've been thinking about your date with your ex all day. I figured you'd chosen him."

Avery's throat felt thick. She stepped in closer to him, putting a hand gingerly on his cheek. "No. I should have told you how that went. I didn't mean to leave you in the dark."

Art's brow was furrowed, his demeanor now somber. "That's where I've left you since I met you. I'm sorry. I don't mean to."

"I know that." He was trying, she could see that, especially with his revelations earlier today.

"I'll cook," he said. "Let's eat here, and I'll tell you what happened with the NYPD, why I left the city, all of it. If we ever do start dating again, I want you to meet my sisters. I want to stop locking you out."

Avery closed the gap between them, wrapping her fingers around the back of his neck, and kissed him. She couldn't stop herself. He kissed her back, softly, hesitantly at first. Art's arms went around her waist, one hand opened wide at the center of her back, holding her firmly, the kiss deepening, gaining urgency. Rational thought intruded, needling her; she couldn't. They couldn't go down this road, not now, not skimming past everything that had broken them up in the first place. Her eyelids fluttered open and she drew back, working to slow her breathing.

Art let go of her. He held her gaze through heavy-lidded eyes, chest rising and falling rapidly like hers.

"I shouldn't have done that," Avery said. "I'm really sorry."

One corner of his mouth turned up. "I'm not mad."

She looked away, her cheeks burning. "It was still out of line."

"Avery."

She met his eyes.

"I make a great Mediterranean baked chicken dish. You babysit the cats, and I'll cook."

# Chapter Thirteen

Art's baked chicken with tomatoes and capers was the best thing Avery had eaten in months. Maybe ever. He'd placed a small baking dish hot from the oven between them, and now it was almost cleaned out.

"You can cook. I mean, I knew you could cook, but this is a little fancy. It was amazing." She speared the last cherry tomato from the pan and popped it in her mouth before he took it to the sink with their plates. "Mmm."

"I figured it was something you could eat without breaking your race prep rules."

"So thoughtful," she said, smiling.

"I haven't said much about my time in the city because I hate thinking about what I did," Art said. He paused, sliding a lone paper napkin beneath his hands. He folded it in half and in half again, pressing the seams.

Avery folded her hands on the table in front of her. Whatever he'd done, it still tormented him years later. But she knew him—she knew his character. She waited, careful to maintain a neutral expression.

"When I got the NYPD job right out of the academy, I wanted to make a good impression. Obviously. You want them to know you're capable, smart, not a liability. My police academy application disclosed the fact that I'm dyslexic. It doesn't have anything to do with intelligence," he added. The napkin under his fingers had become a dice-sized square, which he then turned over and methodically unfolded and refolded as he spoke. "For some reason, it didn't make it into my file on the force. The assistant chief—that's my boss, who works under the commanding officer—didn't have that information. When I signed my papers, it wasn't listed, and I didn't add it. It's my responsibility to disclose any disability that could interfere with me doing my job, and I didn't. If I had, my error would've been caught. I might have been put on different assignments or had different protocols to compensate, but I kept it quiet. And I got my partner shot." He took a deep breath and went on.

"Dyslexia isn't what people think. It's not just flipping letters or numbers. There are a few types, and each one has its own challenges. You learn early how to compensate, or you try to—triple-checking everything, running what you're going to say through a filter first, little tricks. My partner and I were hitting a drug house, part of a bigger operation, and I transposed the address digits. We ended up at the house next door, which tipped off the gang holing up at the correct address. We didn't realize until they started shooting."

"Art, I'm sorry, but that could've happened to anyone, for more reasons than dyslexia. Human error, for example. You're carrying so much guilt for—"

"It gets worse," he said, grim, his jaw set. "We were taken off guard, but there's still procedure to follow. All Denny needed to know was which corner to go around. That's it. Because I could see from my position behind the trash cans. Left was clear, a path to our car, but to the right, these guys were spilling out of the back window like rats from a flood. In my head, I said left. I thought it, said it first to myself, shouted it. Left. But I didn't." He'd begun shredding the napkin, one thin strip at a time, staring past Avery into what sounded like a nightmare. "Denny was shot three times. Ear, shoulder, kidney."

She gasped, putting a hand over her mouth and then regretting it. She gave up trying to control her reactions. He looked tormented, summoning the will to continue. She started to speak, to say it was an accident, unintentional, but he raised his hand, shaking his head. "I need to finish, I'm sorry. Avery, you're going to look at me differently now. I'm not the person you thought you knew. When Denny was shot, I didn't come clean. Even then. I went and saw him in the hospital and didn't tell him. I visited him after his kidney surgery and never said a word. He was home recovering by the time I did, but I was too much of a coward to tell him to his face. I reported myself to my chief. He suspended me, and when I came back, I was useless. Crippling anxiety. I fell apart the first time back in the field. I resigned that same day. Spent weeks trying to figure out what I could do for a living other than what I was trained for, which mostly was me sleeping and my wife running out patience. It gets old fast, you know? You aren't supposed to have a midlife crisis before you hit thirty. That's it, I guess." The kitchen was quiet but for the steady thrum of the rain.

Avery leaned forward, her elbows on the table. "Art." He met her gaze. "I'm looking at you the same way I always have. You made one bad decision. I know there were major consequences, but—were you supposed to be perfect?"

"When you're dealing with life and death, yeah. Not perfect, but responsible. I'd do everything different now if I could."

"I think that's what matters," Avery said.

He shook his head. "No. What matters is that I withheld a vital piece of information that almost got my partner killed. I don't want sympathy or forgiveness. I did what I did. I have to live with it. Thank God Denny pulled through—his wife sends me a Christmas card every year since then. Denny doesn't speak to me."

Sheesh. She suppressed the urge to say what she wanted to—that she was sorry he'd gone through such trauma. He didn't want sympathy. "What made you leave the city altogether instead of finding some other kind of work?"

"My sisters happened." He gave her a wry smile. "They had sort of an intervention, which pissed my wife off even more. They got me moving, made me apply for work, all kinds of jobs, didn't matter. I got offers, I could have stayed in the city, but by then my wife had pretty much moved on. She was over it. The miscarriage was a year earlier, and then my stuff happened, and we were too far gone to save. So when the Springfield Sheriff's Department job came up, I took it. With full disclosure about my dyslexia. My sisters pushed me to find a place in Lilac Grove because it's in the middle of the three of them."

"I'm glad they did," Avery said. "It's awful for you to have to retell all that happened; I'm sorry. But it's an important part of you, your story. I appreciate you trusting me with it."

He frowned. "You don't have to thank me. Look, I did the same thing with you that got me into trouble in the first place in the city. Don't thank me for being honest. If I hadn't been trying to hide this piece of my past, trying to keep you from seeing the ugly parts of me, you'd have had the full story months ago. Maybe you'd never have dated me. I thought I'd grown after what I did to Denny. Now I'm not so sure."

Avery scooted her chair around the table so she was beside him. "Do you think I showed you my ugly parts when we first met? Does anyone do that? Art. Hey." She waited until he looked up from the pile of tiny napkin pieces in front of him and covered his hand with hers. "You are still the same person to me. Nothing's changed. I promise. You did nothing with malice." She reached down and scooped up the tiger-striped kitten who'd squeezed his way through the playpen slats for the third time in five minutes. "One more thing, and I say this in all seriousness. You may need to sleep down here with the cats tonight."

He turned his hand palm up in hers, giving it a squeeze. He let go and went into his laundry room off the kitchen, returning with duct tape and cardboard. "I'll cover the holes, but I have a feeling it'll be a temporary solution."

She and Art made popcorn and found a scary movie Avery'd been wanting to see on Netflix; the thunder and lightning outside made for a perfect ambience. Halfway through, the rebel orange kitten somehow found his way out of the playpen they'd brought into the living room with them. He climbed up Art's leg, sharp kitten nails getting traction in the denim, and snuggled between his shoulder and neck, purring loudly.

Avery forced herself to get going when the movie ended. It would be a short drive home, but she was starting to feel like the kitten. She was exhausted from the long day.

When she rose, Art moved to walk her out. She put a hand on his chest. "Stay. Don't get up. Let him sleep," she said, petting the tiny tabby still lightly sleeping against Art's neck. She leaned down and kissed his cheek. "Good night, cat dad."

*　*　*

Art called Sunday morning to tell her he didn't want to go to the shelter with the kittens; he was going to take another day to figure out what to do. Avery hung up the phone, smiling. She got her run in early, as today was her higher-mileage endurance day, taking one of her handful of alternate routes back from town for the last two miles. After she'd had her protein shake and a shower and applied new Kinesio tape to her calves and left hamstring, she headed back into town in her car. She owed Rachel an appraisal.

Mixed Bag wasn't open yet, but Rachel was waiting for her. "Here," her friend said, looking over her shoulder as Avery followed her through to the back of the shop. "You can use my desk for your equipment."

She unpacked several items from the large protective case: dichroscope, loupe, and her benchtop hyperspectral imaging system that came apart for transport. She attached the platform and plugged into the power strip on Rachel's desk, then connected the spectrometer's cables to her laptop. The imaging system was a sophisticated tool used frequently in her profession. There were many types, but the benchtop machine looked a bit like a microscope with an extended neck—as a twelve-year-old in her parents' lab at the back of their shop, she'd called it the giraffe-scope. She'd been fascinated with it because it produced rainbows. It didn't really—a pixel of the digital image would provide a precise measurement of the portion of light reflected at a particular wavelength. So even jewels that appeared clear to the naked eye could tell a different story using hyperspectral imaging, the end result sometimes showing up on the report as a wide spectrum of color.

She placed Rachel's hairpin on the platform and turned the system on, her laptop screen coming to life as she did. Avery used the camera controller, and the spectrometer lens shifted its orientation to the piece being evaluated. A line graph populated on her laptop screen along with a separate field showing dozens of varying color blocks.

"Whoa," Rachel said. "I have no idea what you're doing, but this is so cool." She pointed at the screen. "You know how to interpret all this?"

Avery smiled. "Sure. I'm getting a very detailed story on each of the jewels in your hair pain," she said, adjusting the camera. "The thermal sensor and multi- and hyperspectral sensors are vital to picking out key features in an artifact, which helps in distinguishing between genuine and knock-off." She reached over and tapped the mouse pad on her laptop, moving the cursor. She wanted to be certain before saying anything else. In her research at the home office, she'd been surprised at what she'd found, but now it was a matter of whether or not the hair adornment Rachel had picked up at an estate sale would turn out to be authentic. She snapped off the spectrometer and reviewed the last few readings on her laptop, then examined the item through her lighted handheld loupe, finding what she was looking for. The hallmark stamp was there, near the hinge on the underside of the clip.

She leaned over and pulled over an extra chair beside her, looking up at Rachel. "I think you should sit down."

Rachel frowned, tipping her head. "It's okay, Avery. I didn't expect it to be real. I only paid twenty dollars for it."

Avery couldn't keep from smiling. "You should still sit down."

Rachel's eyes grew wide. She sat, swiping a wild red curl back toward the very fluffy messy bun on top of her head. "Okay, I'm ready. Hit me."

"This is real." Avery turned the desk lamp so it shone on the hairpin, the jewels glinting in the light. "These two jewels here are real alexandrite gemstones, these are real emeralds, and this jewel in the center is a real, nearly flawless pink diamond. A pink diamond, Rachel."

Her friend's mouth dropped open. She looked up from the jewels to Avery and then back down at the hairpin again.

"I can't believe I get to be the person who tells you this, but this piece is incredibly valuable. Like, beyond-your-wildest-dreams valuable. And on top of that, not that this will matter much, given the worth of the item already, it once belonged to Maude Fealy, the first silent-movie actress." Avery pulled up the article she'd found last week. In it was a black-and-white photo of the actress accepting an award, stylish in a floor-length gown of the era, her long brown curls adorned with Rachel's hairpin.

"But how . . ." Rachel peered at the photo. "It looks the same. But are you sure this is real?" She took the hairpin from Avery's open palm.

"I'm positive. It's the same one she's wearing, the jewels are absolutely real, and if there was any doubt left, the stamp proves it's origin." She pointed near the hinge.

"Oh my God. So what do I do? I almost sold this thing before stopping to think that maybe you should look at it!" Rachel set it down on the desk. "I don't even want to touch it. What if I drop it?"

Avery laughed. "You haven't yet. Even if you do, it's not going to change the fact that you've got a two-point-five-carat pink diamond."

"That's big, right? I've never had a diamond."

Avery relished this. Rachel was one of the nicest, most down-to-earth people she knew. She'd been in Lilac Grove her whole life. She'd worked from the age of fifteen at the diner and then leased the space to open Mixed Bag a few years ago with her life's savings. Avery had helped her move her mother into her small bungalow this past summer after her dad passed away, as her mom couldn't afford to keep the house on her own. Rachel ran the shop seven days a week, which left little time for anything else. Maybe the hairpin would make life easier for her and her mother.

"Let me put this in perspective for you," Avery said. "Alexandrite is one of the most valuable gemstones. It's pretty cool; it can appear to be varying shades of purple or blue depending on the lighting. And everyone knows emeralds are expensive jewels, and these in your hairpin are top pocket. Gorgeous quality. But pink diamonds are rare. For frame of reference, a one-carat pink diamond normally starts at around one-point-two million at auction." She watched Rachel's face, letting that sink in.

It took a moment. Avery expected an elated outburst or jumping up and down, but instead, Rachel's complexion changed from its usual rosy pink to a grayish green, her eyes even wider now above her round cheeks. She slapped a hand over her mouth and shot out of her chair and through a door nearby, slamming it closed behind her. Avery heard water running. She was obviously overwhelmed.

Avery packed up her laptop and tools, fitting everything back into the case, and waited. When she was really starting to worry, she crossed to the door to knock on it, but Rachel came out first. Her hair was damp and pulled more tightly up on top of her head, and her mascara was smudged underneath her eyes, but her color was back. "I am so sorry," she said, sounding embarrassed. "I, uh, that was not what I was expecting to hear." She laughed. "Holy cow."

Avery grabbed her and hugged her, laughing with her. "That was a pretty smart twenty-dollar investment. I'll complete a certification for this, and if you'd like, I can connect you with my partner, Sir Robert—oh, he's not royalty. We just call him that. He handles our contracts with Barnaby's Auction House, and I'm positive this would fetch a nice price for you."

"Um, yes please," Rachel said. "I would love to talk with your Sir Robert, whether he's royalty or not." She giggled.

"Awesome."

"For now, this is going straight to my safe-deposit box at Springfield Bank. I'm guessing you can help me figure out next steps?" Rachel asked. "I feel like you could pinch me and I'll wake up to you telling me it's a twenty-dollar hairpin."

Avery pinched her arm. "You're awake, I promise."

Rachel laughed again. "I owe you one helluva wine night."

* * *

Avery, Tilly, and William spent Sunday afternoon making lasagna for dinner for Aunt Midge and Wilder. At quarter to five, Halston let the trio know their guests had arrived, his whole body wagging excitedly while Avery opened the door.

"Come in, come in," she said, wrapping her arms around tiny but mighty Midge. "I miss you living here, Auntie."

The older woman gently placed a hand adorned with several sparkling rings on Avery's cheek. "Of course you do. We three made the most perfect team, didn't we? But we still have our slumber parties now and then. We'll have to plan another that isn't centered around poor Tilly losing a tooth." She handed her a square bakery box tied with string. "Our traditional cannolis from the White Box."

"Thank you. Wilder," Avery said, moving to hug him next. "We miss you too. It's been too long."

Wilder Mendelsohn and Midge had been friends since college in the late 1970s. He was a professor of philosophy at Columbia University, twice divorced, and had been a regular presence in Avery's and Tilly's lives since they were born. Quiet, calm, and reserved, Wilder was the yin to Aunt Midge's yang. It was an unspoken truth in their family that Wilder had been in love with Midge for decades. Avery wasn't sure her aunt knew or accepted the strength of the torch he carried for her, but it was apparent to anyone who saw the two of them together. Somehow, Wilder seemed to have found a way to be content simply being in her orbit.

Wilder smiled. "It's good to see you. How's everything here? This fellow looks like he's recovered well," he said of Halston. He bent to run a hand down the dog's leg, now completely mended after he'd broken it while protecting Avery during last spring's break-in.

"Halston's a superhero. I can't believe he doesn't even have a limp."

Over dinner, Avery broke the news to Midge about Duke Pennington's riding accident.

"Yes," she said, surprising Avery. "I spoke with Lord Percy this afternoon. A bit of good news—Nicholas has cleared all of his scans and miraculously only has a bad sprain of one ankle. He did suffer a fairly severe concussion."

"I'm relieved you already knew," Avery said. "Wait, Auntie, how did you know to check in on him?"

"Oh, I didn't. His assistant called to let me know he was in hospital. Mathew's a darling," she said. She raised an eyebrow at Avery, obviously reading her perplexed expression. "I'm his ICE, of course. His *In-Case-of-Emergency*, dear? You must know; it's a designation in one's cell phone. If you haven't set yours up, you really should. I have you and Wilder listed as mine."

Avery chuckled. "Naturally. Of course you're Duke Pennington's emergency contact."

Tilly scooted her chair closer to Aunt Midge, handing her iPhone over. "Can you show me, Auntie?"

"Absolutely. I'd be pleased to show you how to do it, just as soon as we're through enjoying this scrumptious lasagna. Phones during dinner are a nuisance. I do have a pressing question, though, and appropriate for dinner table conversation, I think. Do you agree, Tilly?" She winked at the girl. Tilly took a deep breath, widening her eyes, and winked back.

Avery frowned, glancing at her dad. He shrugged, looking as clueless as she felt. "What's the inside joke, ladies?" she asked, looking from her aunt to her sister.

"It's certainly not a joke," Midge said cryptically.

Tilly cleared her throat. "I haven't been sure how to say this. I know how hard you guys all worked to help me apply and get into the conservatory. And I know I screwed everything up. I—" She took another deep breath, looking toward the ceiling and blinking fast before continuing. "I know I can't undo what I did or fix it. And I'm saying this because it's something I've been thinking about since August, before I even left for London. This isn't just because of everything that happened there." She gazed earnestly at her father and then Avery, then at Wilder.

Aunt Midge took Tilly's hand on the tablecloth. She gave her an encouraging nod. "It's all right, dear. We're your family, and we trust your intentions. Go ahead and share what you've been thinking."

"I've submitted my application, essay, and transcripts to Juilliard." She swallowed hard, looking down at her plate. "I also applied for every scholarship offered through the school, and also seven other scholarships from outside foundations. I know it's a long shot. I know they only take, like, amazing talent, and my track record in London will probably hurt my chances, but I did ask my semester-one voice professor for a letter of recommendation, and she said she sent it yesterday. I don't want to go back to London." She raised her gaze, imploring William and Avery both. "Please."

"Wow." Avery stared at her little sister. She checked their dad's reaction before saying more.

"I'm impressed," William said. He was nodding. "What you've done shows great initiative, Tilly. I think it's a good plan."

Tilly frowned, as if she hadn't explained it right. "It might be a terrible plan. I know I've wasted this semester. Even if Juilliard grants me an audition, I still might not make it in, and even if I do get in, I wouldn't be able to start until next semester in January." Tilly rushed on. "And that's if there's an opening. I might not be able to start until next fall. I could lose a whole year."

"I hope you get in," Avery told her. She got up and went around to Tilly's side and gave her a quick hug and kiss on the temple. "Even if you don't, I know you'll make something else happen. I'm proud of you."

William laughed. "Your sister's gotten good at the parenting stuff in my absence. I was just going to say—I'm proud of you. You're aware of what you did wrong. You're taking responsibility for it. I doubt you'll ever do anything like that again. And you're finding a path forward." He paused. "Your mom would be proud of you too."

Tilly bit her lower lip, eyes filling with tears. She was out of her seat now and nearly knocking her dad out of his, her arms tightly around him.

At the end of the night, in the foyer for good-byes, Wilder offered his perspective, always a welcome point of view, given his occupation. "I hope you know," he said to Tilly, "there is no such thing as a year lost or wasted. We experience and learn even when we don't realize it. You aren't in a race. Your only competition is your past self." He shrugged. "Your aunt sometimes accuses me of talking in circles. I'm just pointing out that there are valuable lessons gained in every step of your journey."

Avery walked them out to the car. Wilder got in and started the engine while they said good-bye. "Auntie," Avery started, meaning to ask again why Midge and Wilder weren't a couple.

"Oh!" Midge put a hand on Avery's arm. "So rude of me; I'm sorry to interrupt you. But you know, at my age, I don't want to forget this, and it popped into my head when we were discussing Duke Pennington. You'd mentioned that that poor housekeeper who was killed was related to one of the manor staff, that he helped her get the job?"

Avery frowned at her. Midge was only sixty, and Avery had never once heard her refer to her age in a negative manner. "Yes, she and the groundskeeper are cousins. I guess the other housekeeper left a year or so ago."

Midge shook her head. "No. Oh my. I hope you'll pass this bit of information on to your detective. I believe he may find it useful. The previous housekeeper didn't resign. Nicholas told me when I met him for brunch in Rio, July of last year, that his poor housekeeper had recently passed away. It was the strangest thing. The woman was found dead in the lily pond outside the manor. I believe her name was Tia."

# Chapter Fourteen

Avery was wearing a path in the floor of the temporary lab at Pennington Manor Monday morning. Micah and William were already upstairs working on appraisals, and she needed to get started, but she was waiting for Art.

Aunt Midge was impossible to stay ahead of. Last night, Avery knew she'd cut her off on purpose, using her "advanced" age of sixty and claim of memory problems as an excuse, all to avoid having to answer what she was about to ask: why Midge and Wilder Mendelsohn weren't a couple. There wasn't a thing wrong with Midge's memory, not if she could recall a random detail from a brunch a year earlier. The Pennington Manor housekeeper being found dead a year ago could not be a coincidence. It explained what Mrs. Hoffman had meant in the kitchen Saturday when she'd fretted that Lord Percy could end up like *poor Tia*. Avery gasped. That wasn't even the first time she'd referenced the former housekeeper. Hadn't Lynn Hoffman also remarked that the housekeeping position at the manor was cursed? It made sense now.

What Avery wanted to know now was why Art's colleague didn't already know about the incident. She'd called and told him what Aunt Midge had said right away last night, and he was on his way to the manor now. She moved about the lab, getting her case organized, so she'd be ready to get back to the appraisals once he arrived; partnering with him throughout the manor was the best way to keep his identity quiet. She refreshed her email one last time before closing her laptop and was excited to see a response to the message she'd sent to the major museums of antiquity across the country. She perused the email from the curator at Detroit Antiquities Institute, sucking in her breath. Avery grabbed her phone.

Sir Robert picked up on the first ring. "You've reached Antiquities and Artifacts Authenticated; this is Robert Lane speaking. How may I help you?"

"It's me. Would you check up on Raul Cordoba again? We really need to talk to him. Today, if possible," Avery added.

"Good morning to you too, Avery! How are you?"

She smiled into the phone, forcing her racing mind to a manageable speed. "I'm sorry. I'm doing well. And how are you today, Sir Robert? Anything new at Barnaby's?"

"Ah! Since you ask, yes. A porcelain trinket collection is coming in next week for us. I'm told it was originally an engagement gift given to the queen mother herself, but I'm sure you and Micah and your father will discover its true worth."

Avery was impressed. "Nice one. You've really catapulted us forward getting the auction house contract. I have some news as well. The DAI saw my email. They have two of the stolen items from the manor—the Thomas Tompion clock and the candlesticks. And guess who submitted them?"

"Hmm. I'll say Raul Cordoba in Brooklyn. Oh my," Sir Robert said. "Oh, one moment." Avery heard a muffled rustling sound and then Sir Robert again, not speaking to her. "Happy Monday, Mrs. Kensington. I'll be right with you. Please help yourself to a fresh pastry; I picked them up at Magnolia this morning."

"Not fair," Avery murmured into the phone. "Why don't you ever bring in sweets when I'm there?"

"Because you won't eat them. I've tried!" Sir Robert said. "I must run, but I will place another call to Mr. Cordoba the moment I'm free. I'll keep you updated."

Avery sent a quick email back to the curator in Detroit, thanking him and asking if he'd ever worked with the submitting dealer before. She closed the laptop and set it with her case just as Art finally arrived.

"Tia Swenson," he said, coming through the door from the reception room. "Last year's dead housekeeper was Tia Swenson, assumed accidental drowning until the coroner found ligature marks on her neck." He slapped a folder on the table in front of Avery. "It's all in there. Why are you smiling?"

She shuddered. "I got a chill. You sound like Detective Stabler on *Law and Order*."

He stifled a laugh, shaking his head. "Let me guess, you're a Detective Benson wannabe."

"Oh, hardly. I could never fill those shoes. So." She placed a finger on the folder. "We have a housekeeper murdered by strangling made to look like an accident—or suicide—and a housekeeper murdered by being thrown off the roof made to look like an accident or suicide. Did Detective Carter not come across this during his investigation? That seems so strange."

Art leaned toward her. "I had to dig for this," he said, dropping his volume. "It wasn't attached to the manor or the Pennington name at all. Going through coroner reports to locate this information, I have a theory that somebody was paid off. The address the body was found at is missing from the paperwork. I only found it because Tia Swenson's residential address on the death certificate is the same as the manor's. Suzanne Vick probably moved into the same room vacated by Tia when she was killed."

"Oh my God. Okay, if someone was paid off, that was either done using family money, by one of the sons or Annabelle, or using money earned in the sale of the artifacts that are missing." She gasped. "Remember finding out about Lord Percy's, er, yacht theft last year? Aunt Midge mentioned Nick making sure it was kept hush-hush. He wouldn't . . . you don't think he did the same thing when Tia died, do you?" She stared wide-eyed at Art.

He frowned. "It's possible. I'd say him or Lord Nico. He's basically been groomed to handle the family's business dealings and the like. Somebody covered it up, or Detective Carter would've immediately latched on to that similar death at the beginning of the investigation."

"This just keeps getting worse," Avery said. "Was Tia Swenson involved in the thefts? Or was she killed off so

Suzanne could be installed as an insider to swap out valuables for fakes?"

"We'll find out," he resolved.

Avery picked up her equipment case and laptop. "I've got to get started." She turned to head out with Art. She froze— Lynn Hoffman was standing in the doorway, holding a tray of fruit and biscotti.

"I'm sorry to interrupt," she said, her voice coming out as a whisper. "You're starting early today, and I thought your team might like—" She shook her head, confusion crossing her features and wrinkling her brow. "I thought . . ." She didn't finish.

"Mrs. Hoffman, come in for a minute, please." Avery waved her in, moving to close the door behind her. She shot a quick look at Art. What now?

Art took the tray from her hands. Mrs. Hoffman looked down, as if she'd forgotten she was carrying it. He cut to the chase. "What did you hear?"

"I, uh, I don't know. Are you the police?" She scrutinized Art and then Avery. "Like, undercover? Does anyone else know? What about your partners upstairs?" She placed a hand on her chest, eyebrows going up. "Oh my goodness, does His Grace know too? The appraisals have been a ruse?"

"No," Avery said.

"Nobody knows anything except for you," Art told her. "I really need to keep it that way. I'm a detective working with Detective Carter. Ms. Ayers and the rest of her team are all antiques appraisers, I assure you."

"I have to tell Ira." She sat down heavily, shaking her head. "Don't look at me like that; you can't expect me not to. We've been married twenty-four years. We don't keep secrets from each other."

Art met Avery's gaze over Mrs. Hoffman's head. He looked back down at the woman. "I can respect that, but it could compromise the case. We need a little more time before anyone else learns that I'm not an appraiser."

"Mr. Smith—Detective—is Smith your real name, sir?" Mrs. Hoffman asked.

"Yes, but please just call me Art. Or Mr. Smith."

"Oh my. I'd never want to compromise the investigation, I promise. But I swear, my husband and I had nothing to do with Suzanne's death, or Tia's death, for that matter." She paused, searching his face. "I did hear Suzanne talking to someone the night before she died. She was upset. I didn't tell Detective Carter because I wasn't sure it mattered, but maybe you can make sense of it?"

Art pulled a chair up in front of her. "What did you hear, Mrs. Hoffman?"

"I was in the kitchen, getting the casserole ready for the next morning. It helps, you know, to prepare as much as I can the night before. If I have breakfast for the house planned ahead of time, it's easier in the mornings. Especially if I'm making a hot dish, which I'd planned to the next day, and the casserole prep takes a good hour or more to feed the family and staff."

Avery caught the pulse of Art's jaw muscle, the slow, exaggerated inhale and exhale that he was probably not even aware of. Mrs. Hoffman was trying his patience.

"I had just turned off the mixer when I heard someone crying. I poked my head out the door and it got louder, so I went exploring. I was worried. Most of us get along—we're like a family ourselves here when the Penningtons are gone. The crying was coming from in there." She pointed. "Suzanne was in the reception room, talking with someone. I think she must have been on the phone, because I never heard the other person."

"What did you hear her say?" Art asked.

"She said something like, 'I have to. It's going to be obvious; I don't have a choice.' Maybe it was the reverse of that, 'I don't have a choice; it's going to be obvious. I have to.' It's hard to say exactly because she kept repeating it, like someone was telling her not to do something, and she kept saying she had to." Mrs. Hoffman glanced at Avery and back at Art. "Does that mean anything to you? It proves I'm innocent, doesn't it? My husband and I had nothing to do with that pocket watch disappearing or poor Suzanne. I swear it."

Art rubbed one hand roughly across his jaw, thinking. He left her question unanswered. "Then what happened after you heard that end of the conversation? Did you see her leave? How sure are you that it was Suzanne?"

"I'm very sure. I didn't see her leave, but the only other women here besides me are all from Valle Charme. The duchess, Lady Annabelle, and Miss Gretchen. They all have that lovely accent—I think it's a little bit French and a little bit something else. Valle Charme island accent, I suppose," she said, smiling.

"This information helps, Mrs. Hoffman. Thank you." Art stood. "I'd like to ask that you give us a day or two, please. Don't say anything about our conversation, not even to your husband. It may be our best chance at catching Suzanne's killer, and I know you want that, right?"

The woman sighed. "A day?"

"Or two. Yes," he said firmly.

She looked up at him, her brow furrowed with worry. "All right. I don't want to interfere with the killer being caught. I'll try not to talk to my husband about any of this until it's solved."

"Thank you." He walked with her to the door. "One last thing. I wonder if you happen to remember who was at the manor the day Tia Swenson died last year?"

"Oh, that was horrible. Tia was a sweetheart. To think that she killed herself—it never made much sense to me, but the detective that came to the house said that's what it looked like. What did you ask again?"

Avery swore Art was speaking through clenched teeth, as kind as he tried to make his tone. "Do you remember who was here the day Tia died?"

"Oh, right, sorry. Ira and I were here . . . Jerry Wolf's the one who found her floating in the pond. Greg was out there working on the shrubs and came to get us. Jerry's son Bryan must have been here too, I'm sure; the groomsmen are always together. Lord Nico was here on business, just him and Roderick. The girls and Lady Annabelle don't normally travel with him. That's all."

"That's helpful too," Art said. "I appreciate it." He pulled the door closed behind her this time.

When she'd gone, Avery spoke quietly, paranoid now about being overheard. "Did Detective Carter search Suzanne's room? I know his forensics team went through the manor, but were they able to go through the staff's living areas?"

"Only Suzanne's. There was no warrant for the other rooms, not without specific evidence pointing to an employee or family member."

"Could we take a look? I mean, I'm sure they were thorough. But we know more now about her, her relation to Greg Lightfoot, and honestly, what Mrs. Hoffman overheard makes it seem like she was about to confess something. Theft? Another instance of an affair? We already know Lord Nico is involved with the nanny. What if . . ."

"I wondered the same thing. I know, I don't blame you for not wanting to say it. What if Nico was seeing someone else in addition to his wife and the nanny? Or what if, as you pointed out, Suzanne was the inside source switching out the items? If she was working with her cousin or the groomsmen or even someone like Lord Percy to make a profit, it'd certainly help to have someone inside the house with access to all the valuable heirlooms. Think about it. If a family member was involved—"

"They'd have needed an on-site partner to do the grunt work," Avery said, finishing his thought. They were virtually whispering now. "Between Lord Percy, Lord Nico, Mathew, Roderick, even Annabelle, none of them were here often. What if it was two people, an insider getting the items out to someone else who could take them to the dealer in Brooklyn?"

He nodded. "I think we both know who we're talking about. If Suzanne wasn't just an innocent victim but part of the theft operation, her cousin makes the likeliest partner."

"That's why I'm thinking there may have been something missed in her room," Avery said, agreeing.

"Let's hope we can figure out which room was hers without having to answer any questions. It's a big place. Easy to get lost while looking for an heirloom," Art said, giving Avery a wink that stirred all the warm flutters in her chest from Saturday night.

Down the long hallway leading away from the living quarters of the manor, the only antiquity on the appraisal list was *Ara Eros*, the god and goddess statues in the pool area. Avery was gambling on anyone she and Art might encounter not knowing that. So far, they were in the clear; the hallway was deserted. Avery drifted close to the first of the doors they'd discovered opened to bedrooms the other day. She boldly pushed it open and stepped in. "The inventory says the painting has a gilded frame—" She stopped, seeing the room was empty.

An unmade bed sat in the center of the room, dark-green comforter matching the curtains. "Horses," she said, glancing up at Art. The room was filled with horse paraphernalia. A row of horseshoes was displayed on a long, painted plaque, hooks on each one holding sweatshirts and jackets.

"Not the room we're looking for," Art said. They stepped out, Avery ready to loudly announce that they must have their directions wrong, but the hall was still empty, the smell of chlorine hanging in the air.

She repeated the same routine at the next room but cut herself off right after she'd said *inventory*. The groundskeeper stared back at them, one hand in the bottom drawer of a desk by the window.

"Oh!" Avery's tone was genuinely surprised, and on the heels of that, immense relief set in that Art was right behind her. She could be in the presence of a killer.

"So sorry. There's supposed to be a painting in here for us to appraise. It's got a gilded frame. It's called the, uh," he said, beginning to fumble.

"*The Dark and Stormy Night*," Avery supplied quickly. "It's a Matisse. But . . . I wonder if we've got the wrong room? I'm Avery Ayers, this is Art, we're the appraisers. This isn't the master bedroom at all, is it?" She put a hand on her forehead, trying to look embarrassed.

Greg Lightfoot had straightened up. He had gray circles under his eyes and several days' beard growth. They'd met him briefly on a couple occasions, but this man could be Lightfoot's father, he seemed to have aged so markedly. "No, it's not the master bedroom. That's upstairs." He sighed. "It's—I'm the groundskeeper here—Greg Lightfoot. I could call Mrs. Hoffman to take you up, if you'd like."

"No," Art said, "that's all right. We'll find it. We're sorry to have disturbed you."

"We didn't mean to barge into your room," Avery added.

"It's not my room. I'm clearing out my cousin's things."

The room looked as if it'd been gone through—by the forensics team at first, and maybe again by Lightfoot. The mattress was askew, dresser drawers were pulled out or half pulled out, and the items on the night table were in a jumble—perfume bottle lying on its side, a stack of books knocked over.

Lightfoot must've caught Avery looking. "I should have come prepared," he said, misinterpreting her perusal. "I've got boxes in my car. She's, well, she won't be coming back. She's passed away." The man's voice hitched at the end, and he looked down, drawing in a deep breath.

"Oh no," Avery said. Her mind raced. She'd been there the day Suzanne died. Did Lightfoot not remember seeing her? Should she pretend to be shocked and sad for him? Or let on that she knew? "Suzanne," she blurted. She couldn't see Art—he was behind her—but she swore she felt his stress level rise. "This is Suzanne's room, then. I'm so very sorry. I didn't know she was your cousin. We'll go."

He nodded. "Okay." He looked as if he might cry at any moment.

"Sorry for your loss," Art said, pulling the door closed behind them.

Avery leaned against the wall. "Oof. That was brutal," she whispered.

The poolroom door whooshed open at the end of the hall, and laughter carried to them. Lady Annabelle, Gretchen, Lucy, and Ava came toward them, wrapped in white terry cloth robes, hair dripping. They barely glanced at Avery and Art as they passed.

Avery stared up at Art, waiting until the group was a good distance away. "She doesn't know," she whispered.

He tipped his head in their direction and started walking. "Come on, we need to get out of this hallway. And yeah, I agree with you. I do think she knows Nico's running around on her, but she doesn't know who with."

Avery jumped as her phone buzzed in her pocket. All this sneaking around was making her twitchy. "Sir Robert," she spoke into the phone. "Did you reach him?" She gripped Art's arm as she heard his reply.

"Got him. Raul Cordoba can see you at noon today. I hope that gives you enough time to get to Brooklyn."

# Chapter Fifteen

Avery filled in her father and Micah, who were immersed in a detailed examination of the items in the manor movie theater. They chose to keep working, and Avery promised to update them. She left after Art, who would meet her in Brooklyn.

Cordoba's office was one of several in a quaint old red-brick building in Cobble Hill. The antiquities dealer emerged from the inner office space and ushered her in. He was about to close his office door when Art and Detective Carter came in.

"Oh good, we made it," Carter said. "I'm Detective Carter, and this is Detective Smith. Mr. Cordoba, I presume?" He crossed the room and shook the man's hand.

"Yes." He glanced at Avery. "Sorry, I thought this was about the *Ara Eros* submission to MOA? Is there some kind of problem?" Raul Cordoba looked to be in his forties, a handsome man in an expensive Italian suit.

"That's what we hope to find out," Carter said. "You don't mind if we join you, do you?"

Cordoba raised his eyebrows and held the office door open wider. "That's fine. Let me grab another chair."

When they were seated, Avery handed a slip of paper across the desk to the dealer. "We are here about the *Ara Eros*, but I'm actually in the process of hunting down seven antiquities that have been stolen. *Ara Eros* is one."

The dealer's eyes widened. "No. I saw the certificate myself when I acquired the *Ara Eros*. That's not possible. I don't deal in stolen antiquities." The man seemed genuinely stunned.

"I'm afraid it's true," Avery said. "My partner and I appraised that piece for the museum; we didn't see any red flags with the chain of ownership either. If you wouldn't mind going over this list"—she pointed—"maybe you could tell us if you remember any of these other items?"

Cordoba placed a finger on the page, confirming what Avery already knew. "The Thomas Tompion clock. I placed that with the DAI in Michigan, along with the French empire candlesticks. Oh good Lord." He continued reading silently, finally sitting back and sliding the paper away from him in disgust.

"I take it you know the other pieces as well." Avery leaned forward. "Did you handle the deals for all of these?"

Raul Cordoba put his hands up in a helpless motion, shaking his head. "Each of these were genuine artifacts. I use a variety of appraisers all over the country, but they're all reputable. I've used your company before," he said, nodding at Avery.

"Yes, I learned that," she said. "You'd worked with my partners on a piece of art from the *Titanic*. Amazing find."

"And that one was authentic and certified as well." He bristled.

Avery put a hand on his desk. "Mr. Cordoba, I'm not suggesting you've knowingly sold stolen pieces. None of us are." She glanced at Art and Detective Carter beside her, appreciative that they were letting her run point with the dealer; after all, they worked on opposite sides of the same coin in their profession. "What we're hoping is that you'll share with us how you came by these items. Were they all brought to you by the same person?"

The dealer leaned forward on his elbows and read through the list again. He turned, pulled a thick, leather-bound ledger from a desk drawer, and methodically began flipping through pages. One by one, he jotted notes down beside each item on Avery's list. He pushed it across the desk to her when he'd finished. He then turned the open ledger so it faced Art and Carter and slid it over to them.

"Detectives," he said. "I assume you'll be subpoenaing my records, so I'll try and save you a step. The ledger before you contains an itemization of every purchase I make, the submitting layperson or collector, notes on the provenance or certification, estimated worth, and final disposition. I cannot part with that, but I will provide you with copies of each applicable page from the ledger as well as the transaction and acquisition notes I keep in my safe. I keep meticulous records, going back to when I founded my business. Will that work? I don't knowingly deal in stolen artifacts. I never have."

Avery stared up at him from her list. "Beside every item here but two, you've written the name Gregory Lightfoot. Do you know this man?"

Raul Cordoba sat back down, looking defeated. "Not really. He was sent to me by a friend of a friend."

"What friend would that be?" Art asked.

The dealer groaned. "This doesn't make any sense. I've never had trouble like this. I run a legitimate business."

Detective Carter spoke. "We want to believe you. So far, we do. It'll help if you tell us who vouched for this Lightfoot. And do you know the collector you got the *Ara Eros* from? This—" He leaned over to check Avery's list. "Johnathon Smith? Wait a minute, you've written nothing next to the Petrova pocket watch here. That hasn't passed through your hands?"

"No, I don't know of that piece. Only these other six items; I've listed here which facilities acquired each of them. But no pocket watch."

Avery shook her head. After all of this, the pocket watch was still unaccounted for. She glanced at Art. "That kind of—" She stopped. They didn't know for sure that Cordoba wasn't in on all of this. She'd wait until they were outside to voice her thought.

"John Smith?" Detective Carter asked. "Really? Do you know how many of those there are? He's a John Smith," he said, jerking a thumb toward Art beside him.

"Hey," Art protested. "I mean, it's true. But that's my actual name."

"All right," Carter conceded. "John *Arthur* Smith. I'm just saying." He turned his attention to Raul Cordoba. "You were obviously given an alias."

The dealer shrugged. "Not necessarily. It didn't even occur to me. He's an antiquities collector, as far as I know. He's the one who vouched for Greg Lightfoot, who brought me the pieces on your list except for the first one, the *Ara Eros*, which came from Smith himself. As you can see from my notes, I only met Smith once. A mutual acquaintance of ours connected us."

"Who's the mutual acquaintance?" Art asked.

"Her name is Francesca Giolitti."

Avery gasped, her hand flying up to cover her mouth. She stared at Cordoba.

The dealer frowned at her, looking perplexed. "Francesca had acquired items from me in the past. When she recommended I take a look at the *Ara Eros*, I had no reason to doubt the submitting collector. He was quite knowledgeable about the piece. So when he called me a few weeks later and said a good friend of his had some items he was looking to sell, of course I said I'd meet with him—that was Lightfoot," he said, pointing at the list.

"Do you remember what this John Smith looked like? Roughly?" Carter asked.

"It's been months, and I met him once. Uh. I don't know—medium height, brown hair."

"That's it? Really? Age? Fat or thin? Tattoos, marks?"

The dealer scowled at Carter. "I didn't know I should be memorizing every feature, Detective. He was an average guy. Could've been in his thirties or forties or even late twenties, I don't know. Not fat or thin, medium build. He had on jeans and a baseball cap, I think. I remember wondering how Francesca knew him. He didn't strike me as her, uh, type of guy."

"What kind of identification do you require from the collectors who bring their antiquities to you?" Art asked.

Cordoba shrugged. "It depends. They have to fill out a form with their mailing address, and I have to have a way to pay them." He turned in his chair and tapped a few keys on his computer. The printer behind him whirred. He handed two sheets of paper to Art. "Here. The submission forms for Smith and Lightfoot. They were both paid by money order, made out to cash. It's not unusual for collectors to request that form of payment," he added, obviously anticipating the next question.

The detectives stood, and Avery took their cue. "You've been very helpful, Mr. Cordoba," Detective Carter said. "We'll be in touch."

Art stopped in the doorway. "By the way. Have you had any recent contact with Francesca Giolitti?"

"No. Not since she connected me with Smith."

"It'd be smart to notify the authorities if she does try to get in touch."

Cordoba maintained his neutral expression. "I'll keep that in mind, Detective."

Outside in the parking lot, Avery started to speak, but Art touched her arm. "Wait. There's a coffee shop around the corner where we can talk." She followed his gaze to the brick building, where they could see Cordoba fifty feet away through his ground-floor office window, sitting at his desk. It was chilly for October thirty-first, Halloween, but several of the office windows were open a crack, including Cordoba's.

Avery, Art, and Carter took an isolated table at the back of the nearly deserted coffee shop, Art sliding in next to Avery with Carter across from them. She leaned forward, elbows on the table, careful to keep her voice quiet. "Do you believe he knows nothing at all about what happened with Francesca?"

Carter shook his head. "No. He may not be involved in this apparent crime ring at Pennington Manor, but I'm positive he's not clueless about Francesca. You'd have to live under a rock not to know what happened. Especially in the world of art and antiquities."

Art was nodding. "I have a feeling that ledger he gave us is only going to confirm all of his dealings are legit."

"A John Smith—sent by Francesca Giolitti—brings him an ancient, highly valuable statue set of a Greek god and goddess and presents some kind of forged certificate of authenticity, and you're telling me he doesn't take a moment to question it?" Carter took a swig of his coffee and made a face. He set the forms Cordoba had given them on the table and took out his phone, opening the map app. "Let's see where John Smith lives."

"Francesca," Avery said. "I can't believe there's still fallout from her shady dealings. You guys have no info on her whereabouts? Not you guys. I mean, like, law enforcement."

"It's an international matter now. She was sighted in Monaco, the last time I checked, but it's been a couple months since I looked into it."

Detective Carter spun his phone around on the table, turning the map toward Art and Avery. "As I thought. Smith's address doesn't exist. But Lightfoot's address on his form matches what's on file with the DMV. I'll take what we've got to the judge and get the warrant for Lightfoot's arrest. We've got enough to bring him in, and hopefully he'll give up this John Smith. Without Smith being in the picture, I'd have said Suzanne Vick was Lightfoot's accomplice, she was the insider at the manor, and then I assume once she got the items out to him, Lightfoot would take them to the dealer to sell."

Avery spoke. "What about the former housekeeper, Tia Swenson, Detective? Is it crazy to think she was killed so that Suzanne could get the job as housekeeper?"

"Not crazy at all. Not that we can prove it yet. But after seeing how the coroner's report was mismanaged, I'm certain there was some kind of payoff orchestrated to keep that scandal out of Pennington Manor's history and away from the family name."

"They're launching an internal investigation," Art said. "It may end up pointing back to your friend Nick." Her eyes widened. "Not the murder of the former housekeeper. The duke was in Valle Charme at the time. But this family has a history of keeping their skeletons very deeply in the closet."

Avery sighed. "I'm learning that. So where does John Smith fit in? The way Cordoba described him, it almost sounded like a disguise—medium everything, baseball cap, average right down to his name." She chuckled.

Art sat back and stared at her. "And again. *Hey.* You two really expect me not to be offended every time you insult my name?"

Avery bumped her shoulder against his, smiling. "It's a pretty generic name. But not on you."

Art smiled.

Carter raised an eyebrow, gaze moving from Art to Avery, but he refrained from commenting.

"So, fake John Smith knows Greg Lightfoot," Avery mused. "He had to meet with Cordoba at least once so he could send Lightfoot to him and Cordoba would trust him."

"If Lightfoot won't give us Smith, we'll have to weed him out some other way," Art said. "We'll need to look into his circle, friends, other family members he might have involved besides Suzanne." He addressed Carter. "Did you get any specific hits on any of the men at the manor you questioned? If Suzanne's death is related to the thefts—say, if she was about to confess the scheme to the Penningtons, which goes along with Mrs. Hoffman overhearing her saying, 'It's going to be obvious, I have to'—we can deduce that John Smith killed her to save himself. Technically, Smith could be any of the men who were on-site the day she was murdered."

"Almost," Avery said. "It can't be the people who were out near the body seconds after she fell. But when we were talking the other day, we realized that even Lord Nico could have done it; he came through the maintenance room door outside moments later, which he could have accessed really fast from the roof."

Carter spoke. "Nico, Percy, Mathew, Roderick, Hoffman, and Jerry Wolf. Avery, you'd said Bryan Wolf, the son, ran over to the stables to the body when you came out, right?" She nodded. He continued. "Lightfoot was on the ground with Suzanne, and the duke and his wife were outside too. But that leaves literally every other male occupant of the manor as a suspect."

"Mrs. Hoffman said her husband was with her," Avery said. "I guess I know that doesn't matter; she could be lying. But . . . I have a hard time believing they were involved."

"We can't throw out the possibility that Suzanne was killed by a jilted lover or a jealous spouse," Carter said. "I know, I hate to be the voice of reason here, but no good ever comes from connecting dots without proof."

Art nodded. "Right. From that angle, it'd point to Lord Nico or Annabelle. Or Gretchen, if Avery's theory is correct and Nico was sleeping with both the nanny and Suzanne. That's a potentially messy triangle. Or actually a square."

"One last angle, though I'm not sure yet it goes anywhere," Carter said. "When I interviewed Lord Percy, I was surprised at how forthcoming he was. Okay, for frame of reference, the rest of the royals were markedly reserved. One- or two-word responses to all my questions. Nico, his wife, the duke, and Duchess Mariah were all polite but stoic. Very private, very minimal information offered. But Percy spilled all the dirt between him and his brother and their father. Not that I can really do anything with it."

Avery frowned. "He was going on about something regarding Nico the other day. Art probably filled you in. He was drunk and not making a lot of sense."

Carter nodded. "It might make some sense now. Percy says he and Nico had an agreement that his brother has now gone back on. I guess Percy was a record-breaking polo player in school, and then continued to do well when he went away to Cambridge for college. He'd been working on convincing Duke Pennington to allow him the freedom to pursue an actual career in it here. Percy was even scouted by two of his U.S. dream teams. Nico had agreed to back him up and help convince their father to let him go."

"Oh wow," Avery said. "I mean, I think I get the magnitude of that kind of arrangement. Lord Percy has obligations to the family in Valle Charme, right? Like, responsibilities as Nick's son in their kingdom? So he was hoping to get away from all that?"

"Exactly," Detective Carter said. "The deal between the brothers was that Percy would have Pennington Manor to himself in the States and Nico as the eldest son and primary heir would stay in Valle Charme. Percy threw it all away last year when he got suspended from Cambridge's polo team. He was reinstated for the last stint before he graduated, but the scouts didn't want a potential liability on their teams. The offers dried up."

"The stolen yacht," Avery said. As she relayed to Carter what Aunt Midge had told her, the detective nodded.

"Right. The stolen yacht and evidence of smuggled goods. Since then, without any prospects of a good team here for Percy, Nico's sided with their father. Percy says he begged Duke Pennington for a little more time; he's still scrambling to get one team to look again at his stats. But the duke wants him home in Valle Charme, and he's moving forward on listing the manor, as you know."

"And the fallout from all of that is Lord Percy acting out, as Mrs. Hoffman said," Avery mused. "Getting in fights and coming home drunk isn't going to undo his bad judgment or get his polo career back." She shook her head. "I know he did this to himself, but it's still sad."

"Percy's rant makes sense now," Art added. "I don't buy that it's motive for theft or murder. Not even to get back at his brother or try to profit off a few items, when he's from a family that's arguably worth billions."

"I'd have to agree with you there," Carter said. "Anyway. I'll get the warrant as quickly as possible, but I want the arrest to take place at the manor. You said he's back to work, right?"

"Yes, he was there today cleaning out Suzanne's room," Avery said.

"We'll shoot for tomorrow; it's already late in the day today. My guys combed that room pretty thoroughly the day she was killed. If Lightfoot was looking for something, I'd say it's already gone," Carter said.

They separated outside the coffee shop, and Art caught a ride with Avery back to Lilac Grove. "Why is he waiting until tomorrow to arrest Greg Lightfoot?" Avery asked.

"It'll take the afternoon today to get the warrant," Art said. "My guess is Carter wants the arrest done in full view of the Pennington manor staff and family. He's hoping our so-called John Smith will make an impulsive move and out himself."

"Smart."

The time on the road with Art passed too quickly. He asked how Tilly was doing, and Avery filled him in on her sister's tentative plan. She asked about Art's sisters, and he surprised her by going into detail about each of the three of them.

She already knew that he was the youngest; she'd guessed that a while ago based simply on how protective they sounded. But by the time she turned into his driveway, she'd not only learned the basics about each of them but also knew that the oldest, Katherine, had tried for eight years before having her first child last year at forty; that Jeannie, the second oldest, had just gotten a new car; and that Claire, the sister two years older than Art, was getting married in December to Phoebe, who taught at the same high school with her.

Avery couldn't resist following Art inside to see the cat family. He opened the pen and scooped up a black-and-white kitten, handing it to her. "I know you need your kitten fix," he said.

She saw he'd replaced the plastic Tupperware bowl of cat food with a cute, paw-print pet food and water caddy, and now instead of the old comforter on the bottom of the play pen, there was an extra-large dog bed. "You've really embraced them adopting you, huh?"

"For now. My sister says she thinks they're around five or six weeks old, still on the young side to be away from their mother. Ow!" He reached down and grabbed the rebel orange kitten that was clawing its way up his pantleg, settling it against his chest. "They have a vet appointment next week, and then when the vet says they're ready, I wondered if your offer to help me find homes for them still stands?"

Avery was thrilled. "I'm so glad you're keeping them here for now. I'd have worried about them at the shelter. What about you, though? Will you find other homes for all of them?"

Art tipped his chin down, where the orange kitten was rubbing its head on him. "I don't see how I can get rid of this one," he laughed. "I was thinking of maybe keeping two. So they aren't alone all day when I'm at work."

She hugged him impulsively. "Perfect." She let the orange kitten sniff her nose. "So you and a buddy will get to stay with Art!"

"My sister Claire might want one too, I'm not sure yet. And you and Tilly could have first choice . . . Halston might like a friend."

"I've actually thought about that. Let me talk to my dad and Tilly about it. All right." She kissed the tiny kitten on the top of its head and then did the same to the one in her arms, setting it down. "I've got to run. Literally. It was so cold this morning that I couldn't bring myself to go, but I can't completely skip it. I'll just wear layers. I can't start slacking now."

He walked her out. "About your marathon. Do you think your family would mind if I met them there, to cheer you on?"

"Yes! I mean no." She laughed. "No, they won't mind, and yes, please, I would love that. Thank you." She hugged him one more time, loving the way he didn't loosen his arms at first when she tried to let go.

"I'll see you in the morning," Art said. "I could pick you and your dad up, if you'd like."

"My dad and Micah aren't going tomorrow. Work is getting backed up at the shop, and we're almost done with the manor's appraisals, so it'll just be me."

"Perfect. See you at eight."

* * *

Tuesday morning's dark, overcast sky and frigid air would've been the best kind of weather for snuggling under the covers and sleeping in, but Avery was outside on her run by six AM, dressed in layers. Halston greeted her in the driveway when she got back, and William was in his winter parka on the porch.

"Not quite winter yet, Dad," she teased, tugging at his sleeve. She began her stretches on the porch before going in to shower. Art would be here soon.

"If they're arresting the groundskeeper today," William said, "and they know that might trigger the killer into some kind of rash action, I'd rather you just come with me to the shop today. Nothing is so important with the Pennington job that it can't wait another day or two."

Avery pursed her lips. "That makes sense. If you really want me to, I'll cancel going. I don't want you to worry. But . . ." She joined him on the porch swing. "I really don't think anything's going to happen. Detective Carter isn't positive Suzanne's killer is one of the staff or family. It's one possibility, but even so, there'll be plenty of law enforcement there when they make the arrest."

He didn't answer.

"Dad. I'll call Art and cancel. When are you heading into the city? We can deal with the manor job in a few days or whenever this is all resolved."

William toed the porch floor, making the swing move. He scrubbed a hand through his hair and looked at her. "They don't tell you, when you're a parent, that there's no cutoff age for when you get to stop worrying about your kids. I thought when you and Tilly grew up, it'd be a breeze, no worries. You'd be adults, doing things on your own out in the world, and that built-in parenting radar, the need to know your kids are safe and healthy, would just sort of go away." He shook his head, smiling. "I don't think it'll matter if you're sixty and I'm eighty-five. I'm still going to worry."

Avery rested her head on his shoulder. "Try not to. You and Mom raised us to be smart and self-sufficient. Which I think you'd have to acknowledge after this past year."

He patted her knee. "I have no doubt about that."

She stood. "I need to catch Art before he starts heading over here."

"No." Her dad stood up too. "What do you want to do? I trust your judgment."

She put her hands on her hips. "Is this a trick? I feel like it's a trick."

William tipped his head back and laughed. "I swear it's not a trick."

She narrowed her eyes, studying his expression. "Hmm. Well, if you really mean that, I'd still like to go. I think it'll be fine. But I will respect whatever you want me to do. I mean it."

He nodded. "Go. I'm sure you're right. And as you said, there'll be a police presence today."

"Right." She kissed his cheek. "Please don't worry."

# Chapter Sixteen

As Art's truck rolled down the long, curving drive to the manor, Avery let out a long whistle. "Whoa. Are those thunderclouds?" The sky to the northwest over the house was filled with rolling gray clouds. "We must be getting rain today."

He shrugged. "The weather's been weird all week. Look." He pointed. "No horses. They must all be inside with the rain coming."

"Oh," Avery said, her memory jarred. "Aunt Midge said Nick came home last night. He has an air cast for his sprain, and it sounds like he's fine other than the headaches from the concussion."

Art chuckled. "Your aunt definitely has her finger on the pulse of what's going on with her friends, doesn't she?"

"And family," Avery said. "She comes off as a little stern sometimes, especially when Tilly gets cheeky—which happens a lot—but she has a huge heart." She realized she could be describing Art as well. "Hey. You don't have any kind of deadline Sunday after the marathon, do you? Nothing you have to run home for?"

He parked in the circle drive and looked at her. "Just cats."

"Well, obviously. So, I'm spending the night at Aunt Midge's apartment Saturday so I'll be in the city early for the race. She thought it'd be nice if we all came back for dinner afterward. Would you come?"

Art's face broke into a wide grin. "Sure. I'd love to."

"Awesome."

In the lab through the manor's reception room, Avery and Art worked side by side in near silence on their laptops for the first two hours of the day. While Avery was uploading all the documentation so far on the antiquities she and the team had finished appraising, editing and then getting it all compiled into an easy-to-read spreadsheet to add to their full, detailed report, Art perused as many websites as he could find, using public domain sites as well as law enforcement access-only sites, looking for a connection between Greg Lightfoot and one of the other manor occupants on their suspect list.

Avery saved the last file and scooted her chair over to Art's computer. "Anything?"

He shook his head, scowling. "I've given up on him and switched to Suzanne. Lightfoot's circle is shockingly small. He doesn't share a bowling team, doctor, dentist, accountant, gym, or anything else with anyone here besides his cousin. Let's hope Suzanne was more interesting."

Avery had an idea. She pulled up the Pennington Manor page she'd located before they'd begun this assignment and found the listing of manor employees. She read through the brief résumé-like bio for Gregory Lightfoot and was gratified to see her memory had served her well for once. She scrolled further, jotting down notes on the other manor staff, and got stuck when she came to Mathew and Roderick. Why were they not listed? She turned to Art, about to get his input, and then realized—of course they weren't listed. They weren't manor employees.

Her next website search was for the Valle Charme Pennington estate. There she found a plethora of employees listed. Among them were Mathew Nolan, valet and personal assistant to Duke Nicholas Pennington, and Roderick Chamberlain, Pennington family driver. She jotted down notes from their short bios and opened a new browser window to check something else.

"What are you doing?" Art had moved his chair over next to her now.

She clicked back to the Pennington Manor employees. "I remembered reading about the family and the staff here when we first met with the duke for the appraisal job. Each employee's bio gives a quick summary of professional and personal info. Most of these list universities or trade schools along with experience, and I thought I remembered seeing a school listed in Greg Lightfoot's bio. I did, right here." She pointed.

"Academy of the Arts in Paris?" Art raised his eyebrows. "Did not expect that. But he's from here, right? At least that's the information I have. And I didn't hear an accent at all."

"Yes, I think so. But look." She clicked back to the Valle Charme estate employee page. "Roderick also went to that school. That'd be a weird coincidence; they must know each other."

He pulled his laptop over and began quickly typing. "I'll have Carter see what he can pull up on the two of them at that school. If they knew each other prior to their roles working for the Pennington family, that could lead to something."

"Wait, don't send your email yet. There's another connection he should look into too." She opened the other browser window and scrolled down. "This is crazy. This is an article from five years ago in a Paris newspaper; the first couple photos are just Lord Nico and Lady Annabelle . . . Lady Annabelle holding baby Lucy . . . Nick and the duchess holding the baby . . . but look at this last photo. That's Saint Antoine cathedral, and on the front steps, you can see Lord Nico and Lady Annabelle holding a baby, and—let me zoom in again."

Art leaned forward, reading the caption. *"Duke Nicholas Pennington and Duchess Mariah Pennington at the traditional baptism of Lord Nico and Lady Annabelle Pennington's first child, Lucille Josephine Pennington. Also pictured are—"* He touched the screen. "Is that Greg Lightfoot? In Paris, at Lord Nico's daughter's baptism? Okay, you're a genius, Avery. Explain this to me."

"I can't," she said, shrugging. "Why is he there? Is he, like, a longtime family friend or something?"

"I obviously need to hone my internet deep-dive skills," Art said, leaving her question unanswered. He resumed reading. *"Also pictured from left to right are Gregory Lightfoot, Mathew Nolan, Lord Percy Pennington, Roderick Chamberlain, and Rowena Benoit.* This lady, Rowena, she must be part of the Valle Charme staff," Art said, pointing.

"She is; I checked," Avery said. "But this means Greg Lightfoot can be connected not just to Roderick, but to the whole family. He must have known them somehow before his job as a groundskeeper here, to be at Lucy's baptism. But how?"

Art was quiet, staring at the screen. "I don't know. Hold on; let me send this to Carter. While he's waiting around for the judge to approve the warrant, he can check that school, and then I'm also asking him to look for any connection to Mathew. I can't wrap my head around him being chummy with one of Nick's sons; he doesn't have that kind of demeanor around them at all. Mathew and Roderick are the only two working-class people in this photo. You may have just eliminated our stateside suspects," Art said.

"I guess we'll see what Detective Carter can dig up before we knock Hoffman and Jerry Wolf off the list. Would there be any reason to look at shady contacts of Greg Lightfoot outside of work? Or are you and Carter positive the killer lives or works on-site?"

Art hit send on the email to Carter. "We're waffling on that. Without a solid lead, we can't rule anything out."

Avery stood. It was already past eleven, and she hadn't done any hands-on work yet. She gathered her equipment case and laptop and checked the inventory of items still left to appraise. "There are three antiques in Nick's office we haven't gotten to yet, so I think I'm going to start there."

"I'm going to drift," Art said. He dropped his volume, even though the door was closed this time. "But I'll stay close. I'll let you know when I hear from Detective Carter;

he's going to shoot me a text when he has the warrant in hand and ready to go."

Working in Duke Pennington's office at the end of the second-floor hallway, Avery kept an ear out in case there was any more drama from Lady Annabelle's quarters. The place was eerily quiet today. Mrs. Hoffman poked her head in near lunchtime, letting Avery know there was soup and sandwiches in the dining room.

"Thank you so much," she told the woman. "I completely lost track of time. It's kind of secluded and peaceful back here in the duke's study."

"That it is. I'm sure that's why he likes this spot."

Avery left her kit and accompanied Lynn Hoffman down-stairs, Art joining them from the other end of the hallway as they went. "How is he feeling today? It was awful, seeing him be taken away in the ambulance," Avery said.

"You can ask him yourself. I told him I'd serve his lunch in his room, but he sounds irritated with being in bed. He's already in there." Mrs. Hoffman held the door open for Avery and Art and then hurried back to the kitchen.

Duke Pennington was seated at the head of the table, looking every bit himself except for the chair with a pillow in front of him where his leg was propped up.

Avery took the seat on his left. There was no one else here yet. "How are you? You have no idea how much you scared everyone, Aunt Midge included."

"I'm well. Truly. My ankle doesn't hurt at all with this thing on it." He waved his hand at the bulky gray plastic boot covering his right foot and leg. "The headaches aren't pleasant, and there's a bit of dizziness, but I believe I'm fortunate my injuries aren't more severe."

"I think you're right." Avery glanced at Art and then back at Nick. She'd better ask what she'd been wondering now, before anyone else showed up. "Nick, do you mind if I ask why you let the groomsmen put you on that horse? They said it's one of the younger, more spirited animals. Couldn't you have gone for a trail ride on that older black mare?"

He looked sheepish. "I suppose I could have." He sighed. "I purchased that stallion myself. He's a thoroughbred, like most of my son's polo ponies. When we thought Percy might pursue it professionally, we added to our string of horses a few years ago. I got it into my head that I'd like my own stallion. I call him Clive, a shortened version of his proper name. As you saw for yourself, Clive's a gorgeous animal, majestic, fast—and smart when he's inclined to be. It seemed a shame to send him away with the others without enjoying one last ride with him."

Avery couldn't conceal her surprise. "So no one convinced you to choose Clive for your ride?" She mentally crossed off Jerry Wolf from the possible John Smith list. If Nick had chosen that dangerous horse all on his own, it answered the question of whether the Wolfs were trying to harm the duke for their own agenda, leaving no real motive for killing Suzanne or stealing artifacts.

The duke registered surprise at her question. "Of course not. No one convinced me. I assure you, I make my own decisions. I'm the only one to blame for what happened."

Avery was almost finished with her soup when Art tapped his foot against hers under the table. "We've got several more antiques to appraise before we're finished today," he said. "We'd better get back to it. Ready?"

She took two more quick spoonfuls of the cream of broccoli. "Mmm. Yes, I'm ready. Mrs. Hoffman, you're a magician in the kitchen," she declared, smiling at the woman, who had just set a tray of cookies on the table.

"Well, I thought soup sounded perfect for today, what with the snow already falling. It'll warm us all up."

Avery frowned and moved to the large, curtain-covered window on the far wall. "No way," she breathed. "Art. Did you see this?" She drew the curtain back. In the three or four hours since they'd arrived, snow had covered the ground.

He moved to stand beside her. "Well, that's different. It's November first—a little early, don't you think?"

Mrs. Hoffman laughed. "Tell that to Mother Nature. I think it's pretty."

"It's beautiful," Avery agreed. Art nudged her with his elbow. She'd almost forgotten he was trying to signal her to get going. "Back to work. Thank you for the delicious lunch. And Duke Pennington," she said, "I'm so relieved you're all right."

She followed Art down the hall. He looked around, making sure they were alone, and stopped in the vestibule, handing her his phone. On it was a message from Detective Carter. She read it, raising her gaze to his. "He's asking if you can confirm Lightfoot is here today?" she whispered.

Art scrolled up and pointed to the previous message. "He's got the warrant. He's leaving soon, but he wants to be sure he's here. He says the roads are a mess," he whispered back. "Have you seen him?"

She shook her head. "But would he be outdoors working in all this snow? Maybe he went home."

"I'm not sure. I know the staff are allowed to park in the garage; he may have done that if he knew we were getting all this snow. I need to do a quick walk-through and to see if I spot any sign of him, but you've got to stick with me. I'm not leaving you alone here."

Under any other circumstances, Avery would've disagreed with his misplaced chivalry, but she appreciated it now. "But," she said, glancing down both of the hallways in her line of sight, "that seems risky. We're just going to stroll around the manor?"

"Same story as before if someone asks, but we'll switch it up," he whispered back. "We were looking for the library and got lost."

"Let's check Suzanne's room first. There isn't really any-where else indoors Lightfoot would be."

"You read my mind," Art said.

Suzanne's room looked emptier than it had yesterday. A few half-packed boxes stood in the center of the room, the closet and drawers in disarray, the contents of Suzanne's bookcase and dresser top even more of a mess than they'd been before. "He must be here," she said. "This almost looks like he stopped in the middle of packing and is coming back. And what's with all that?" She pointed to the dresser, where a jewelry box was turned upside down, the back panel pried off.

"He's looking for the pocket watch," Art murmured. "I'm sure of it." His head jerked to the right—a shout had come from the end of the hall. He took a step in that direction and then stopped, pointing at Avery. "Stay right here. I mean it."

She peered out into the hallway after him, seeing nothing but Art disappearing into the alcove for the pool entrance. She'd heard the shout too, but now it was dead silent. She took a few steps toward the alcove. "Art," she called in a stage whisper.

A gunshot resonated through the hall. Avery flinched and ducked instinctively, her hands coming up to cover her ears. She started running. "Art!"

Reaching the alcove with the key-code-protected door, she was shocked to see the glass shattered and the swimming pool inside a shimmering pink color. Heart racing, Avery rushed through the glass-fringed doorframe and darted toward the pool. She gasped, freezing abruptly on the slick tile, Art's arms grabbing her before she fell into the water.

Floating facedown in the center of a slowly spreading cloud of red was Gregory Lightfoot.

# Chapter Seventeen

Art leapt into the pool.

Avery dropped to her knees and helped him pull Lightfoot out, turning him over onto his back on the pool deck. "Oh God." Lightfoot's eyes were closed, and she couldn't see him breathing. He was nearly as white as the tile he lay upon.

Art clamped his hand firmly over the deep slice at the front of the man's neck, the blood continuing to leak from under his fingers. He met her eyes. "My phone was in my pocket; do you have yours? Call 911."

She did, following Art's furtive looks around the room while she gave the operator the address.

"This just happened," Art said. "Whoever did this could still be in here. Give me your hand."

Avery sucked in her breath but presented her hand to Art. He quickly swapped his for hers, pressing her hand down firmly over the wound on Lightfoot's neck. "Don't let up on the pressure." Art got to his feet and ran over to the outside exit door, throwing his jacket back and placing a hand on the revolver he must've used to shoot the lock on the pool area door. He shoved the exit door open and leaned out. He did the same with the locker room and sauna doors.

While he searched, Avery maintained pressure on Lightfoot's neck, but she had a sinking feeling they were already too late. The man was ghost white now and lifeless under her fingers. The swimming pool had turned a pale red, and she knelt with Lightfoot in the center of a large puddle of blood. She used the first two fingers of her other hand to check his pulse below the corner of his jaw, where she checked her own when running, and found nothing.

"Art." She tried to get his attention, but he was back at the exit door to the outside again. He'd propped it open with a chair and was staring down at the snow. "Art," she called again. "He's gone."

He came back inside and moved toward her. "I know. There are footprints in the snow leading away. But I think he was in the locker room first. The garbage can is knocked over, and a bunch of the lockers are standing open."

"No." She stared up at him. "Lightfoot's gone. He isn't breathing, and there's no pulse. He's lost too much blood."

Art bent down, hands on his knees, peering at the dead man. "Christ." He stood up, his eyes growing wide. "Avery. Come on, I have an idea. Hurry," he said. He was already at the glass-shard-filled door out to the hallway. She followed him through. He was at the opposite wall, running his hand over the wallpaper. "We need to be quick. Where's the latch?"

Avery moved to the wall and looked back, checking to be sure she was in line with the pool alcove. She slid her hand along the wall at hip level and found the latch. She opened the door, and Art pulled her through to the hidden passage, closing it behind them. He went up, taking two stairs at a time. He looked over his shoulder at her. "The snow's coming down hard, but we should be able to see almost all the way around the property from the third floor. We might be able to see where he went."

Avery caught up to him and then passed him on the stairway up to the roof. She paused, checking back on him. Art was limping slightly, favoring his bad knee. She tried the doorknob at the top of the steps. She hoped it hadn't been a fluke the other day that it was unlocked. The door opened, and she and Art jogged to the edge, between parapets, and peered over. Art moved to the left, Avery to the right, scanning, and a minute later Art called out. "There. Footprints."

Avery crossed to where he stood, following his outstretched arm. "I see them too." The footprints led away from the pool's outdoor exit and curved out and then back in an arc, ending at the brick exterior of the manor. She leaned over farther, craning to see. "That's . . . is that the door outside from the maintenance room? It looks like—" Art's arm slipped around her waist and pulled her safely back from the edge.

"We're not having another Suzanne incident," he growled. "Be careful."

"I am," she retorted, hearing a trace of Tilly's sass in her own tone. "I am. Sorry. But I think he must've circled back inside. That's what it looks like, right?"

He leaned over the edge where she'd just been, though not as far due to his couple-inch height advantage. "Has to be. Hold on." He pulled out his phone and swiped. As he did, tiny shards of the shattered screen fell off. Art jerked his fingers back. "Damn!" A large drop of blood was forming on the tip of one finger. He wiped his hand impatiently on his pantleg and tried again to use the phone, to no avail. "Ugh. It's all pixelated and glitchy. I must've smashed it on the side of the pool, getting Lightfoot out."

"Here." Avery offered her phone to him. "Do you want to call Carter?"

He took it, meeting her gaze. "Yes, but I don't know his number. It was in my phone. I can almost remember it." He looked down at the keypad on Avery's, moving a finger back and forth but not dialing.

"Maybe just try. It might come back to you."

He nodded. "I'm thinking."

"Well, the ambulance will be coming, and I'm sure they'll send police. They know it was a stabbing."

Art went back into the stairwell, holding the door for her. "If Lightfoot's killer did leave the pool and then come back inside through the maintenance room, we're not going to find him now." He led the way down the steps.

"What do you think he was after in the locker room?" Avery asked. She was a few steps behind him as they descended to the first floor. His limp was still there but much less pronounced. Going up must be more painful.

He looked back at her. "I don't know. I'm not sure if there are marked lockers for everyone or just a bunch of empty ones that anyone can use. I think Lightfoot spent his last couple—" Art had just stepped through the secret door through to the main floor hallway when it slammed closed, his last few words cut off.

Avery threw herself at the door, pulling at it, using her weight as leverage, but the latch on the outside held. She put her ear against the door, catching the sounds of Art struggling against whoever'd locked her in. Scuffling noises, grunts, a shout, a thump, and then the door she was hugging thumped under her ear, making her jump, as someone must have been thrown against it. She screamed, kicking the door as hard as she could. Silence, followed by the heavy sound of a body hitting the floor. She shouted again, calling Art's name. Silence. Nothing but silence, a horrible lack of sound. She immediately saw in her mind's eye the hallway on the opposite side, the way it almost always was: empty. Deserted. Nobody was going to find him or hear her until who knew when. She spun and darted up the steps toward the second-floor landing, then froze as she was plunged into darkness.

Tendrils of panic tried to worm their way into her thoughts. She widened her eyes but literally couldn't see her hand in front of her face. The killer had gotten Art, locked her in, and then cut the power. Her cell phone! She could call for help. She tried to grab it from her pocket, but it wasn't there—she'd given it to Art. "Oh God," Avery whispered, pressing her forehead against the cool wall. She listened. Nothing. There was no sound from outside the stairwell. What had happened to Art? So many had died already; she couldn't bear to think of him in that kind of danger.

Her heartbeat pounding in her throat, Avery forced herself to get moving. She kept a hand on the wall and climbed the last couple steps to the second-floor landing. Maybe she could still help him. Maybe the whole manor wasn't dark and it was only this stairwell. Avery fumbled with the latch on the door out into the second-floor hallway. It suddenly gave way, swinging open, and Avery's eyes struggled to adjust as a black-clad figure filled the doorway, backlit with dim grayish light from a window somewhere nearby. She tried to focus, but there was nothing to focus on: a black ski mask obscured any detail. He raised something in his hand, and she lashed out, striking forward on impulse in an attempt to deflect whatever he was about to hit her with. She felt his hand clamp like a vise around her throat, and she flailed, her hand contacting his skin. She felt the attacker's guttural shout beneath her fingers at the same time she heard him. Avery gripped and dug her fingertips into what felt like his neck where it met his jaw, scraping and clawing and trying to hurt him enough to make him let go, and then fireworks exploded behind her left temple. She was falling backward, tumbling, grappling at the walls, and then her world went black.

\* \* \*

Avery's eyelids fluttered open slowly, then closed again, then opened. She was staring into nothingness. She put a hand out and miraculously caught the trail of her arm moving; the faintest sliver of light peeked in from beneath the hidden staircase door. Art. Was he still out there? Or had the killer already taken care of him? The little vision she had blurred with tears, and her throat was suddenly thick. If he was out there, if he was alive, he'd already have gotten in here to help her. Her breathing sped up as the panic from earlier threatened to creep back in. How long had she been lying here?

She became aware of her orientation at the base of the stairs, flat on her back, one leg underneath her and the other twisted, caught under the lip of the bottom step—she'd never be able to do the marathon now. If she even got out of this alive. What if her leg was broken? She couldn't feel her foot. Jesus, if her leg was broken, she'd never get out of here. She turned and sat up, groaning, and got her legs straightened out. Her foot immediately began tingling, little needles zinging up her leg. What were the odds it was just asleep? She could see almost nothing, but she rolled both feet in a circle from the ankle, flexing and pointing; so far, so good. Avery slowly stood, gratified that her legs held her and seemed fine. Her head was another story. The throbbing she'd woken up with was magnified now that she was on her feet. She slid her hand across the wall and found the latch on the door. She pulled, throwing her body backward, trying to force it, but it had to be firmly locked on the outside. She didn't have a choice.

Avery carefully made her way up to the second-floor landing, déjà vu hitting her hard. She had to be smarter this time. She located the latch on the door and crouched down low, gingerly pulling at it—it wasn't locked. She opened it just a hair, peering into the second-level hallway. She saw no one; no one blocked the door or came at her. Staying low, she opened the door enough for her to slip through and closed it noiselessly behind her, her pulse racing as if she'd just done a sprint. The power was still out, leaving the manor cast in an eerie dim grayish light from the windows. She stood up, listening.

She heard conversation coming from somewhere below, a few people, but couldn't discern what was being said.

She hurried silently to the stairway, stopping to peer down into the vestibule. Her heart leapt—Detective Carter and his partner were speaking with Lord Nico and Duke Pennington, the foursome with their heads close together, Carter nodding. As Avery watched, the detectives moved toward the front door, Carter pausing and turning back to speak to Nick and his son.

"We'll check at his house. I'd hoped he was here working today, but if no one's seen him—"

"Wait!" Avery shouted. She rushed down the steps, registering the three men and the female detective staring up at her in surprise. She was almost to the vestibule when she suddenly felt light, as if she were drifting rather than walking. The group before her receded in front of her eyes, becoming the only thing she could see, a faraway, pinpoint image, and then blinked out as her eyes closed, her legs folding in slow motion until she felt the steps against her back and then nothing . . . and then snapping, an irritating noise near her ear. She opened her eyes to find Detective Carter's concerned face too close to hers. She drew back, trying to sit up.

"Are you all right?"

"What happened? Did I pass out? For how long?" She tried to calm her breathing; this was too much, and she had no idea where Art was.

He shook his head, the trio behind him watching her with worried faces. "You were out a few seconds," Carter said. He gave her his hand, helping her sit up, and she pulled herself to a standing position. He motioned to the left side of her head. "You're bleeding."

"I am?" She reached up and cringed as she touched near her temple, pulling her fingers away from the drying blood and matted hair.

Carter frowned, his voice stern. "What's going on? Should I call an ambulance for you? Why isn't Art with you?"

She was so confused. "What time is it?"

Nick checked his watch. "I've got quarter past three. It's been a couple hours since we finished lunch. Ms. Ayers, come, sit down." He motioned to the bench near the fake Federico portrait. "Tell us what happened."

"I don't want to sit down. It's three? We have to find Art. We called an ambulance; where is it? I don't understand." She stared at Detective Carter. "You know what happened to Lightfoot, right?"

He shook his head slowly, looking spooked, which only confirmed Avery's sense of urgency.

"Okay." She took a deep breath, trying to ignore the throbbing in her head. "Greg Lightfoot is dead in the pool. We found him at like, one thirty, and called 911. They should have been here over an hour ago. We saw footprints in the snow and used the hidden staircase by the pool area, and the killer grabbed Art and did something to him and locked me in the stairwell, and when I tried to get out, they hit me and I must've blacked out. That was right when they cut the power to the manor."

Avery looked from Carter to his partner to Nick to Lord Nico, impatient with the time it seemed to be taking them to process.

"The storm knocked the power out," Detective Carter said. "It's out all over the Hudson Valley. There's a huge pileup on the highway, twenty-two vehicles at last count, black ice under the eight inches we've gotten so far. Dispatch should've sent out a call for a new—"

"Detective!" Avery cut him off. She was almost jumping up and down, she could hardly control the fear that Art was lying alone somewhere, dying or already dead. Her stomach flipped over, tying itself in knots. "I'm sorry, but we have to find Art. Please. Come on, I'll show you where we were."

Carter started to follow her but then stopped, speaking to Duke Pennington. "We still don't know who Lightfoot's accomplice is," he cautioned. "Stay together. Where are the children?"

"Gretchen and Annabelle took them to the reception room to play dolls. It gets more light than the rest of the house," Lord Nico said.

Detective Carter nodded, and Avery caught a silent exchange happening between him and his partner, and then she addressed the duke. "It might a good idea for you two to check on Lord Percy." The detective turned, heading toward the kitchen while typing something on her phone.

Carter hesitated, eyes on the two Pennington men. "Just— be on guard."

He fell into step with Avery as they headed down the length of the long hallway toward the pool. "I still don't trust Nico," he grumbled. His phone buzzed and he checked it, typing a message back. "Good. Zane—my partner, Detective Zane—is going to do an inventory of staff, starting with the kitchen. Based on your great eavesdropping experience the other day," he added, glancing at Avery.

She nodded, checking over her shoulder. She couldn't help it. Where the hell had the killer gone? They couldn't assume he was off the premises, not in this weather. Carter spoke. "I've texted Art several times, but he hasn't answered." He stopped at the first door in the hallway filled with closed doors. He put an arm out and then rested a hand on his holstered revolver. "Stand back." He knocked twice and opened the door, going through gun first.

Avery stayed in the hallway as he'd told her. When he closed the door and moved on to the next door, she followed, silent, keeping her eyes on each direction of the hallway. It'd be a wonder if her crazily beating heart ever settled back down to normal when this was over. She couldn't stop imagining Art—she squeezed her eyes shut. Neapolitan. Okay, she could get through this. Cookies and cream. Lemon sorbet. Dr. Singh's advice drifted through her mind. Orange sherbet. Raspberry chocolate chip. She knew how to dial down her stress response when her adrenaline was in overdrive. Mint chocolate chip. Chocolate chip cookie dough. Her pulse was beginning to drop, alleviating some of the nauseating dread. Peanut butter fudge.

"—like this earlier today?" Detective Carter's question drew her back to the here and now. He was staring into Suzanne's room. "Have you seen anyone in it since yesterday?"

"No. Call my phone, Detective. Art had it when we were separated. You can't reach him because his phone's dead." She rattled off her number too quickly and had to repeat it after he had his phone in hand.

He held it out in front of them, the two of them falling silent. She'd hoped to hear ringing somewhere along this godforsaken hallway, but there was nothing besides the quiet ringtone of the outgoing call. It went to voice mail and Detective Carter hung up. He hit redial before she could suggest it. "Here, keep trying," he said, handing her his phone.

She pointed into Suzanne's room. "We didn't see Lightfoot or anyone else in here today, but it's a lot messier than it was yesterday morning when he was packing up her things. Art and I both had the impression he was searching for something, presumably the pocket watch."

They moved forward to the alcove and the door framed with broken glass, Carter drawing in his breath and blowing it out in a stunned huff. "Damn." He bent down, examining what was left of the destroyed secure-entry door handle.

"Art shot it. Look, before you go in there." Avery pulled his attention back to where she stood against the wall opposite the alcove. She slipped her fingers under the latch and pushed the wallpaper-covered door open. "I was in there and Art had just stepped through here when the door was slammed closed and locked. I heard a struggle, and then someone had to have been knocked down, right here." She stared at the floor.

Detective Carter crouched down, scanning the carpeting. "Find the flashlight app on my phone and turn it on," he ordered.

She did and handed it to him. She watched him move the light over the carpet slowly, holding her breath, uncertain if she should hope he found nothing or something.

"Damn," he said under his breath, but Avery caught it. He snapped a photo and then took a white canister the size of a large spool of thread from his jacket pocket. He pulled a long, thin white strip out and touched it to the carpet, holding it up. He reached into his other pocket and placed a yellow card with a black number one on it near the spot and then straightened up.

She was shaking her head. "That's not Art's blood," she whispered.

He frowned. "How do you kn—"

"Because it's not," she hissed at him, tears threatening to overflow. She took the phone from the detective's hand without asking, hit redial, and turned, going through the glass-shard-rimmed door into the pool area. She was immediately assaulted with a metallic stench, Greg Lightfoot's body a few yards from her in a pool of his own blood. The room was freezing. Her gaze went to the door on the other end, still propped open with a chair. A small mound of snow had blown in and was piling up inside.

Detective Carter was beside her, looking down at Lightfoot. "You and Art tried to help him."

She nodded. "It was too late." She glared at Carter's phone as the ringing ended, and the call went to her voice mail again. She hit redial.

Carter had moved to the open door and stepped outside. He was back in a moment. "No tracks. The snow's coming too fast." He bent suddenly at the waist. He continued back toward her that way, hunched over, peering at the tile. He motioned Avery over, grabbing the phone from her hand and turning the flashlight back on. "Look." A sparse trail of tiny drops of blood led across the tile, easy to miss with the lack of lighting and many of the drops blending into the black-and-tan marble. There were a few, and then none, and then a few more, and the trail ended in the middle of the tile, across from the sauna and locker room. Detective Carter opened the sauna door, sticking his head inside.

She took the phone back and hit redial again. She wasn't giving up now. Avery nearly dropped the phone when the call was answered after the first ring. A rustling nose came through the speaker. "Art! Hello?" She spoke into the phone but only heard more rustling. The call was disconnected. Avery's heart dropped to her toes. She hit redial. She held her breath. And then she swore she heard it. Her eyes widened as she stared at Carter.

He waited, listening. Faint sirens carried to them from a distance. "It's just sirens," he said quietly.

She waved a hand, trying to shush him. She picked out the ringing, much quieter than the sirens, coming from the locker room. She crossed the tile and yanked open the door, catching the last ring before the call went to voice mail again. She redialed. He had to be in here; the ringing was loud. She followed it through the second short row of lockers. Her gaze dropped. Art sat on the floor, propped against the corner where the bank of wooden locker doors met the wall. His head was slumped to his chest, and his entire middle was covered in blood.

# Chapter Eighteen

Avery fell to her knees beside him. His arms were limp at his sides. She cupped his face in her hands, his skin cold and clammy. "Art."

He groaned, moving his head but unable to lift it. His eyes opened, meeting hers briefly, and then closed again. He mumbled something that she couldn't decipher.

"Carter!" she shrieked.

Detective Carter spoke from the doorway. "Right here." He rounded the corner and halted. He recovered and came over, shedding his jacket and tucking it around Art. He leaned in close to Art. "You're fine. Hear me? You're gonna be fine." He stood. "Stay with him. I'm hoping those sirens are finally the ambulance you called."

The scream of the sirens was much louder when Carter yanked open the locker room door and took off running. They had to be coming here. Avery tried again to wake Art. "Hey. Art. Can you hear me? Help is coming. You're going to be okay."

He rolled his head to the side, opening his eyes again. "Hey."

She half laughed, half cried. "Hi. What can I do?"

Each time he blinked, she wasn't sure he'd open his eyes again, he was working so hard to stay conscious. "He came in here. I saw him. He took something." Art murmured.

"Who? Who was it?" She forced herself not to look at the blood.

"I pulled the cap off, but he got away. I didn't see—" Art cringed, drawing one long leg up close and bending forward. He groaned. "Christ, it hurts."

Avery put her arms around him as best she could, loose enough to hopefully not jar or hurt him, tight enough to lend him her strength. There was so much blood. "You'll be okay. I promise."

He nodded, not speaking.

Hours seemed to pass before Detective Carter reappeared along with a cluster of first responders. Avery stood back, giving them space to help Art. She noticed that a brass name plate adorned each of the polished wooden lockers in the unisex locker room. Three narrow doors to the right, the brass plate read **Suzanne Vick.** Most of the lockers were standing open, including hers, which Avery could see from here was empty. A quick perusal of the other block of lockers revealed that one row was for Pennington manor family and the other row was for staff. She was betting that whatever Lightfoot hadn't been able to find in Suzanne's room, either he or the killer had recovered from her locker.

She spoke quietly to Carter, who stood beside her watching the medics work on Art, sharing her suspicion.

He nodded. "You could be right."

"Detective, when you went out to meet the ambulance, did you happen to see anyone with marks on their neck? Scratches or red marks or even someone with a Band-Aid or two? I know I hurt whoever it was that hit me at the top of the stairwell."

"I thought about that too. I only saw the duke and the two sons and they all looked fine. My partner said most of the manor staff was in the kitchen. I did fill her in though, she's got an eye out."

Before they wheeled Art out, he gripped her arm. He was now clearly in a lot of pain. The paramedics had explained they could give him something for pain the moment they got his blood pressure up enough; it was dangerously low due to the blood loss. He motioned her toward him and croaked, "Take care of my cats."

She laughed and then clamped her lips closed, feeling like a horrible person. "Of course. I will, I promise, but only until you're back home." She walked alongside him and spoke to the paramedics. "Can I stay with him?"

"Up to him, ma'am."

On the gurney, Art nodded. "She's with me."

In the vestibule was a crowd of first responders. Through the open door, Avery spotted two ambulances and two Westchester County patrol cars. Family and some of the household staff spilled outside as Duke Pennington hobbled his way through on his walking boot to wish Art a quick recovery. Avery scanned the clusters of people, scrutinizing everyone she could get a decent view of. She'd grappled with her attacker well enough to grab hold of the skin around his neck and jawline. She had to have done some damage to someone in this crowd.

A hand closed around her upper arm, and Avery spun around, ready to fend off another attack, but saw it was Detective Carter. "Sorry. I need you to look to your left, ten o'clock. Right in front of the entryway window, next to the door."

She looked. Carter's partner, Detective Zane, was staring at Avery near the window. She stood slightly behind the Pennington's driver, Roderick. Even from here, Avery could see she had one hand on her gun.

Carter spoke near her ear. "She herded the staff out here for us, told them they'd need to make statements about Lightfoot."

"It's him," Avery said. "The red scrapes over his left jaw and neck. Those are mine."

Carter gave his partner one quick nod and moved through the crowd toward her. Roderick had already appeared uneasy; as Detective Carter closed in, Roderick turned and darted out the front door. Avery let go of Art's hand, leaving him with the paramedics, and followed, sliding across the exterior stone steps that were now coated with ice and snow.

Roderick must have done the same. He was on his belly at the bottom of the steps, Detective Zane kneeling beside him while she handcuffed him. The scuffle had caused a hush to fall over the gathering. Zane read Roderick his rights and got him to his feet with help from Detective Carter. Avery carefully descended the steps, taking Lord Percy's outstretched hand to steady her.

"This is unlawful," Roderick shouted, as Detective Carter pulled gloves on and patted him down. "You have no cause. Let me go!"

Detective Carter pulled his hand out of Roderick's jacket pocket, holding a white handkerchief wrapped around something. "Are you sure about that?"

Duke Pennington had come out and stood on the porch leaning on his cane. Avery spotted him in her peripheral vision. She followed his gaze, expecting his attention to be glued to the small item Carter was unwrapping, but his eyes were on Roderick. He looked completely crushed.

The detective dropped the handkerchief and held up the Viktor Petrova pocket watch for Nick to see. He brought it over to him, holding it on his palm. "We'll need a moment to confirm fingerprints before I hand it over, but I assume this is yours?"

The duke nodded. "It is. Oh my." His face crumpled. He moved to the edge of the porch, addressing Roderick. "All this time, it was you? You were part of my family."

Roderick spat onto the ground between them. "I was never. I'd have been a lord if my parents had just stayed in their miserable marriage like all of you. Instead, I had to bow to you every day. Same with Greg! You promised him a post in Valle Charme and then went back on your word. You don't even need that," he said, eyeing the pocket watch.

Nick shook his head sadly. "It's not about the money." He started to go on but seemed to think better of it and turned, heading inside with an arm through Lord Percy's.

"It's always about the money!" Roderick roared. He got no response from the duke as Zane and Carter helped him into the back of the squad car.

"Ma'am!" Avery's attention was pulled to the ambulance that now had Art loaded into the back. The paramedic leaned out, holding on to the one open door. "Leaving now!"

She grabbed the door and climbed in. She took a seat near Art and slipped her hand into his. His eyes drifted open, and she smiled. "Hey there, cat dad."

# Chapter Nineteen

Avery had waited for over a year to run the New York City Marathon. She'd spent months wishing it sooner, counting the weeks and then the days, dealing with bursts of anticipatory excitement and nerves. But arriving at Aunt Midge's Upper East Side apartment Saturday evening, she was incredibly relieved that she'd had four long, boring, event-free days to recover from Tuesday's Pennington Manor trauma.

Her run-in with Roderick could've turned out much, much worse, but she still had a low-grade headache from whatever he'd hit her with. She'd been lucky not to break any bones in her fall down the stairs, and exceptionally fortunate not to end up like Roderick Chamberlain's other victims. Including poor Art.

The emergency room doctor had checked Avery's head wound and sent her for a CT scan Tuesday while Art was rushed upstairs to surgery. She was relieved to be diagnosed with a severe head contusion rather than a concussion—the triage nurse had warned her that if her scan showed a concussion, she'd have to withdraw from the marathon.

Avery stepped off the elevator on the seventeenth floor, pulling her little travel case behind her. She looked back, making sure William, Tilly, and Halston were with her, and knocked on Aunt Midge's door. Wilder opened it almost immediately. "Hello, welcome," he said, exchanging hugs and kisses and bending to give the dog a good scratch around the ears.

Halston meandered over to the staircase where Aunt Midge was descending, securing another petting, and then turned in a circle and settled onto the plush, fluffy white rug in front of an oversized peacock-patterned ottoman.

"We've got the bedrooms all made up for you," Midge said, joining their group. "Wilder's ordered in; we'll be having Thai food. Avery, I ordered exactly what you chose last time, no frills. It won't do to derail you the night before the race after all you've weathered. I also added one of my blackout sleep masks to your pillow. You may find it helpful, though very little light peeks through those curtains." She held her arms wide, smiling. "Having all of you here delights me so."

Midge occupied the southwest corner of the luxurious high-rise on Fifth Avenue between Eighty-Fifth and Eighty-Sixth Streets, with a view overlooking Central Park and the Met Museum. The apartment encompassed every shade of white, with splashes of color—a red chintz chaise longue, velvety red couches, a peacock-blue tapestry on the wide stairway wall just past the baby grand piano. The massive windows were devoid of window treatments, allowing plenty of natural light in, the living area opening onto a formal dining room that would accommodate their dinner party tomorrow night after the marathon.

Midge took both Avery's hands in hers and held them out to the sides, the older woman's pink silk and chiffon caftan fluttering at her arms as she did. She examined her from head to toe and back, reaching up but stopping short of touching Avery's left temple. "Good gracious, child. Does it hurt? More importantly, are you truly all right? And don't even think of lying to me."

"Auntie, I'm perfectly fine. I promise. Pinkie swear," Avery said, holding up her little finger.

Midge took her up on it, wrapping hers around Avery's. She nodded. "Good. I can still hardly believe what you've gone through. And poor Nicholas. Now, tell me about your detective," she said.

Avery joined her on one of the couches. Wilder and William moved to the kitchen for drinks while Tilly took a phone call she'd just gotten outside onto the terrace, which afforded an amazing view of Manhattan.

"Art is a lot better than I'd have expected," Avery told Aunt Midge. "When Roderick stabbed him, he missed every vital organ. The surgeon said he should play the lottery, he's so lucky."

"I'm sure he doesn't feel very lucky," Midge remarked. "What a kerfuffle, and all during that early blizzard. And now it's already all melted and dry, thank goodness."

"I was worried about the snow," Avery acknowledged. "Glad it's gone. And you know," she mused, "Art surprises me. I saw him Friday after his sisters brought him home from the hospital, and he's seriously just happy to be home and okay. He'll be off work for a while, but he was up and moving around without too much discomfort on Friday. I think the kittens are helping with his spirits."

"How will he manage them on his own, in his condition?" Midge's brow furrowed in concern. "He realizes they could go to a shelter, doesn't he? Maybe that'd be best."

"He doesn't want that. His sister Claire is staying with him for a while. She'll handle the cat situation until we can start finding homes for them. Art insists he's coming to spectate tomorrow," Avery said, shaking her head. "He's ridiculous. I forbid him from showing up."

Aunt Midge laughed. "I like that. I hope he abides, for his own sake. And now, are you all finished with Nicholas's appraisals, one hopes? I don't imagine you relish the thought of being at the manor."

"Dad and Micah spent the last two days finishing up with everything. They let me off the hook. Duke Pennington now has a full report, and he'll be getting his stolen antiquities back except for the ones he chose to simply be reimbursed for instead. Did you know he visited Art in the hospital? I was there. He told us that Roderick is a second cousin twice removed. Roderick and Greg Lightfoot were roommates at an arts college in Paris. When a job for Lightfoot didn't pan out at Valle Charme, Roderick convinced your duke to hire him for the Hudson Valley house. It sounds like bitterness ate away at him and drove him to do what he did."

Aunt Midge shook her head. "Oh my. How very sad. To think he murdered an innocent woman to further his ambitions, and then another one to avoid being found out."

"And, in the end, even his own friend for profit," Avery added. She lowered her voice. "I have to tell you, Duke Pennington is one of the nicest men I've met. Right up there with Wilder, Auntie. You have an instinct for good men." She smiled. It was as close as she could come to saying what she wished she could, if her aunt wouldn't accuse her of being cheeky and disrespectful.

Midge patted Avery's hand. "You're right, my dear. Wilder is a truly wonderful man, solid and sweet and reliable. I could set my watch by him. I don't know if I love his brilliant mind or his exceedingly kind demeanor more."

Avery raised her eyebrows. "And?"

"And what?" Midge stared back at her blankly.

Avery sighed. "You know what I'm asking, Auntie."

"Wilder and I have the most perfect relationship. We have caring and companionship and the pleasure of each other's company. Isn't that enough?"

Avery wasn't certain it was enough for Wilder, but that hadn't stopped him from being a constant in her aunt's orbit. She gave in. "Yes. You're right. It's more than many people have."

"Avery?" Tilly spoke up, having just come in from the terrace. "I, um. Come upstairs with me." She crossed the room and ran up the steps two at a time.

Avery stood. "I've been summoned," she chuckled. "Ooh! For me?" She took the mocktail from her dad, noting he and Wilder held real cocktails. Wilder handed Midge her signature perfect Manhattan with a Luxardo maraschino cherry.

Avery followed Tilly upstairs, nearly running into her in the hallway. "What's up?"

"Okay, I don't want to step on your big day or anything, but I have to tell you something and ask you something."

Avery nodded encouragingly. "Go for it. You aren't stepping on anything."

"Juilliard granted me an audition—I just got the email."

Avery shrieked. "Oh my God!" She grabbed Tilly and picked her up, hugging her. "Yay! When?"

Her little sister beamed. "December. And here's my ask. Noah called me as we were walking in. He's outside, A. He wants to talk. How does he even know I'm here? Ugh, Micah must've told him we'd be in the city. I *know* he was home last week when I tried to see him, and he ignored me. I'm still mad. I can't really tell if he's still mad at me too or why he wants to come over, but oh my gawd, I cannot deal with all the questions and awkwardness if he comes up here. And I don't want to, like, come running just because he suddenly feels like talking to me. I told him maybe I'll consider meeting him, but I can't go alone, A. You have to come with me."

"Running out for a sec; we'll be back before dinner," Avery called from the foyer, pulling the door open. "Tilly wants coffee."

Tilly smacked her arm. "Why would you throw me under the bus?" she hissed.

"Coffee now?" their dad asked. "It's almost six."

Avery tried not to laugh. Tilly rolled her eyes at her and mouthed *thanks*. "I have a, um, another scholarship essay I need to finish, need some fuel," Tilly said. "Be right back!"

Outside, Avery walked with Tilly around the corner to the coffee bar on Madison Avenue. Noah Abbott stood outside, hands in his pockets, kicking the toe of one sneaker against the pavement nervously. He'd always been a little more comfortable with books than people. He was a year older than Tilly and had been oblivious to Tilly's longtime crush on him until last summer. Something had shifted, and it seemed that once he'd finally looked at Tilly through a different lens than their lifelong friendship, he'd fallen head over heels for her. Avery still thought it odd that he'd distanced himself from her sister so hurtfully when she was already paying for her terrible mistake. She followed Tilly over to him, trying to hang back.

"Hey," Tilly said.

"Hi," he returned. "Oh. Hi, Avery. Do you want to go inside?" he asked Tilly.

"I came to see you at your house," Tilly said, not budging from her spot on the pavement.

"I—"

"Don't act like you didn't know," she added.

"I was mad at you. I should've answered the door." He looked down. "Sorry."

"I know you were mad. Are you still? Do you even know what those girls put me through after I got caught?"

"Why did you do it?"

"I tried telling you, Noah. I was failing. I didn't know what else to do. That was my one shot at finding a way to use my voice, and I blew it. I lost everything I've worked for since I can remember. So if you think you had to punish me by breaking up with me, that was just mean. I'm already being punished."

He stared at her, silent.

Avery spoke. "Hey, Tilly, want to go get a table? It might be easier to—"

"No," Tilly said.

"We're broken up?" Noah asked, his voice small. "I thought we were in a fight. Why would you think—is that what you want now?"

Avery's eyes widened, and her gaze darted to Tilly.

"Is it what *you* want?" she asked.

"No!" Noah moved toward Tilly. "I was mad. I thought you were into that guy, the one who wrote the paper for you. I mean, are you? Into him?"

"What?" Tilly's voice was loud and incredulous. "Are you crazy? I paid for a paper that—jeez, why do I have to say it out loud again?—I paid him to do a paper I couldn't do because it was the only way I had a chance at not failing, and I'm an idiot for doing it. It's, like, what he does for money. Or did. I'm pretty sure he's getting kicked out because of me. I'm not into him. I'm not into anyone but you," she said.

Noah wrapped his arms around Tilly and hugged her. "I'm sorry," he said, turning his face into her neck. "I'm really sorry I was such a jerk."

"Yeah, you were," Tilly mumbled. She tightened her arms around him.

Avery took a step backward, and then another, drifting toward the corner. "Hey, Tilly," she said softly. "I'm just going to, ah . . ."

Tilly opened her eyes and met Avery's gaze over Noah's shoulder. She sniffled, smiled, and gave Avery a thumbs-up and went back to hugging him.

* * *

Sunday morning on Staten Island, Avery began her run with two of the women she'd been chatting with online through the Swifties website. The crowd of roughly fifty thousand was overwhelming at first. Runners found their pace and began to spread out, and Avery's mind drifted to all that had happened in the last two weeks and the last few months before that, worry about her dad and Tilly and Art creeping into her stride. She forced her focus back to the moment, the present, another gift of wisdom from a past session with Dr. Singh. Avery had asked for advice during her most recent session, filling the psychologist in on her dad's trouble adjusting. William had immediately agreed with Dr. Singh's suggestion of a few family therapy sessions for the three of them. Their first appointment was next week. It was a start.

Now she concentrated on her soles hitting the pavement, the in-and-out rhythm of her breathing, the music of her heartbeat strong and steady in her ears. She didn't struggle until around her fifteenth mile, crossing the Queensboro Bridge into Manhattan. The uphill trek made her calves and hamstrings ache. She pushed through, surprised to find that even though she'd always preferred running solo, knowing her fellow runners were going through the same thing helped propel her forward.

When the route took them through Harlem down Fifth Avenue, Avery knew she could finish. She could see Central

Park. In the final mile, she heard her name and spotted Tilly and Noah waving wildly at her. She laughed, nodding at them and raising a hand. As she came into the finish line, the cheering from the grandstand was near constant. She scanned the crowd. Auntie Midge was seventeen stories above Central Park, watching the race from her terrace with Wilder. But Midge had used her connections and snagged grandstand seats for William, Micah, Sir Robert, and Tilly—who apparently wasn't in hers.

Avery crossed the finish line in triumph, her longtime goal of experiencing the New York City Marathon now fulfilled. She had no interest in her time; that had nothing to do with why she was here. She found the grass and started to pace, slowing to a walk, and had begun stretching when she heard her dad's voice.

She turned and William pulled her into a hug. "I'm so proud of you, Roo." His voice was thick. She saw when they separated that he was smiling widely, his cheeks damp.

She kissed his cheek and grabbed one more hug from him. "It was for both of us, Dad. You're with me next time."

Tilly and Noah joined Micah in congratulating her. Someone from the race committee handed her an aqua recovery bag. She looked up from peering inside to see her medal, and Sir Robert was in front of her.

"Congratulations, Avery. Job well done," he said, holding out his hand to her.

She laughed and hugged him. "Thank you, Sir Robert."

"Oh, by the way," he said when they'd stepped apart. "You'll be pleased to know, Barnaby's has your friend's hairpin on the slate for next week's auction. Bidding starts at one point eight million."

"Oh my goodness. Have you told Rachel yet?" she asked.

"I can, if you'd like. I thought I'd let you handle that." He smiled.

"Avery." A voice came from behind her, sounding just like Art, but it couldn't be. He was in no shape for something like this.

She turned and found Art smiling at her. With him was a pretty brunette Avery recognized from the family photo at his house as Claire, the youngest of his three sisters.

"Art!"

"Congratulations. You did great. I'm always impressed by you."

Warm tingles zinged through her at his words. She shook her head. "What are you doing? You can't be here." Her gaze dropped to his middle, where she knew a thick gauze bandage was securely fastened over a six-inch, sutured incision.

He raised his eyebrows and then looked down at himself. "I seem to be all right. Avery, this is my sister Claire. Claire, this is my—Avery." He cleared his throat.

Claire tilted her head, looking up at him. "This is *your* Avery, hmm?" She smiled, holding out her hand and shaking Avery's. "That was amazing. I'd pass out if I tried to run a mile, and you just did twenty-six," she said, grinning. "Anyway, it's so nice to meet you. I have heard so much about you."

Art scowled at her, color rising in his cheeks. "What the hell, Claire? This is why I wanted Jeannie to bring me."

Avery grinned. She already loved Art's sister. And judging by this one, his other two were probably just as awesome. "Is he actually okay, though?" she asked Claire. "How's his incision?"

"*He* is right here," Art grumbled. He looked down at his sister. "Give us a minute, would you? I'll be just as okay if you're over there." He pointed away in the distance.

"Sure. Only because I see cotton candy for sale." She left them alone.

Avery closed the space between them, her brow furrowing as she glanced again at Art's belly. "How are you on your feet this long? Doesn't it hurt?"

He shook his head. "Not right now." He slid an arm around her waist, and his face scrunched up in pain with the movement. "But yeah, I probably have another seven minutes left before I need to sit down."

She supported him gently around the waist and slowly led him to an open spot on a nearby park bench, relieved when he lowered himself to a sitting position. She rested a hand on his shoulder, standing in front of him. "Do you feel up to coming to dinner at Aunt Midge's? Claire is welcome to come too."

"She's busy. She has cats to take care of; thanks anyway. But I wouldn't miss it."

"Be nice to your sister," Avery ordered.

"I am. She really is busy; she has a wedding-planning thing later tonight."

Avery placed a hand on his scruffy cheek. "I'm sorry you got roped into the Pennington job because of me."

He gazed up at her. "I'm not sorry. Except for this." He rested his hand lightly on his abdomen.

She bent and quickly kissed him, mindful of the fact that her family and his were likely watching. She straightened up. "I have zero future assignments involving murder plots and stolen antiquities. I think we're in the clear from now on, Art; don't worry."

# Chapter Twenty

The first thing Avery noticed, coming through the gates to Pennington Manor, were the horses. She counted seven—no, eight. They were all out in the pasture near the barn. She'd never seen so many of them at once before. Rehoming horses was clearly an ambitious undertaking; it was probably a long process. She wondered how many of these were Lord Percy's polo ponies, and she felt a twinge of sympathy again at his situation.

Art's truck rolled to a stop beside Aunt Midge's powder-blue T-Bird. She'd told him she would drive, but he'd insisted he was fine. In the nearly three weeks since he'd been stabbed, he'd been recovering well, and he was exceedingly stubborn and independent. Avery straightened the flouncy black skirt she'd finally had an excuse to wear, centering the slim, satin belt that matched her pink chiffon blouse. She was growing to love the feeling of dressing up once in a while. Art handed her the bouquet of flowers she'd brought, a thank-you to the duke and duchess for their generous dinner invitation.

"Looks like Midge and Wilder are already here, and Micah and Sir Robert," Avery said, tipping her head toward the other car. "I think my dad and Tilly were only a few minutes behind us."

"This should be interesting," Art said. "Is the whole family here? Or have they flown back home by now?"

Avery slowed her pace to match his as they approached the manor. He could kid himself into thinking he was healed and back to normal, but he couldn't fool her. "Nick didn't say. How are you feeling? Does it hurt?"

"I feel great. Really." He met her gaze. "Stop worrying."

She chuckled. "Sure, okay." She rang the bell.

Nicholas Pennington himself opened the mammoth front door. "Avery. Detective Smith. So wonderful to see you." He welcomed them in warmly, kisses on cheeks all around. "Shall we? We aren't in the dining room tonight."

Mrs. Hoffman hurried into the foyer, drying her hands on her apron. "Oh my, Your Grace, you're too fast for me. I thought I heard the bell. Hello, hello, you two!" she exclaimed, beaming widely. "How are you feeling?" she asked Art, her brow wrinkling in concern.

He smiled wryly. "I'm fine, thank you. No worries."

She nodded. "Good. Okay folks, follow me." She led them down the hallway in the opposite direction of the dining room, chatting as she went. "We're still waiting on the boys; they'll both join us shortly. We thought the reception room might be perfect for dinner."

Avery drew in her breath as they entered. Her father and Tilly came in a moment later, chatting quietly. Somehow, being here as a dinner guest allowed her to see the space as if for the first time. The textured white-on-white decor, the skylights intersecting the arced panels in the high, domed ceiling, and the panoramic view of the Hudson Valley and the river at twilight were lovely and peaceful. An expansive, white linen-clad table took up the center of the room, aromatic, steaming serving platters at the ready on a long sideboard. Most of the family was already around the table, including Lord Nico's wife and two daughters. Lucy and Ava had their heads together, giggling softly. Avery smiled, taking her seat across from them beside Aunt Midge. Wilder was absent this evening; she'd thought her aunt had said he was coming. She was about to inquire about him when Lady Annabelle spoke, taking her by surprise.

"Ms. Ayers, we must thank you and your team for your excellent work. We truly hope you're both fully recovered by now?" Her gaze moved from Avery to Art and back.

"Oh! Yes, we're doing well, thank you." Avery couldn't help it; she was waiting for the other shoe to drop. The woman had been nothing but brusque at every encounter.

Lady Annabelle cleared her throat. "I . . ." She glanced at her daughters beside her. "I'm so grateful no harm came to my girls. I hadn't realized how dire the situation was here. When I think of what might have happened, well . . ." Her voice trailed off, and Avery was shocked to see tears in her eyes.

Avery leaned forward. "I'm glad we were here to help," she said earnestly. "Your girls are darling, Lady Annabelle. You're all safe now."

Lady Annabelle smiled. Avery realized it was a first; she'd never seen the woman smile before. "Thank you," she said again.

Avery noted the empty chair beside Lucy. "No Gretchen today?" she asked. Maybe staff wasn't to be part of the meal, Avery mused.

"No Gretchen," Lady Annabelle confirmed. "Nanny Gretchen has been dismissed; she wasn't needed anymore. I'll have these two little pigeons to myself for a while, and that is a wonderful thing," she said, meeting Avery's eyes.

Lord Nico pulled out the chair beside Lucy and took his seat, touching Lady Annabelle's shoulder as he did. "Family first," he said. "We're off to St. Tropez in a week, just the four of us. It'll be nice to relax and reconnect."

Lady Annabelle turned an adoring gaze on her husband, and Avery instantly understood. She knew about her husband and Gretchen. She was choosing to move past it; from the way she stared at Lord Nico, Avery didn't think there was any alternative for her. For Annabelle's sake, she hoped things would be different from now on. When Avery caught her eye again, she gave Lady Annabelle a reassuring smile. She wasn't horrible. She was insecure and lonely and trying to be brave.

Lord Percy burst through the doors just as Mrs. Hoffman began circulating with the first course. He was wearing a crisp white dress shirt and black trousers, and his hair was hair was wet and combed back as if fresh from a shower. Avery'd seen him that first day wearing a bowling T-shirt, then later in swim trunks, and of course on that unforgettable morning staggering half dressed from the Tesla. He looked like a different person tonight. He flashed his dazzling smile as he joined them, taking the seat beside Tilly. "I am so sorry for my tardiness. Practice went long. It couldn't be helped. Hello." He tipped his head toward Tilly. "We haven't met. You must be the voice virtuoso."

Tilly returned his gaze, wide-eyed. "I am," she said, smiling. She shook his hand. "Practice for what?"

"Oh," Duke Pennington spoke up, just as Percy began to answer Tilly. "Apologies," Nick said, nodding to his son. "I hadn't had a chance yet to share with the group. Go ahead, Percy, it's your news."

Lord Percy shrugged, but he was unable to keep the grin off his face. "It's nothing, really. I've just been accepted onto New York Java, a top ten sponsored U.S. polo team. I'm in a probationary period, obviously, because"—he broke off, rolling his eyes and gesturing with both hands toward his chest—"you know, but after sixty days I'm fully instated. Tournaments begin January second."

Avery clapped her hands together. "That's amazing, Lord Percy! Congratulations." Seeing Lord Percy this joyful warmed her. She hoped he'd turned a corner and left his willful indiscretions in the past.

"In light of the happy news and pending the results of the probationary period," Duke Pennington added, his stern gaze locked onto Lord Percy, "we've decided to keep the manor in the family. For now. Percy will stay stateside while the rest of us return to Valle Charme."

Lord Percy returned his father's stare unflinchingly. When he spoke, his tone was quieter, humbler. "Thank you. I won't let you down."

As Avery lifted her fork, she paused and turned to Aunt Midge. "It's a shame Wilder couldn't make it tonight, Auntie. He'd have loved seeing the manor."

Midge nodded. "Yes, so true. He was sorry to miss it. It's not like him to drop out of plans last minute. He called this afternoon to say something urgent came up and he had to fly out unexpectedly. He's in the air as we speak."

"Hmm." Avery took a bite of her salad. It was hard to imagine anything urgent happening in the life of Wilder Mendelsohn, but perhaps there was more to him than met the eye. "Well, I hope everything's okay."

"I'm sure it is," Aunt Midge said. "Now, tell me about the new friend my Halston is getting soon—did Tilly fib, or are you really adding a kitten to your household?"

Avery winked at Tilly. "No fibs. We're adopting a little tiger-striped kitten from cat dad here," she said, tipping her head toward Art. "We can't wait."

As the evening was winding down, after a delicious meal and too many desserts to choose from, Duke Pennington motioned Avery and her team over to the glass display case on the other end of the reception room. Under the illumination of the overhead spotlight, the Viktor Petrova pocket watch was now in its rightful place on the bed of black velvet, surrounded with the gleaming cuff links, diamond tie tack, and monocle with gold chain.

Avery couldn't help saying what was on her mind. "It's gorgeous. But are you certain this is the best place for such a valuable heirloom?"

He nodded. "I think it is. Detective Carter did let me know that a copy of the key was found in Roderick's belongings when they searched his room. We aren't sure whether he filched mine or Percy's to make the copy, but it wouldn't have been difficult for him, as our driver. So we've added a security measure." He pressed his fingertip to a smooth square of black glass Avery hadn't noticed on case's top corner. There was a beep and then the click of a latch, and Nick opened the case, demonstrating.

"Ah," William said. They were all gathered around, watching. "That's smart."

"Well, nothing's foolproof, I suppose," Nick admitted. "But it's an improvement. I won't wear it except for perhaps very special events, and I don't want to part with it or lock it away somewhere. So here it will stay."

"Your great grandfather would be happy to know it's so cherished," Avery said. "I'm glad you've been able to recover all of the stolen items."

"Thanks to you. Expect a few calls," Nick said. "I'll be letting my friends here know who to turn to for antiques appraisals. And if you ever grow the company into Europe, you'll have as much work as you can handle."

"Excellent!" Sir Robert said. "That's definitely something to consider."

\* \* \*

It was late by the time Avery and Art got back to Lilac Grove. The mid-November night was chilly, the clear black sky filled with millions of stars as they climbed Avery's porch steps. Halston heard them; distinct whines and then a howl came from the other side of the front door.

"Jeez. Hold this please," Avery said, handing Art the scrumptious take-away package of pastries Mrs. Hoffman had prepared for them. She unlocked the front door and released the dog.

Halston bounded past Avery to Art for ear scratches, then sprinted into the yard for his frisbee, fur flying. Art laughed. "I hope your new kitten is tough. Halston's going to have to slow down when you bring the cat home."

"Aunt Midge had a cat when she got Halston, and he was sweet to it. I think he's going to love Watson."

"Why Watson? You never said how you chose that name."

"Tilly chose it," Avery said. "She's obsessed with Sherlock Holmes stories—she's gotten me into them too."

"I should have known." He moved closer, his face half in shadow. His deep voice was quiet when he spoke. "Have I told you how beautiful you are?"

Her cheeks burned, making her glad the lighting was dim. "I can't remember. Maybe you should, just in case you haven't." *Cheeky*, Aunt Midge would've said. Avery closed the gap between them, resting a hand lightly at Art's waist.

He dipped his head, his lips near her ear giving her chills. "You're gorgeous, from your beautiful mind down to your runner's feet."

She laughed, turning her face toward his. "Really? My mind and my feet, that's what you like?"

He dropped his gaze to her lips. "Well, everything in between is pretty great too."

She kissed him. Art wrapped an arm around her and pulled her close and kissed her back. His fingers glided over her neck and into her hair and she let herself melt into him, breathing him in. He was everything she'd never known she needed.

Avery finally loosened her arms around him. She nuzzled the sharp line of his clean-shaven jaw, trying to calm her racing pulse. She felt him smile against her temple and drew back to look at him.

"Avery."

What *was* it about the way he said her name? There would be no slowing her wild heart around him. "Yes?"

"Two questions. Have dinner with me tomorrow? Fratelli's, just us."

"Absolutely yes. And?" she asked.

"How do you feel about weddings?"

She raised her eyebrows. "Um. I like them?"

"Good, because I'd love for you to be my date for my sister's wedding in Niagara Falls next month. But," he rushed on, "I'll warn you now, my family's not small. And they're going to drive you crazy with questions. They've been dying to meet you. So brace yourself."

Avery smiled. "That sounds perfect."

# Acknowledgments

A very Ayers and her world wouldn't exist without the fabulous mind of Fran Black. Fran let me borrow the loose concept of a gems-and-antiquities appraiser and a few of her cohorts to weave into the Avery Ayers Mysteries. Thank you, Fran, for your wonderful support, advice, advocacy, promotion, ideas, links, edits, and all-around awesomeness. I'm lucky to have you in my corner.

Faith Black Ross, a world of thanks to you for publishing *Peril at Pennington Manor* and loving Avery Ayers. I so appreciate your sharp eye, your great catches, and your unfailingly spot-on advice for making the work stronger. I am truly honored to be part of the impressive Crooked Lane team.

Thank you to that team: Melissa Rechter, Madeline Rathle, Rebecca Nelson, Rema Badwan, and editor Rachel Keith. I'm grateful for all that you do to help this process run so smoothly and create such a beautiful end result!

I am not by any stretch of the imagination a runner, but I'm in awe of runner girls everywhere. Thank you to my sister Julie Velentzas for sharing with me what makes you love running so much; watching you run track in school and beyond and fearlessly pursue goals I'd never dream of inspires me. And thank you so much to friend Shana Barmoy for the invaluable advice and education you provided me on the intricacies of running. Also, Avery appreciates the supercool shoes you helped choose for her!

My husband is the best man I know. Thank you, Joe, for always supporting my dreams. Even when I'm not sure I believe in them, I know you do.

Our kids are the best of us. Thank you, Katy, Joey, and Halle, for being the glue that binds our family together. As you move forward into adulthood, I hope you continue to embrace the fiercely independent, driven, brave attitudes I see in you now. You inspire me.

Thank you to my concert wife and friend, Ann, for your fashion sense and styling help and early reading; to my kind and generous friend Rocsana, for your reading and support; and to my mom, for telling me all those stories about the talking plants, Delores and Larry. I'm certain you created the spark that set the storytelling fire in me.

Thank you, Dad, for free access to your shelves upon shelves of Nancy Drew and Hardy Boys mystery books. I wish you were still here to see that you created a lifelong reader.

And thank you, wonderful reader. I hope you love *Peril at Pennington Manor*.